CHRIST ON A BIKE

CHRIST ON A BIKE

by Orla Owen

Bluemoose

For Ian, Carys and Erin

Copyright © Orla Owen 2024

First published in 2024 by
Bluemoose Books Ltd
25 Sackville Street
Hebden Bridge
West Yorkshire
HX7 7DJ

www.bluemoosebooks.com

British Library Cataloguing-in-Publication data
A catalogue record for this book is available from the British Library

Paperback 978-1-915693-12-9

Printed and bound in the UK by Short Run Press

ONE

When the hearse pulled up outside the house, Cerys knew it was real. Gwen was gone. Until it appeared she hadn't been sure, but that's the way of an unexpected death. The grief muddles usually-clear thoughts. Before Cerys saw the brown wicker box inside the glossy black car, she'd thought it must all be a terrible mistake and she would definitely get to see Gwen again, one day.

She wished the front room was empty so she could fall to her knees and weep like a lady in a film from the olden days when hair was hot-ironed into waves and people were slim because of the war, the walking everywhere, the home cooked meals rather than the fast food fat burgers and sugar, sugar everywhere. But it was the new days so she stayed standing up. Her knees buckled. Nausea rose which she swallowed down, so well-practiced at keeping things just about under control.

People chatted quietly behind her. They ate biscuits and drank tea, saying how sad it was, how much they'd miss the old lady. Not that old. Wrinkles spread like fireworks from the corners of her eyes, but she hadn't reached an age where you expected a person to die from natural causes. Cerys closed her eyes, bowed her head, and let the sun fail to soothe her through the blinds.

~

The guests sat in their cars, ready to follow the limousine which was parked behind the hearse. Cerys got in last, after Seren and

1

Seren's husband, Mark. Their two young sons were at home. Cerys was glad. She found her nephews whiney and full of tantrums. A few hours in their company made her relieved she didn't have to spend all of every day with them. She pinched the skin between her eyebrows to stop herself thinking bad things when someone so good was being buried. Gwen would be ashamed if she saw the inside of her brain, tut-tut at the meanness.

~

Mourners were clustered at the edges of a square room. No incense like in church, just a whiff of various perfumes, their scents clashing. Chairs were lined up round the sides, their wooden backs against the walls, but people were standing stiffly rather than sitting down. Even the elderly lady with wide ankles, clumpy veins and a walking stick chose to stand. There was the odd mumble or murmur but little chat. That was the love, the shock, the disbelief that Gwen's dead body lay in the room next to them.

An old man in a black suit smiled at her. She nudged Seren. 'Who's that?'

'Mark's Uncle Tom, her brother. Jesus, Cerys, how many times have you met him?'

A man with a full head of silver hair came over to Mark.

'Would you like to view the coffin?'

'No. Thank you.'

Seren squeezed her husband's arm in support but he didn't acknowledge her. Cerys hadn't realised that was an option. What was it like, seeing a dead body? She never had, not once in her life, never in all her years. It might make her accept the finality of the death if she saw her.

'I would.'

Seren tilted her head as she and Mark looked at her. They didn't realise how much Cerys had loved her brother-in-law's mum.

'Please. If that's okay? I don't want to...'

Mark shrugged as if it didn't matter to him. Seren frowned in the same way her husband had a few minutes earlier. Cerys knew she'd have got a sharp *no* if they hadn't been in front of people. The funeral man smiled kindly at Cerys, making her want to hug him, but instead she followed him through a door that led to the room the service would be held in.

They walked past rows of red velvet chairs to the coffin. Cerys felt sick. She nearly turned back but the lady, the humanist who was sitting next to the open casket, gave Cerys a look of such absolute understanding that it pumped the courage she needed through her veins and propelled her forwards.

Her stomach scrunched up tightly as Gwen's head came into view. It was nearest the seats. The top of her head faced the congregation, the soles of her feet pointed to the wall. Cerys had imagined her facing the other way, looking towards the room when it was full of her friends, family and work colleagues. A muslin cloth covered her face making her a ghost at her own funeral, features blurred before the mourners, not quite forgotten, not yet. Her green eyes were closed, curly hair styled flat in a way she'd never have worn it when alive and her lips were coated in a matt pink lipstick, bright, so bold it took attention away from the rest of her body. Cerys crumbled. She held onto the table the coffin rested on, couldn't take her eyes off Gwen's lips. It was a colour she'd never have worn. She liked mascara, not lipstick. She thought her lips were too old, too thin, didn't feel confident enough for colours that brought attention to her face, to what she was saying.

Cerys wanted to wipe the lips clean. A noise escaped from her mouth. So loud, making primal, desperate noises. The humanist sat still, gazing at her hands that rested on her thighs, unfazed by the grieving banshee. Cerys swayed from side to side. The fact that Gwen couldn't tell them *no, I don't wear that colour, I don't like pink, that's not me...* It was wrong, so awful that she'd had no choice over what they did to her body. Even if it wasn't to be mean. It was a kind gesture but they'd made such a terrible mistake. Cerys should tell someone before the service started, get them to change it. She looked around the room for the man who was in charge.

'Are you alright?' asked the humanist.

'It's so unfair isn't it? She was such a good person. One of the nicest, kindest people you could meet. She was so lovely. It's not fair she's dead. Sixty-three's too young.'

She would let it be. Gwen was more than the colour of her lipstick.

~

The seats filled up, every single one full of love for Gwen. So many people wanting to say goodbye. Cerys sat down in the second row from the front. She hoped the silver lining to the vast cloud that had hung over her since the phone call with the terrible news, was that the full room meant Gwen was getting a proper goodbye, whereas if she'd lived until the ripe old age of ninety-nine who knew which mourners would have made it. Cerys's brow furrowed as she tried to imagine her own death, her method of passing.

'Okay?' Seren mouthed to her sister.

No. Yes. Just about. Cerys nodded, then focused her attention on the circle of cream and white roses resting on the now-closed coffin.

Seren turned to face the front. She was glad she didn't have to comfort the older one. They weren't close, as in sisters-hugging close. They'd never been for a coffee or enjoyed a meal out just to catch up, *how are things, you look well, did you get your hair done*? Which was fine. Their friends found it odd but Cerys and Seren were used to it. And why pretend? Not every

4

set of siblings was destined to be secret-and-problem-sharers, especially after big things happened. After dramatic events people could go either way: close, so close, too close, or really rather distant. Seren and Cerys had chosen the latter as their lives had veered in opposite directions. They each enjoyed the company of their friends and neither of them was desperate for their sibling relationship to be different. They didn't dislike each other. They simply weren't similar, or keen on becoming over-familiar.

Seren's voice wobbled through the first reading. She managed to hold in her tears and get the words out. As she walked back to her seat Cerys mouthed *well done.* Seren sniffed as she got a tissue from the sleeve of her black top. She blew her nose, then got another tissue from her bag which she used to wipe the tears off her cheeks, smearing pale patches through her blusher, making her skin like a sunset sky with airplane trails running across it.

Mark began to read his mother's favourite poem. Even though she was watching him intently, all Cerys could picture was the body with the wrong lipstick on the dead lips and her being so quiet. That was wrong. Gwen had a warm laugh that made others giggle. Cerys stifled a laugh at the memory, which turned to full-on crying when the humanist said 'her daughter-in-law's sister, Cerys' as one of the people Gwen loved. That was kind of Mark to have included her. She reached forward, squeezed his shoulder, and when he turned round she mouthed *thank you.* She hadn't expected to be name-checked, though it was true. Gwen had loved Cerys, Cerys had loved her back, and to feel the love of a mother when yours was gone, that was precious, not taken for granted.

She shouldn't worry about the lipstick. Gwen wouldn't, because according to her there was no afterlife. Ghosts and spirits didn't exist. There was no high-and-mighty maker as far as Gwen was concerned, hence a humanist giving the eulogy, so no need for Cerys to fret. She felt hands on her shoulders, pushing down, stroking her collar bones as they let go. The weight was lifted.

~

Teenagers dressed in black trousers and white shirts carried empty plates and glasses through swinging double doors marked *staff only*. Cerys bit back more crying when she heard Seren ask the receptionist to call their taxis. Gwen was gone and that was that. She was over. It was over. They were over.

Seren sat down next to her.

'Could you give us a lift tomorrow, to the solicitors? I'm not up for driving and Mark keeps drinking so much the alcohol will be in his blood for days. He needs to see them before we go back. They all do.' Mark swayed between his brothers. 'There's lots of paperwork. They'll have to sell the house. No-one lives near enough to look after it. God, that'll be weird, horrible. We always go there for Christmas. It's where everyone gathers, you know. Wales is the good place, her house the one everyone looks forward to visiting.' Her lower lip wobbled.

Cerys touched her sister's arm for a second, ashamed that was all the physical reassurance she could offer, wishing for a moment they were like normal people and her instinct was to give her a hug, have the hug accepted, squeezed back even stronger, to stroke her hair and kiss her cheek, maybe.

TWO

Not many people want to visit a remote Welsh beach in the rain, when the drop in temperature proves that the warmth enjoyed over the last few days was merely a passing moment. Winter still owned the air, the soil, the sea. But that didn't matter to Cerys.

She drove slowly down the single-track road. The muscles in her arms loosened with relief when the lane opened up so there was enough room for cars to pass each other without the risk of scraped edges, battered wing mirrors or, even worse, having to reverse down the road to let another car pass, swerving from left to right as she swore like a bastard.

Seren tutted in the back seat. Mark was silent in the front. They'd both agreed to the trip, some coastal air to clear their heads following the meeting with the solicitor but, as Cerys turned into the car park, her passengers wished they'd made their own way back to the house where Mark's brothers had gathered. They needed to seethe, rant, question why Gwen had funded three cruises and five holidays with an equity release scheme, meaning there was little to be shared once the house was sold. The percentage of the property the family owned was tiny compared to the amount a company registered in Leeds would be getting.

~

The solicitor shifted in his seat, resisting the temptation to fill the silence. Let it sink in. Give them time to process what he'd told them.

'I'd have lent her some money. We all would have,' Mark exclaimed. His siblings nodded in agreement. 'Or I'd have told her to live within her means. Jesus.'

The brothers were glad Mark had said what they were thinking, what they and their wives were all thinking. The solicitor pursed his lips, sympathetic. The shock for the children, on top of the grief. It wasn't a good thing. Now there was anger mixed in with the love, memories tainted, creating a painful confusion. A poor decision. Why hadn't she spoken to her sons if she needed money, advice about her finances? And the assumption that the house would be left to them, that was fair. What parent wouldn't want to help their children?

Gwen's boys sank down in the faux leather chairs. Tim, the youngest, looked like he wanted to punch something as he tapped his heel up and down. The realisation that some company would be getting what their parents had worked all their lives for, what their father had worked for, because let's be honest Gwen had only been a housewife... To think that strangers would be given all their dad had worked forty-five years for, passing away before he got the chance to enjoy even a day of his retirement, it was diabolical.

'You'll need to put it on the market as soon as possible I'm afraid. And empty it of all her things. I'm so sorry, but these companies are pretty ruthless once the person who signed the contract is no longer with us.'

~

Cerys turned on the engine when she saw them emerge single file through the glass door onto the high street. Mark slammed the passenger door shut.

'Don't ask,' Seren said as she clicked her seatbelt on in the back.

'Hang on a minute.' Mark ran into the Spar, returning with a packet of cigarettes and a purple plastic lighter. His wife didn't tell him off for buying them like she normally would.

Cerys took her sister at her word and kept quiet, biding her time. As soon as they were on the dual carriageway it started.

'I mean for fuck's sake. Really? What was she thinking?'

'Don't,' said Mark.

She was his mother. She was dead. You weren't meant to talk ill of the dead. Though why not if they'd been stupid?

'You know I loved her. I really did. We all did but honest to God, that was such a silly, selfish thing to do. And for what? To sit around the same pool each day then get ripped off when she disembarked, paying even more money for three hours on a guided tour of some busy, shitty city. And destroying the planet. Totally unsustainable. We'd have taken her on holiday with us. It would have cost a hundredth of the amount she's given that company.'

Mark wound down the window and lit a cigarette. Cerys didn't dare ask him to please not smoke in the car, it's a hire car, you're not meant to. Angry grief changed the rules. She checked Seren in the rear-view mirror. Her sister was staring at Mark whose eyes were pinched as he watched the fields, sucked hard on the nicotine.

'What happened?'

'Gwen did one of those equity release schemes. You know the ones you read about all the time in the Money pages where they warn you not to do them because they're a total rip-off. Seventy per cent of the house is gone. Some company in Leeds owns it and wants it sold asap. So most of what she had is gone. On nothing.'

'Not on nothing,' said Mark. 'On holidays. On memories. She really enjoyed them.'

Seren bit back the swearing she wanted to throw at her husband. She'd loved Gwen, hadn't ever wanted her to die but for Christ's sake... She pinched her fingers together, ashamed of her fury, that it showed up the fact that in the back of her head she'd thought when her mother-in-law died, not yet, many years in the future, there'd be something for the family. A little sum to ease the loss and help with the onward march of the mortgage, the bills, the kids. Not too little, enough to erase some of the worry. And they'd have handed most of any inheritance straight to their boys because god knows how they'd ever be able to afford their own home. Seren burst into tears at the madness of it all. Mark lit another cigarette.

~

Cerys checked the parking machine and decided to risk not paying the Welsh Woodland Trust four pounds, because who'd be checking windscreens for stickers at this time of year. She opened the driver's door and leaned in.

'Coming?'

'No,' said Mark.

'Me neither,' said Seren. 'It's going to piss down with rain. Look at the clouds. That's the problem with Wales. It always bloody rains.'

Cerys was glad. She didn't want their bad energy weighing her down. She understood why they were upset but needed to not be a part of it. When she looked back Seren was talking nineteen to the dozen at Mark whose eyes were shut, his forehead resting against the closed window.

As she crossed the road that separated the car park from the fields, Cerys put her hood up to keep off the sideways drizzle that had started to fall. Always. Always as soon they got out of the car the rain that had been threatening to fall on the journey would come down and soak them, a running joke from their childhood holidays.

She stood at the start of the path to take in the view of the church to her left and the hill to the right, behind it. It was a hill she'd always found too steep to climb, too scary the way its edges disappeared over the cliff with nothing to save you from falling. Between the church and the hill was a pale brown path that led to the beach, just as she'd remembered it. Oh happy melancholy.

The path curved left then right, tipping Cerys gently towards the cove, the sand, her beach with no-one else on it. The best body-boarding, the best cave for exploring, the best place to feel the wind race around you, wrap around you. And so few people. Even on the hottest days of summer there would only be seven or eight families with what felt like miles of sand separating them, which was the way with Welsh beaches. They gave a person peace and space, unlike the South Coast sandy beach she'd visited once and never again thank you very much. The crowds had made her want to scream, made her feel like she was stuck in a page from one of her nephews' *Where's Wally* books.

Cerys walked towards the water, her arms raised in the air like Jesus talking to his dad, showing off to his people.

'Peace be with you,' she called out, thrilled at her eccentricity.

She breathed in more deeply than at any yoga class, that fresh salty air. The joy of being alone after full rooms at Gwen's house. Thank God, if there was one. From the tide's edge, Cerys looked out to sea. Was there a more soothing sound than the water as it rolled in and out again? It was reassuring, the planet carrying on, ignoring the nonsense of all the humans.

She strode to the cave that was moulded into the cliff face, clambered on all fours over the seaweed-covered rocks to reach it, wiping her wet hands on her jeans as she peeked in the entrance. When she was little it had seemed huge. Now it looked more like a deep dent in the side of the cliff rather than an actual cave. She climbed back down, slowly, jumping onto the sand, walking the whole way across the beach to the other rocks, her rocks, their rocks, the ones they'd always run

11

to and bagsy because her family were regulars. They knew there was a patch behind them where the wind wouldn't get them, and when the sun shone it was as warm as being on a foreign holiday. Your damp towels dried out in a jiffy.

'Who needs aeroplanes and tummy bugs when you've got this?' their mum would ask.

At that moment Cerys would agree, sitting on a warm rock eating a mint choc chip cornetto.

'It would be nice one day though, Mum. Everyone else does it,' said Seren. 'Lucy's gone to Corfu. She said they've got three swimming pools to choose from and one even has a bar in it like in a film. You'd like that, Dad.'

Cerys had tried to imagine such opulence. They'd never been on holiday anywhere with a pool, had never flown in an aeroplane. Their mum sniffed and turned her nose up.

'You can't beat Wales,' she said. 'It's the most beautiful country in the world. Why would you want to go anywhere else? Sometimes I don't understand you.'

~

The sun came out. Joy. Proof it was right that Cerys was there at that moment in time. She pulled the bottom of her coat under her bum and sat on the edge of a rock. So. Many. Memories. How had life passed by so quickly? There was Gwen, gone in a moment with no warning. She didn't drink, had never smoked, which showed it could happen to anyone. To Cerys even. So what was she doing? Why did she live where she did, in an expensive flat, spending fifty hours of her week working in a job that was stressful, awful on a bad day and meh on a good one?

'Hey.' Seren sat next to her but far enough apart that they wouldn't happen to touch one another. 'Sorry about that. Being so angry. It's just all so shitty.'

'Don't worry. No problem.'

They both closed their eyes to let the sun momentarily heal them. Drizzle replaced the rays. When it turned to rain, they walked back to the path. Cerys raised her head. There was a man standing on top of the hill, his red windcheater puffed up by the breeze as he looked right at them. She waved. He didn't wave back.

'Is that Mark?'

'Where?' Seren followed Cerys's gaze. 'I can't see anyone.'

Gone in an instant. No-one there now.

'Let's go to the church,' said Cerys.

'Can we not? We've been here ages.'

'It'll only take a few minutes. Please. Remember how much we used to love looking at the gravestones, how Mum would always look for the oldest one and—'

'You go. I'll head back to the car. Mark's shattered; it's been a tough few days. Don't be too long, yeah?'

Seren dipped her head and hunched her shoulders forwards as she stomped over the field. Cerys turned through the gap in the wall where once there was a gate, into the graveyard. She checked for recent flowers on the graves of the local people, going back hundreds of years, their marriages, children, wives, husbands. She found the children's graves the saddest: Bronwyn, one year and seven months. Heart breaking. Rhiannon, four years and three months, too little. David didn't even make it to a year. But it must be nice being part of a community where everyone knew you, so different to the sprawling mass of London.

The circular metal handle on the church door groaned as she turned it, lifting the rusted latch. She pushed on the heavy wood, tempted to hug the worn flagstones before her. It was part of her, that place. Powerful, full of memories she rarely let herself think about. A visitor book lay on the table opposite the door, bound in brown leather, attached to the dark wooden table with a chain, a shabby string of red silk marking the open page. There was comfort to be found in nothing changing.

'The most beautiful church we've ever seen.' Doris and Michael from Dorset.

'Thank god it was open to keep us dry from the constant rain!!!!!!' Lauren and family.

'Preety. Niceeee.' No name, instead a row of black biro love hearts.

Cerys smiled, agreeing it was the most pretty, the most niceee. She flipped back through the years but the book started in 2015, long after her childhood. She looked under the table and on the shelf in the alcove but there were no other books full of names and compliments. She walked down the aisle, soaking up the musty smell that was wiped away sporadically by the sea air that blew through the door when it was open, that seeped between the gaps in the leading of the ancient windows. The whitewashed walls meant the room was bright and they were so thick that even on a wild winter's day it was warm inside. She stood still and looked up at the wondrous stained glass window above the altar she loved. The altar that made everyone gasp when they saw it. Good. Welsh. Slate. A good Welsh slate altar. That's what her dad used to say. And that's what she'd come for. She needed to touch it, to feel the cold, smooth stone beneath her palms to see if it channelled her mother and her father, the innocence before the bad thing happened, which she never usually wallowed in but today she'd let herself think about it. The death of Gwen had made her feel like it was the right time to indulge in some sadness. It was as if the planet was all powerful around her and she was merely on it, a fool to think she was ever in charge of her own destiny. She needed to embrace the altar. But in front of it, between her and it, was a metal stand that wasn't usually there, and on top of that, sat an open coffin.

THREE

Cerys held onto the back of a pew as she retched. She should leave. The mourners might arrive any minute and she'd be in their space, destroying their private moment. But the altar. She'd come so far to see it. Would it be wrong to sneak past the coffin? Would that be selfish? If only there was a lid on it. She didn't want to go from never having seen a dead body to knowing what two look liked in the space of twenty-four hours.

Death was exhausting. And this was a person she didn't even know, had no connection with to be wounded by. Which made her curious. Was it a man or a woman, old or young, some tragedy perhaps? If they were being buried in this graveyard it must mean they were local. You couldn't ask for a more beautiful spot. She'd like that, for her final resting place to mean she was nestled behind the stone wall, able to hear the sea, smell its freshness. That had to be a good start to a death, knowing your last spot on earth was somewhere so divine, your friends and family able to mix a visit to your grave with a day at the beach, a walk along the craggy coastline. And when tourists visited as daylight lasted longer each day, your ghost could watch them, so there was entertainment as well as peace when you needed it. Presumably you wouldn't be cold when you were dead, so the rain, the biting winter wind, more rain, always the rain just as you thought the clouds were clearing, that wouldn't bother you. People wouldn't bother you. She shouldn't bother the body.

Cerys walked on tiptoes as if sneaking up on a living person. Quietly. Toe to heel of her rubber soled trainers so she made no noise. She held her breath without meaning to. She'd make a good ninja warrior. Ankles sank into polished black shoes, a man's pair of shoes. She saw a dark grey suit leg and the hem of a matching jacket. He was facing the same way Gwen had been. That must be a thing then, facing the altar and God rather than the congregation. Who knew? She went to the side of the coffin. There was no muslin cloth. He wasn't scary though. It didn't feel like he was about to come alive and grab her. And he was old, which was a relief. He'd had his years and his time, proven by the deep wrinkles, the skin sagging under the sides of his chin as he lay down. His arms were by his sides rather than resting on his chest like Gwen's had been. Cerys nearly put her hands on his as a blessing but the thought of germs and diseases stopped her. Who knew what he'd died of? There were no marks on his body. Could be a heart attack, an aneurism, cancer, or quietly in his sleep like everyone on the planet wanted. Should he have a cloth over his face? It seemed odd that he didn't when Gwen's had been covered in one. No lipstick. No make-up on the man to cover the dark shading under his eyes that looked bruised, like he hadn't slept in days or weeks even. Blood spots contrasted with his paleness. His nails were neatly manicured, nicotine stains between the second and third fingers of his right hand.

A loud bang of a door made her jump, the door that separated the main part of the church from the entrance. The noise quietened as it increased in frequency, as it settled down to resting shut. The wind. The strong sea breeze. Goosebumps erupted over her arms.

'Shitting hell. Sorry. Sorry, don't mean to be rude. I'm so sorry. I hope you're okay now, at peace, and that it didn't hurt when you died. Rest in peace and God bless you.'

Cerys didn't like pain, for her or for anyone, couldn't bear to see people suffer. She stepped away from the dead man and ran her fingers over the altar. That chilled, dark grey, smooth Welsh slate. She laid both her hands on it to soak up the coldness. Though cynical of hocus pocus psychic feelings and the like, she closed her eyes as if she was a witch in order to let the power of it in, in order to make sure the history of it flooded her soul. The church had seen so much, felt so much for so many hundreds of years. She liked to think it was cocooned from the horrors that had been played out over the hills and inland. It was hidden. People didn't know to visit it unless they were told of its existence. And that was in this day and age when roads had been built. In years gone by strangers would have had to ride a horse for days over mountains and moorland to reach such a remote cove. She hoped the locals had been kept safe by their isolation, able to grow the crops they needed, catch fish they could cook over their fires, and sleep peacefully at night, sitting in the small, bright white church for a rest every Sunday. She remembered her childhood. She remembered the funeral. She remembered the prayer they'd memorised, a line each at the front of the church, all the adults crying, saying how brave they were. She recited it for the stranger.

> *Eternal rest grant unto them,*
> *O Lord, and let perpetual light*
> *shine upon them. May the souls*
> *of all the faithful departed, through*
> *the mercy of God, rest in peace.*

The door that had been shut by the wind flew open.

'Cerys! Come on. For Christ's sake. We've been waiting ages.' Seren stopped halfway down the aisle. She made a sign of the cross and murmured *Rest in Peace*. 'Come on. Hurry up. Mark needs to get back to his brothers.'

Cerys wanted to stay there, to hug the altar, sit in a pew, relish the quiet time, but instead she hurried down the aisle. She stopped behind Seren in the entrance. A second book was now sitting next to the main visitor one, even older looking, the open page crinkly, faded yellow paper like the scrolls they had to

17

make for school projects when they'd soaked the paper in tea, the teacher's top tip for ageing it. The lines on this book were the palest grey, barely visible, and a navy ribbon lay down its centre separating four columns on the empty right hand page with the headings Name, Address, Prayer of Remembrance, Message, and to their left, a note in the most elegant, old-fashioned style of handwriting though the words were modern, easily legible.

'This is the body of Thomas Morgan. He died with no friends or family alive. If you have been kind enough to say a prayer for him, please leave your details so he and the church may be forever grateful. Respectfully yours.' Cerys couldn't read the signature. Her shoulders drooped, her heart weighed down with sadness. That was so awful, not having any friends or family alive, the opposite of Gwen's funeral yesterday. Was it because he'd never married, not had children? Was he an only child so there were no nephews or nieces? Or he could be so old that all his friends had died before him. That must be it. No-one could have absolutely nobody to care whether they were alive or dead. That would be so wrong. It was all about the timing.

'Cerys, come on. Honest to god, Mark's going mad. It's not fair. He needs to get back. Please. It's not right. If we'd known how long you were going to take we'd never have come with you.'

Look at all the support Mark and his brothers had compared to the old man. They had each other plus their children for hugs plus their partners, even their neighbours had brought round food in big silver casserole dishes, lasagnes all snug in stainless steel platters. Look at them with their whole chain of carers.

'He died all alone Seren. It's so sad.'

Her sister shrugged. In that moment Cerys hated her, the lack of empathy. Psychopathic nutjob. She picked up the pen and filled in her details, just the name of the prayer rather than all the words plus a message Thomas could take to the afterlife he believed in.

Dearest Thomas,

I hope you are at peace and having a wonderful time in heaven. You look very smart in your suit and this is the most beautiful place on earth I can imagine for a final rest. I feel honoured to have seen you, to have prayed for you. Know you are loved. Rest in peace and take lots of care. Cerys. x

She didn't know him to love him but she did want to send him all her love in that moment. She would have hugged the dead man if he was alive. She absolutely meant it.

FOUR

The postman rang the doorbell. And again. He walked down the path, squinting when the sun hit his eyes as he put the envelope back in his satchel.

'I'm in. Sorry. I'm here. Hi! Sorry. So sorry.'

Cerys had to run down the two sets of stairs from her bedroom to the front door, always a rush when she heard the bell ring. The postman sighed and turned back, holding out a brown A4 envelope with an orange label. She wedged it under her armpit as she signed the screen of his black electric box with the black plastic stick that was attached to it.

'Thank you so much.' The postman nodded. 'Have a good day!'

She wanted him to think she was a polite customer, someone he should like because she was nice, said please and thank you. She wasn't one of those rude, expectant people who looked down on others.

Cerys sat at her dining table and looked out over the parked cars. The hours she'd whiled away watching people, buses, cars, knowing they couldn't see her. It was the best view. If only she'd bought the flat when she'd had the opportunity. Look at her thinking it was expensive all those years ago. Fool. Stupid idiot. Seren had. She'd bought a place in Zone Two. She'd told Cerys buy now, then in twenty-five, thirty years, you'll have no rent to pay and know you've always got a roof over your head. It's important. Do it. But Cerys hadn't bothered. Because who knew if she even wanted to stay in that area, who wanted to be tied down, who knew where life would take her? Nowhere. That's where. She still lived in the same flat in the same borough, worked in the same job and, every day, wished she'd listened to her little sister.

The kettle clicked off. She filled the cafetière with Marks and Spencer's Italian coffee, thirty-five pence more than the one in Sainsbury's but worth it to her for a perfect flavour. Leaving it to rest in the sink, she took a white mug from the cupboard then pushed the plunger down, poured, added two sugars and to her shame, the secret ingredient she enjoyed when no-one else was there to witness it: a large scoop of double cream whipped to a soft peak, never mind the heart disease, twenty seconds in the microwave to transform it into a bubbly white coating that sat on top of her drink, quick stir, big sniff, her favourite smell, there we go. Her morning comfort.

She pulled down the sash window ready for a warm day. She'd go for a walk round the park sooner rather than later and try not to get cross with all the people, so many children on scooters. She remembered the years when it was virtually empty. No-one had heard of Victoria Park. They'd sneer *where* scathingly when she told them it was in Zone Two but there wasn't a tube station. Now they didn't sneer. Now their eyes opened wide as in what are you doing living there, you're old, not a trendy one but you must be rich, living in such a place, lucky you to have bought all those years ago. Sometimes she'd admit she rented, usually after a third glass of wine, but that would turn into a bitter rant of *I should have bought, why didn't I buy, I should have bought, ninety-seven grand they offered me the flat for*. The thought of it made her feel physically sick. At other times she'd keep quiet, say nothing, make out as if she did own somewhere, let them think she was a cool cat hipster from the old days before E9 prices rocketed.

First coffee finished, she made another. Two coffees got her going and no food until midday helped her stay slim. At least these days there were no cigarettes. She was healthier than some. And she hardly drank, really. Plus she was virtually a vegetarian. Tick, tick, tick, cross for the double dose of cream and caffeine, huge tick for the rest of her lifestyle. Surely she was due that and if she did die young, younger than most people, so what. She didn't have children she needed to live a long time for, to see married, pay through college, cuddle grandkids with, to offer to babysit for. She had no partner to love, miss, travel the world with. And she'd travelled herself. Years going back and forth to South-East Asia in her twenties and early thirties, hence not buying the flat. Idiot. Idiot, idiot. Now she took an annual two week holiday in Europe. That was her lot. So if cream made her happy, why not? She could even start smoking again. What was there to stop her?

Cerys put the fresh coffee on the table. She opened the brown envelope, expecting a life insurance letter, an energy company offering her a better price per kilowatt, or one of the broadband companies desperate for her to switch. Maybe she would. It always cut out at three in the afternoon, whirring, whirring, whirring as it failed to take her anywhere.

The paper was thick. Cartridge paper. That's what it reminded her of – her mum had balked at the price of it but Cerys had insisted that was what everyone was using for the school project and if she didn't have that particular one people would think they were poor, and did her mother want other children and parents thinking that of them. The shame. Awful child, poor mother for having her.

There was a watermark on the letter like the cream Basildon Bond paper she used to write thank you letters on to her Nana every Christmas.

Dear Cerys Jones...

Her coffee went cold. Oily patches of cream floated on top of the brown liquid. She stared at it. Was that what was happening to her insides? Cream and oil clogging up her arteries, making her primed and ready for a premature heart attack. Was that why the doctors and nutritionists said it was bad for you? She would have to find a way to wean herself off it, now she had a reason, a reason to care about whether she lived or died. Hundreds of reasons, thousands, millions maybe. She reached for her cup. Her hand shook and her heel bounced off the beige carpet as it tapped up and down. Too much caffeine. Too much adrenaline. The two mixed together. She started to laugh then burst into tears as she re-read the letter. My. God. Who would she call, apart from the signee on Monday, as requested. She wouldn't leave the flat until then in case that made it not true, made it not happen. Which friends would she tell? Sam, Ellen, Frankie, Jim, Lucy. Or Seren. This was a life changing event and blood was thicker than water. For some reason hers was the name that kept jumping to the front of Cerys's brain. She'd do it. She'd follow her gut instinct and telephone her sister.

FIVE

Cerys put down the phone, her joy flipped to shame. Not the reaction she'd expected. Scathing. Cynical. Bitter. Was it jealousy or was Seren right to think it was a joke, a scam? If it had been an email Cerys would have spotted the dodgy address it had been sent from and clicked the phishing button. But the letter hadn't asked for her bank details. All they'd asked was that she call them.

'Yes, but it'll be one of those numbers that costs four pounds a minute or something,' Seren said. 'I've read about them in the Money section of the papers. You must have too. You can't be that stupid, not stupid but you know what I mean. You mustn't fall for it. Whatever you do, don't call them.'

Cerys hadn't thought of that. People were so cruel, getting someone's hopes up then scamming them out of their hard-earned money. What was the world coming to? She would call them but from work so it was her company's risk of a big phone bill, astute rather than foolish.

~

The screen outside the meeting room said it was free for the next half an hour. Cerys went inside and sat facing the glass so she could see colleagues approaching. She opened her work notebook as if she was doing very important business then took the photocopy of the letter she'd made at the newsagent's on Saturday, scared that she might lose the details, her rare chance of a different future. The original letter was safely hidden in her

24

jumper drawer wrapped up inside the navy Argyle sweater she never wore because she always got too hot in it but wouldn't give to charity because it had cost forty-nine pounds, an amount that shouldn't be squandered.

The phone was answered on the third ring by a lady's Welsh lilt, which made sense because Cerys had googled the telephone code and it had said Carmarthen, same as the address on the header, same as the postcode. They were clever thieves, all bases covered.

'Hi. Sorry. I wonder if you can help me. I received a letter and was asked to call you.'

The lady waited for Cerys to say more. Cerys waited for her to ask something.

'Hello?'

'Yes, I'm here,' said Cerys.

'Lovely. Thought I'd lost you,' the lady laughed. 'The letter. What did it say? Which solicitor was it from?'

'Oh. Sorry. Of course. Sorry. It's from a Mr Kendrick. Mr Stephen Kendrick. And it says it's relating to the last will and testament of a Mr Thomas Morgan.'

'Lovely. I'll just see if he's available.'

He was.

And it was real.

Could she please come down come to their offices, not a dodgy rendezvous in a car park or down an alley, but to 37A The High Street, to sign some paperwork and please bring her passport plus two documents as a proof of address – a council tax bill, an energy supplier bill, a bank statement, you know the sort of thing.

'You might want to sit down Mrs Jones. It is Mrs?'

'Ms. I am already. I'm already sitting. I'm sorry but why do I need to visit you?'

Her head spun as her heart cha-cha-cha'd. She could get a day off work, hire a car and drive all the way there or get a train as close as she could so it was a more relaxing journey and she

25

only had to drive the last bit. Expensive though. Last minute train tickets were extortionate.

'Right. Lovely. Well then. The reason you've been sent the letter is we believe you wrote your name in the book at the church, that you said a prayer for Mr Morgan?'

'That's right, yes. But I'm afraid I didn't know him.'

She had to be honest in case it was a mistake. Doing bad things meant you brought bad luck upon yourself.

'No, that's fine. That's unimportant. Well now Ms Jones. Mr Morgan, Thomas, he stated in his will that all his assets should be divided equally between those who prayed for his soul when he was resting in the church. He had no siblings, no family alive, God rest his soul, and he was a kind gentleman, always wanted to help others.'

'Wow. Really? I—'

'So. As his solicitor I need to make sure that happens and as your name was in the book, legally that means you, Ms Jones, are a beneficiary of his will.'

She wanted to ask what she'd be getting but that would be rude and callous considering someone had died. Uncouth. Greedy. Grasping. And he'd said assets not money so it was probably an old car or a watch, a kayak as he was from the coast, a chunk of land from a field he'd farmed since he was a boy.

~

No-one was free to go with her. Friends had work, they were tired, they had kids, there were things on and they'd love to but you know busy, busy, busy. There was the swimming, the tennis, the gym class, the football. Fair enough. She got it.

Cerys didn't mention the trip to Seren. She didn't want a lecture, couldn't bear the questions: why are you spending so much money on a train ticket to go on a wild goose chase where you could end up dead in a ditch, an item on the news, that's what you want is it? Jesus, Cerys.

She didn't want the joy sucked out of the fun her imagination was having as it played *what if*, like when she bought lottery tickets and didn't check the numbers for days, weeks, months sometimes. Instead she'd look out of the bus window on her journey to and from work, imagining she'd won from one million to fifty million pounds, always enough to own a flat, her flat. There were the big things she'd buy – homes for her and her friends, a place in Wales because that's where her soul felt wisest. If it was fifty million she'd give up work and spend her time flitting between Wales and London which would be bliss, absolute perfection. January and February were her least favourite months so she'd spend those abroad somewhere warm because as a lottery winner she could afford it. Somewhere luxurious with pristine sheets and an ensuite, a hotel room big enough that it had a sofa and chairs in it. An immediate thing she'd do was go to John Lewis to buy new towels that were fluffy and sheets that were soft rather than thin and faded, plates that weren't chipped, new mugs just because she liked the colour of them, not because they were needed. Just like that. Check amount due, press enter. So much stuff that she'd need to get a taxi home, where she'd then have so much fun unpacking. She'd worry how much of the imaginary money she should gift to her family and friends. She'd keep the actual amount she won a secret or lie, tell everyone she'd won just enough to buy her flat and have money left over to live on as long as she was frugal. Sam had laughed so much when Cerys told her she'd lost sleep over it.

'Oh my God.'

'What?'

'You were up half the night worrying about the complications that might arise if you happened to win fifty million on the lottery. You're bonkers. Absolutely bonkers. That's so funny.'

Cerys laughed too. Sam was right. She was ridiculous.

But that didn't stop her dealing with all sorts of made-up scenarios as the train sped out of the metropolis into the countryside. She worried about how she'd get an imaginary kayak back to London or would they let her keep it in Wales, but would they charge her money for storage? She thought of Mr Thomas Morgan leaving her a cottage by the coast then shoved that out of her mind because it was beyond ridiculous and would only lead to disappointment, like the time she got an email saying she'd won a prize on the lottery and it turned out to be five pounds seventy. She didn't even know Thomas Morgan. And who knew how many people had signed the book plus he probably lived in one of the modern grey brick houses that you saw in the pretty towns at the end of a road, in a cul-de-sac near all the old fashioned gorgeous-looking cottages and you always thought, *ooh no, I wouldn't want to live in that one,* as if that was a choice you'd been given.

The other signees. They might be at the office too. Would she have to talk to strangers as well as Mr Kendrick? Probably. Of course she would. And it would turn out she'd spent £98 on an off-peak train ticket and £58 on a night at the nearest Travelodge only to be told that Mr Morgan had an old Ford Escort and a twenty-year-old caravan in Tenby that was to be divided between seven of them.

Jesus.

Look at her being all ungrateful. I mean, my God, what a kind man to leave his possessions to a stranger. He didn't have to. She wasn't sure that she'd do the same in his position.

~

The brass plaque was at head height to the right of a navy doorway that sat between a bookshop and a gift shop, opposite a cafe. Kendrick and Partners, Solicitors. Cerys didn't know what the letters after their names meant. She couldn't see a buzzer or bell. The door opened when she pushed on it. That would never happen in London. She liked that they weren't scared of who might traipse up the stairs that were covered in a dirty, dark green carpet. She picked up the post from the floor, mainly junk mail.

There was space on the first-floor landing for two people standing. She could go up more stairs to another floor or through a white door with a glass window. She peeked through it and saw a lady at a desk: dark brown hair, pink hairband, narrow shoulders. The room was white and bright, the opposite of the dark hallway. Cerys knocked as she pushed the door open. The woman beamed at her.

'Cerys?'

'Yes.'

'So lovely to meet you.' She stood up and leaned so far over her desk Cerys thought she'd fall over it. 'How was your journey? You live in London is it? But you must be from Wales with a name like that. I always said I'd call my first girl Cerys, if I have one. Better find a boyfriend first, though,' she laughed. 'You must be shattered, travelling all that way. Tea, coffee, water? What can I get you?'

The girl picked at her scalp as she waited for an answer, her jaw twisting from left to right like a cow chewing the cud. Cerys felt zen in comparison. She smiled to help calm her down.

'Water would be lovely, thank you.'

Cerys had spied the tray with a jar of instant coffee on it. She didn't like tea and only drank good coffee, fresh coffee, not granules from a jar like when she was at university, though then she'd bought the powdered stuff that was even cheaper, loading it up with sugar and milk which was fine as the flavour hadn't mattered. Its purpose had been to take away the taste of her cigarettes.

'Stephen,' the girl called. 'Stephen! She's here.'

'I'll be there now in a minute,' a man's voice called back through the closed door to Cerys's left.

'Is that for us?' the girl asked.

'Yes, sorry.' Cerys swapped the post for her drink.

'Where is he then? Goodness me, eh?' the girl said. She shook her head, still smiling as she knocked on the door to her right before popping her head into the room. Cerys wished her office in London was the same – her own space rather than open plan hot desks, a window that looked out over the high street, always something interesting to see and sunshine warming your back or your side or your front, depending on whether you worked there or were visiting. Her stomach gurgled. She coughed to clear her nerves. She checked in her bag again: passport, two bills proving her address, the original solicitor's letter, a photocopy of it safely at home plus another copy in her locker at work in case there was a fire because you never knew with electrics. Before she left for Wales, she'd unplugged everything except the boiler. She'd even switched off the cooker.

The receptionist stepped back from the door and a man in a navy suit, green tie, white shirt, messy hair, grey curls, beamed at her.

'Cerys,' he said with such warmth it was as if he was an uncle who hadn't seen her since she was five, excited they were going to spend some time together. 'Good to see you. So good to see you. How are you doing?'

He held out his arms as if to hug her. She put her hand out to shake. He took it in both of his, one shaking, one grasping, beaming, such a wide *I can't believe it* grin at Cerys, the receptionist, back to Cerys again.

'Tea, coffee, or something stronger?' He winked.

All three of them laughed, the receptionist the loudest and the longest. When Stephen coughed she stopped then grinned again. Cerys adored being surrounded by such positivity.

'I've got a water, thank you.'

'Excellent. Let's get this show on the road then, shall we? Come into my office. Come in. Come in. No calls for the moment, sweetheart.' The receptionist nodded and sat back down in front of her computer. 'Take a seat then Cerys. Take a seat. Marvellous. Let me get the file and we'll get started shall we.'

There were two chairs for visitors facing a large wooden desk that meant Mr Kendrick faced the door she'd just come through. There was a closed door to his right, next to a green tiled fireplace, grey metal mantlepiece surrounding it, similar to her flat but smaller and hers had maroon tiles. She sat in the chair nearest the large window, the sun strong enough to warm her hand and cheek. A good omen, the sun shining in Wales when Cerys was there, a rare and wondrous thing.

'Here we are then. Thomas Morgan. Terribly sad but quick and painless, in his sleep I believe, which is how we'd all like to go, isn't it? Here we are and there's him gone then.' He clasped his hands together and rested them on the desk, on top of the open file. He looked straight at her, his tone now serious. 'So. It was only you who signed the book Cerys. You did something very kind, I hope you realise that. And Thomas, he appreciated it and wanted to show his thanks with something that we, that he, hopes you'll think is a very good thing.'

Just her. No other strangers. No-one else at the meeting.

~

Cerys ordered a coffee and a slice of carrot cake with a thick coating of cream cheese icing after she'd checked it didn't have raisins in it, because otherwise she'd have gone for the coffee and walnut one. As she paid she noticed they served white wine and prosecco by the glass, a picture of a green bottle drawn with chalk on their blackboard with white bubbles surrounding it. She ordered a glass of that too. Eight pounds fifty, just for one glass. But she felt reckless and needed it to steady her nerves. She had a big decision to make, though in her head it was already sorted because really, who would turn down what they'd offered? It was like a lottery win. Better. Even better than a lottery win, because all the decisions had been made for her. She didn't have to take responsibility for any of it. She simply had to think about it and say yes or no. If her answer was yes then she was to go back to see Mr Kendrick and Mfanwy in the morning. Cerys had found out the receptionist's name when she hugged her before leaving. Cerys had hugged her back just as tight, in shock, full of hope, relief, disbelief at what was happening. If her answer was yes and she was absolutely sure about that, it was important she slept on it, they'd insisted on that, then she simply had to go back to their happy office in the morning to sign some forms and it would all be sorted within days, a week at the most maybe.

The girl at the till put the cake and coffee on the tray while the older lady, the manager or the owner Cerys presumed, poured cold fizz into a tall glass that had been sitting in their fridge along with the juice cartons.

'Celebrating are we?'

'Yes,' Cerys said, putting two pounds in their tip cup. The epitome of decadence.

A man in a red sweatshirt stood up to leave the table in the corner near the window, his bushy beard and moustache meaning he wouldn't look out of place back in Hackney. She made a beeline for his spot and slipped behind him, apologising when the tray touched his back but he was too preoccupied with his phone to notice her. As she ate the cake and sipped the prosecco, the bubbles from the milk on her cappuccino disappeared. Cerys wished she hadn't ordered it until after she'd finished her cold drink because now it was wasted. What use was it without creaminess? That was £2.50 down the drain. She caught herself. She should change her thinking. She could afford to do that now. She could afford another coffee if that was what she wanted. She had to get used to life being different, if she said yes and signed the papers they were preparing for her.

There was a house in Newport, Pembrokeshire, not the one in South Wales. Mr Kendrick had shown her a photo, a set of photos. It was one of those Grand Designs-type places with huge windows overlooking fields that led to the sea, a vast garden separating its grounds from the lane behind it that people walked on to get to the beach. It was the sort of village that was so stunning, with such a beautiful beach, that tourists went there for the day or to stay for weeks at a time. And it was a short drive to her beach, the good Welsh slate one. There was parking for cars, plural, and a gate at the bottom of the garden that led to the path that led to the sea because Thomas enjoyed a dip each day no matter the weather. He'd left the whole of the house and the land to her, all for saying a prayer over his dead body. He'd wanted to see if a stranger would provide a random act of kindness and she had. So that was her reward. Hallelujah and praise be.

The house was not all. There was a kayak. She'd laughed at that. It was in a locker by the beach in Aberporth. They sorted out the payments and upkeep so no need for her to worry about that bit. And a car. A one-year-old Toyota, one of the hybrid ones with the high base, sharp lines, fancy lights, and a satnav so she wouldn't get lost; one of the posh built-in ones, two models up from Seren's car, seven years newer.

'Do you drive?'

'I do but I've never had a car, not in London. There's no need for one there. They're so expensive to run and there's no parking of course. I'm rubbish at parallel parking too, that would stress me right out.' She was rambling. 'So I don't have a car, no, but I can drive. I hire them when I need them. I did today, to get here from the station.'

'Excellent. No need to hire one now eh? And no need to worry about parallel parking, it's all driveways and car parks around here. The streets are too narrow for anything else, I tell you. Now. The costs for the car, like the kayak, Thomas made sure everything was sorted out for you so no need to worry about that. The servicing will be done by David down the road. You can pop in to say hello to us when you're getting it done. We've an account with his garage so no need to fret about any sudden expensive exhaust problems. That's what happened to mine. The bill nearly gave me a bloody heart attack, I tell you.'

He tutted and shook his head. Cerys loved how Mr Kendrick wasn't jealous of her getting all these things. She would be if she was him. She'd be thinking *lucky bastard*, not in a good way.

'Do you own your flat in London, Cerys?'

'No.' She shook her head, for the first time unashamed of her answer because it didn't matter any more. She'd be a homeowner in Wales. And what a home, the sort of house someone who owned a Victorian townhouse in Islington would want when they saw it on a visit from London. And it was all hers. She'd be looking down on them, rather than up into their bay window wondering what it was like to have such a beautiful kitchen-dining room.

'Well then. That's lucky isn't it? As in this is something that could change your life, be a really good thing. And it makes things simpler I guess, decisions and the like.' Cerys pursed her lips as she nodded, his soft tone and kindness making her want to cry. If all she needed was money to live off, money for food and bills, she could get a local job, one that wasn't stressful, and live a simple life after making a simple decision, everything so easy. A perfect life just a signature away. 'And finally, there's the annual income.' There couldn't be more. This had to be a dream. Her stomach churned. She swallowed some bile, desperate for it all to be true, this pot of gold at the end of the rainbow that was only a foot away from her. 'An annual income of £60,000, so £5,000 per month, after taxes I might add. And like with the car and the kayak you don't need to worry about the legal side of things, HMRC etcetera because Rhys, you'll meet him if you decide to go ahead with it, he was Thomas's accountant so he'll be yours now and he'll sort everything out for you. Just give us and him your bank details and away you go. I can't believe he's an adult now, to be honest. I used to know him when he was yay high.' He held out his arm, palm below the top of the desk as he smiled, lost in the memory of looking down at the little one. Cerys waited, processed, her insides screaming with joy. She'd won the lottery. After all those years of playing it religiously every Wednesday and Saturday, she'd only gone and done it, differently to how she'd expected but what did that matter. 'Sorry. Ha! Lost in time. Rhys, right then, he'll arrange for the £5,000 to be paid monthly into your bank account. How does that suit you?'

Mr Kendrick beamed at Cerys. She beamed back at him with tears in her eyes, her hands shaking. She looked down at them, at her legs that were bobbing up and down as if she had a twitch, a bad one. It better not be Parkinsons, not when something so amazing had happened. She couldn't get ill now. That would be terrible.

'There is one condition though Cerys. A small stipulation but an important one. And as long as you're happy with it then all of this is yours.' He floated his hands over the papers on his desk like a magician who'd made a rabbit appear out of a hat. She saw the edge of the house, the car, the orangeness of the kayak. 'Whoever receives Thomas's possessions, his estate, his monies, they have to keep everything for themselves. They're not to share their luck, I'm afraid. And there is a reason. He thought that if someone did such a kind thing for him, they're probably the sort of person who always does kind things for others and therefore this time, he wanted to make sure they got everything for themselves. So they don't have to feel bad about it, so *you* don't have to feel guilty or selfish, he made the decision that you're not to give any of the money away or lend it to friends and family. And you can't let them stay in the house rent free for a year or suchlike because you're only using one of the bedrooms. They can visit of course, for a maximum of three nights at a time, that's the rule, and you can buy them dinner on a birthday like you might have done before, but nothing huge, no gifts over fifty pounds in value, absolutely no handing over chunks of cash, that's the main rule that he was very serious about. Thomas wanted to know that whoever received this would enjoy every penny he'd left them. You've worked hard for years, I'm sure. Your job, living on your own, having no back-up, no-one to share the burden, it's stressful isn't it?'

Cerys nodded. No more squishing onto the Central Line at 7.30 each morning. Instead there'd be lie-ins, walks on the beach, the best food, the most beautiful views from her living room. She could afford to shop for food in M&S, eat macarons for breakfast if she so desired. With no worries. There'd be no more anxious thoughts about the future and how she'd pay rent when she was too old for commuting, how she'd be able to keep doing her job as she got older, unable to keep up with the technology meaning the firm no longer wanted to employ her.

'Rhys will help you keep an eye on what you spend. He's very good at that sort of thing. And one other point, a tiny detail really, so far off that you don't need to be thinking about it now but the last thing is that in the case of your death, years from now I'm sure, well then you're to do exactly as Thomas did. You're to lie in the church in Mwnt, casket open, and you're to pass on the house, the car, the money, to whoever says a prayer for your soul before you're buried.'

'Buried where?'

'In the graveyard, the same one.'

'You mean there'll be a plot for me where he was?' Stephen nodded. 'And that's got to be part of the deal, no negotiating?'

'Yes. Is it a problem?'

Cerys sat back. Mr Kendrick scratched his eyebrow, worried the last point was a deal-breaker. You never knew what people believed in, what they wanted, what the after-life meant to them.

'No. Not a problem at all. A blessing if anything, a sign that I should do this. It's something I've always wanted. That's decided then. I'll do it. I'll sign whatever you need. You've got yourself a deal, Mister Kendrick.'

'Ha. Fabulous. Fabulous. But you must sleep on it, my darling. We don't want anyone thinking we bamboozled you into deciding. If you're of the same mind in the morning, if your answer is still yes, we'll be here at 9am sharp, all ready for you.'

~

Cerys spent the night checking the Google Maps street view of Newport and the house. Her house. The shops, the restaurants, the roads, the beach, the cove, the port, the yacht club, the cafes, the walks. How could a person manage to spend five thousand pounds a month on just themselves? She could buy a bag, a Mulberry bag, the oxblood Bayswater design that she stroked every time she was in John Lewis as she imagined one day being able to afford one. She googled bags, expensive jeans, new plates and cutlery. Imagine buying cutlery when you already owned some, just because it was more shiny. Would they deliver to Wales or should she buy it all in the Oxford Street store, hire a man with a van, get it delivered when the house was ready for her? She could afford it, a man with a van for a day, two days and a night in a hotel for him so he had a safe journey. It wouldn't matter what price was quoted.

She only managed three hours sleep but it didn't matter because she'd catch up during all the days she wouldn't be working in the future. She read through the forms, their language a mix of plain text and lawyer speak, nothing she could see that stood out as *don't sign me, I'm going to get you.* But she didn't sign because Mr Kendrick said it must be done in front of witnesses and not to worry because they'd arrange that.

She was outside the navy door at eight fifty, keen, so keen to make sure this dream didn't slip away from her. Mfanwy let her in. Mr Kendrick appeared from the door next to his desk. Footsteps clumped up the stairs, a man and a woman laughing. David the car mechanic man, Cathy who managed holiday lets in the area and her house, Cerys's new home. They were always popping in to witness signings for Stephen.

'Nice to meet you,' echoed round the room as hands were shaken.

It was signed. It was sealed. Mr Kendrick called Rhys, whom he put on speaker phone, who transferred the first payment into her current bank account immediately but suggested the next one should go into a bank that had a local branch, one in their town, that would be easier in the long run, would she be alright with that? He could arrange it all for her.

'Of course. That's a great idea. No problem. Absolutely.' She smiled. 'So kind of you. Thank you. Thank you so much, all of you. I really appreciate it.'

She kept adding a thank you onto the end of her sentences, three more times before she headed out to check her balance at the cashpoint five doors up from the cafe. Five thousand seven hundred and twenty-one pounds. She raised her hands in the air. Thank you, Jesus.

~

Stephen, Mfanwy, David and Cathy watched Cerys head to the bank, on the verge of running, to check if it was real or was she dreaming, some cad playing a cruel trick on her.

'Fingers crossed then,' said Mfanwy, holding up both hands.

'They're all the same,' sniffed Cathy. 'It'll be just like last time.'

'Now, now,' said Stephen. 'You don't know that. None of us do.'

'Ha,' said David, as cynical as his sister.

'David,' snapped Stephen before switching to a gentler tone. 'None of that. We don't know. We can't tell by looking. That's the whole point, isn't it? No pre-judging. No assuming. You know the rules.'

'I'm just saying it always ends up going the same way. Tell me a time when it hasn't and I'll be quiet but—'

'Lots to do. Best get on,' said Mfanwy, her eyes panicked, not wanting more badness to come, wondering what she'd got herself into. 'Whose coat is that jacket lying there on the floor then?'

'Mine. Sorry Fan. Sorry.' David picked it up and carried it out with him.

Mfanwy shook her head. Honestly, it was like looking after children.

SIX

The boys were playing Swingball in the garden. The dishwasher was ten minutes into its cycle. Coffee had been served in matching china cups and saucers, the good ones from the wedding list. Seren and Mark sat slumped in their dining room chairs, exhausted. Cerys felt bad for what she was about to tell them. Her stomach churned up the small portion of lasagne she'd managed to eat. Why was she nervous when it wasn't a bad thing? She sipped her coffee and breathed in the nutty aroma as if it would give her courage. Seren served good coffee and that made Cerys feel a rush of warmth towards her. She sipped again, putting it off, delaying, sip again. Deep breath. Sip, sip. Now or never.

'Do you remember when we went to that church by the beach, when I went in, the day after the funeral but you wanted to get back so you headed to the car then came into the church to find me?'

Seren made her eyes all *why are you mentioning that when I told you he can't talk about it yet, why are you bringing this up now when it's still too painful?* Mark went to the fridge to get another beer. Seren mouthed *nice one* at her older sister. Mark sat back down. Cerys finished her coffee.

'Well? What about it?' asked Seren.

Cerys couldn't look up as she told them. She stared at her fingers that picked at a non-existent stain on her new dark green linen trousers. She'd bought them in Whistles. Not the sale rack she always headed straight for, the only part of the store she usually contemplated buying an item from and even then it had to have at least fifty per cent off before she considered it. Not this time. The guilt at buying them full price, how decadent to walk out of the store with a bag that didn't have the word SALE stamped in red across it. She had to keep reminding herself it was okay, she could afford it.

Seren and Mark shifted in their seats. She could see their feet and legs moving. Mark got another beer before she'd finished disclosing all the details. Seren leaned forward. She talked fast.

'What do you mean he's left it to you? You didn't give them your bank details? How do you know it's not a scam? What have I told you? You're so naive Cerys, such a fool. Your passport. You let them have a copy of your passport? I mean, a house? Show me the house. Show me the photos.' She snatched Cerys's phone off her and scrolled through the eleven pictures. 'This can't be yours. It's beautiful. My god, look at the kitchen. Is that granite? Look at the views, Mark. The furnishings. It's incredible.' He accepted the phone and sank lower into his chair as he flicked through the proof. Cerys wanted to snatch it off him. They were her photos, and what if he went past the house ones into her private business. 'And they said there's no mortgage. Seriously? But how do you know it's real? Have you been to see it, walked around it? Have you got the keys? Did they give you the deeds for it?' Cerys shook her head. Seren sat back, triumphant as she filled her glass with more white wine. 'See. It's a con. They've reeled you in and you've fallen for it hook, line and sinker, giving them your bank details. Honestly, Cerys. You should call them from here, your bank. Call them right now and tell them to put a stop to your cards and any online transactions before you lose too much money. I can't believe it. They've totally scammed you after all I bloody well told you. Honestly.'

'They haven't.'

'They have. You need to get real. I'm sorry but—'

'Can I have my phone back please?' Mark passed it to her. 'There's an annual income too. They've put money into my account already, rather than taking stuff out of it. So it's not a scam, not a trick by cheaters. And there's a car.' She rubbed it in. She rubbed it into her sister's face because of all the times she'd been called a fool by her. She was not a fool. She was the equivalent of a god-damned lottery winner. 'A top-of-the-range one-year-old Toyota CH-R with all the servicing paid for and an automatic upgrade every five years. It's even got a built-in sat nav, one of those big screens in the middle of the car.'

'As if,' Seren laughed. 'A car, a house and money? Are you on drugs? You've got to be kidding me. How much money?'

It was more than her sister and brother-in-law earned working ninety hours a week for forty-eight weeks a year. Telling them the real amount would be a step too far. She'd go with a little white lie. God didn't mind the white lies. That's what they were taught when they were little.

'Fifteen hundred pounds a month. They pay all the household bills so it's enough for a simple life. Enough to keep me going.'

Seren sat back in her chair, arms folded. 'You're getting all of that for a prayer? For nothing, basically?' She wished she could drag hard on the cigarettes she'd given up eleven years ago in order to be healthy when she started trying for a baby. 'But I was in the church too. I saw him as well. I said 'Rest in Peace.' She waited for Cerys to get what she was implying but her older sister just squinted, showing up more wrinkles round her eyes. 'I'm not being funny but doesn't that mean some of it's mine, that it's ours?' She nodded to include Mark. 'Oh my God. It does. You need to tell them. You need to tell them that I prayed for his soul too which means we can share it. Or they might double the money. You don't know do you? Did they say how they worked it out, when it would run out, how many years you'd get it for?' Cerys hadn't thought that her sister would want in on the gift because she'd been there too. Her insides flipped. Should she tell Mr Kendrick about the jealousy that had turned to euphoria in front of her? 'Mark.' Seren slapped her husband's arm with the back of her hand even though she already had his attention. 'This changes everything. Oh my god. It means we don't need to worry so much about the future, the present even.' In a millisecond Seren decided that a sister on her own with no children and no costs, she wouldn't need all that money. It was a waste her having it. She already had spare cash to spend with only herself to think about. Try paying for school shoes three times a year for two growing boys on top of all the bills and a thirty-year mortgage. 'This makes up for all your Mum's will nonsense, no offence. I mean you know I loved her but Christ. Maybe there is a god. Ha! Imagine that. This is a good thing. It is. It's such a good thing. It changes everything.'

Cerys watched her sister, confused that she'd turned the story, the good luck, from being about Cerys into being about her, her husband and the life of her boys. She hadn't listened. That wasn't what Cerys had said or implied and now she'd have to reel in her sister's dream which would make Cerys look like the baddie. From good to bad with a click of a finger, click clack, just like that. Seren's imagination was running away with itself, desperate to escape the present and live in a different future, which Cerys understood, of course she did, she used to daydream about it all the time. That understanding made her more anxious about telling Seren *no that cannot happen* plus *they'd said she couldn't share.* Should she stop her now or let her keep on going? Would that be cruel, lead to even more damage?

'The solicitor said you had to have actually signed the book and said a full prayer. He was very clear about that.'

'Pfff. That's just details. Rest in Peace is a prayer when you think about it. It's just a short one, a blessing. And I did a sign of the cross so you can tell him that too and that I was going to sign the book but you made me leave in a rush, or Mark did. That's it. You say to them that Mark came down just as I was about to sign it. I'd picked up the pen and was going to write my name down but then my bloody husband shooed us out of there.' In Seren's mind that was true, nearly true. If she hadn't been in a rush she would have written her name and address below Cerys's, of course she would. 'You will say that won't you?

43

And don't worry, you can still live in the house and have the car, that's fine. Unless you don't want it. You don't like driving do you? You always get nervous. We can sort that out later though, the main thing is we'll both get the monthly money, that's what's fair. And we'll come for holidays, only when it suits you. Mark, just imagine, four or six weeks a year, all of the school holidays right by the beach in a huge, glamorous house for free. Free! Easter and the May half term when they charge a fortune for places. It'll be amazing. And the money. A bit extra each month for treats. So appreciated because it's so unexpected. I could go down to three days a week at work or both of us do four. That'd be incredible. Call him on Monday, Cerys. Do you want me to be with you? I can phone in sick if you think I should be there to talk to him too, no problem. And if he needs to talk to Mark as well that's fine, isn't it honey?'

~

Cerys hadn't realised a dream coming true could make a person feel so blue.

Lie.

Lies.

Liar.

If that was true she wouldn't have been so worried about telling them. She'd been nervous beforehand and rightly so. Look at how well she knew her sister.

The tube lurched to a stop. She walked from Mile End, not even looking behind her to see if a bus was coming. She must not let her sister spoil this. But she would tell Mr Kendrick about it. If she didn't, she'd always be thinking *what if Seren's right and it's not really mine*. What if she didn't deserve it. If Cerys got the house and the money by cheating she'd have brought bad luck upon herself and be doomed to hell or a terrible future. She didn't want to jinx her good fortune by keeping secrets;

44

she had to be a good and honest person like Thomas Morgan had obviously been.

~

Kind Mr Kendrick was having none of it. His tone was firm when he mentioned *your sister*, back to kind when he told Cerys it was all hers and that was what the heavens wanted, fate if you like. The words Rest in Peace were most definitely not a prayer. Seren hadn't signed the book so that was that as far as the rules were concerned. It was all about the detail, as is often the way in life, and he'd have a word with Seren himself, sort it out, explain everything. It wasn't fair that this had become Cerys's problem. She needed to concentrate on moving house.

'You need to look forward to going forwards,' he laughed.

Mr Kendrick was her solicitor now. He was there to solve her problems and deal with any difficulties. She wasn't to worry about a thing. What was her sister's phone number?

~

Seren put the phone down on *that man*. She did not like him. Not one bit. How dare he? How dare he use such a strict tone as if he was a teacher cross with a cheeky pupil. She wasn't cheeky. She'd made good and fair points. He hadn't listened properly, that was his problem.

She ran to vent her anger. No-one from work lived near enough to catch her pulling the sickie. She sprinted because she didn't have long before school finished, before the boys were home, before Mark came home, before the evening ended and another day began, the same as yesterday, the same as all the days last week and the weeks before them. She held back tears. She could curl up behind the pine trees, bend over and sob, let it all out. What was wrong with her? She needed to be strong.

Why hadn't she signed the book? Such a small, simple gesture. If she'd signed the book their life would now be different, easier. She could work fewer days a week, be less exhausted. All of Mark's wages could go towards the mortgage so it was paid off ten years early. And some of the new extra money would be for fun, she'd have made sure of that. It would have been spent on treats, days out, holidays, nice clothes maybe. They could go on holiday twice a year rather than once for ten days, only eating out one night in the middle of their stay and on the last evening. That was their rule because it was so expensive to eat at a restaurant with a family of four. She could have ensured they had enough money to eat out every night of a holiday if she'd written her name and address in a book, in a column, between the lines on a piece of paper. But she hadn't. She'd missed the present moment because she'd been too focused on getting Mark back to the house, to his brothers. That wasn't such a bad thing was it? It didn't deserve such a momentous punishment. She was kind, looking after her husband who was grieving his newly dead mother, who'd left them each seven thousand pounds after funeral costs and solicitors fees. God-damn it. She pushed herself up the hill to overtake the man running ahead of her. She wanted to scream and wail, had secretly smashed a glass against the wall of the garage. So angry. Disappointed. And hurt, in so much pain from what Mark's mum had done, who she'd loved so very much. Seren didn't understand it.

Her friend Tallulah said at least you were in the will, at least she thought of you. Her father was a c-word, everyone thought so. He'd treated his children like shit his whole life, then when he died he left everything to his new girlfriend of two years who made it clear she wasn't going to give any of his children a penny. Three years later Tallulah still hated her dead dad and now Seren understood why. She empathised when Tallulah ranted and raved, eaten up with anger whenever they saw her.

Seren felt mean, greedy and furious, which wasn't who she wanted to be. It wasn't who she used to be, so why was it overwhelming her now? Because of life. A life of first world problems, she knew that, but work was stressful and she was so tired all the time. There was no respite. Work, work, work, work, the boys, cooking, one night out a month if it was a friend's birthday, money always tight and budgeted so carefully and now the tease, the torture of a dream life she could have had that she'd never be able to forget about.

'Move on,' said Mark. 'It's happened. There's nothing you can do to change it so there's no point in getting so upset about it.'

She'd sighed heavily then smiled and nodded as if agreeing with him. She didn't want him to know how nasty her thoughts had become. If he saw how it was eating her up inside he might wonder exactly who he'd married; a good person shouldn't be thinking the bad things she was.

'At least you don't need to worry about her now.'

'What do you mean?'

'Cerys,' he said. 'How many times have you worried about where she'd live when she was older, in her sixties, her seventies, because she hadn't bought somewhere. You used to say *how will she pay the rent, she'll have to keep working until she drops down dead.* Now she's got a place forever hasn't she, so that's a good thing.'

'True,' said Seren. 'I hadn't thought of that. That's a really good point, you know.'

In the bathroom her face contorted like a mad old gargoyle as she wished she could scream *fuck you all* to the universe.

If she was honest, really honest but don't tell anyone because it's so shameful, what she'd meant was Cerys should buy a place so she had somewhere to live until her dying days, yes, but also part of Seren used to think if her sister didn't get married, if she didn't have kids, then she might leave her home to their boys and that would be them sorted. In a good way, through love, because they loved their Aunty Cerys even if she didn't seem so keen on them because they were a bit of a handful sometimes, but that's because she wasn't used to children.

47

Now that would never happen. Because it wasn't allowed, that was a rule. Cerys could live in the Welsh house for her lifetime but not pass the property on. Fuckers. Seren could never, ever tell anyone about the selfish thoughts spinning through her head because she knew they made her seem like a very bad person. Look at her life, her family's life. She was lucky compared to lots. She didn't feel lucky. The opposite. There'd been a way out of the family's current doldrums but she, the mother, had let them down, missed the chance to change it. Why couldn't luck have thrown her new wealth rather than an annual pay rise that barely covered the January increase in train fare? She'd have been eternally grateful, never taken it for granted. She'd have said a prayer of thanks every morning, honest to God she would have.

Sprinting down their road Seren wished she'd increased her speed earlier to make her lungs hurt as much as her heart. She wished she was twenty-five again, knowing what she knew now. She'd have had the boys later on in life so their central London flat went up more in value, meaning their suburban mortgage was smaller. If only she'd made different choices. She'd done it all wrong. She wasted time worrying about things she couldn't fix, was constantly trying to control the future, and look where it had got her. Nowhere. To the same place she was a year ago and four years before then, meaning that's what her future would be. Whereas Cerys had sailed along not giving a moment's thought to what was ahead, which she should have done because it was up to her to sort it out and be responsible for her life, not other people, and now she'd landed on her feet. More than that. She'd been given the best thing ever and the rude man, that smarmy man, he'd confirmed it was all true. Cerys wasn't allowed to share her winnings: a meal out, yes, but no payment towards her sister's mortgage or car, no savings accounts for her nephews, not even *I've booked a villa for us all in Majorca for two weeks, my treat.* Nothing over fifty pounds. For some reason that was oh so very important. A pittance. A god-damned pittance from the god-damned dirty bastards.

~

Seren locked the door and lay in the bath, muscles tight from the longer-than-usual run, mind exhausted from the bad thoughts that kept churning up her brain, keeping her awake at night, that meant she kept running on near-empty, drained of all energy. Was that why she must not win a good thing, because she thought bad things? Was there a god who could see inside her head, who knew the truth, that she wasn't as nice as her smile and volunteering once a month at the charity shop made her out to be? She tried so hard but couldn't stop the fury, even though it felt like her brain wanted to burst out of her skull to find a different owner.

She imagined winning the lottery in the same way Cerys had but because she was in a foul mood, still unable to shake off the nah-nah feeling, it all got stuck. Instead of a win bringing her joy she went through all the people she knew who she wouldn't share it with. Not to be mean. There were valid reasons. The taxes they'd skipped paying, legally but my god, they paid so little compared to her PAYE job; the inheritances they'd already received whereas look at her and Mark with nothing, de nada; the money two of her friends' parents gifted them each month that they took for granted because it was only £400. Only. Seren would smile understandingly when really she wanted to scream *do you know how lucky you are, go back in time and imagine never having had anything from anyone ever you fucking moaners.*

The f word had come in since Gwen had died. That'll be the grief, the article in the paper had said, it made people all sorts of angry. She closed her eyes. It wasn't her. It was her circumstances, not her fault. It was the death that had done it.

49

SEVEN

Seren stood behind Cerys's friends as they toasted her sister's future, Wales, wished her the best luck in the world, a good friend, a wonderful friend, how we'll miss her but free holidays at the beach, guys. Wey-hey. They all laughed and raised their glasses. Cerys glowed in front of the fireplace with the grey surround and maroon tiles. She beamed, not even a hint of sadness at what, at who, she was leaving behind.

Seren was always surprised at how many friends her older sister had, enough to fill the living room that had two sash windows, a table, a sofa, an armchair, so many friends that they spilled out onto the stairs and down the hallway.

She watched them all, paying particular attention to their eyes. It was the eyes that told her the truth. She spotted Clare and Megan looking at the floor after a few wines, sad, questioning their lives, wondering what such good fortune felt like. The others in the room seemed okay with it. But of course they were. They'd bought homes in Hackney twenty, twenty-five years ago, that were now worth ten times the price they'd paid for them. Seren opened another bottle of wine. She wished she'd stayed in her place in Balham, not had kids, perhaps Mark was still in the picture, perhaps not. Who cared? How easy life would now be. How uncomplicated. No need to worry about anyone but herself, which would make life so very simple. No boys to take to A&E; no parents evenings where she was told they were a bit raucous, a bit bitey; no separating them at home where ninety per cent of the time they fought like cats and dogs and some days, lots of days if she was honest, she wasn't even sure if she liked them. How uncomplicated it would be to not have them and their issues in her life. Just her and work and a central London flat that was tidy because no-one made a mess in it. She'd cook food when she felt like it, not because she had to. It would all be eaten because it was what she wanted. She'd go to restaurants a few nights a week because she could afford to. And to cap it all, she'd have been able to retire at fifty or fifty-five say, rather than sixty-seven.

'Ha,' she said out loud. The man next to her gave an uncertain smile as he raised his eyebrows. She needed another drink. Fuck everything.

'It's very generous of her. So kind,' Seren pointed at the table covered in what Mark had noted were very expensive wines: red, white, rosé and champagne, Taittinger no less, fifty-something pounds a bottle according to Google. She counted thirty-six bottles including the ones that were under the table plus there were empty ones in the kitchen when they'd got there. And the catering, organic curries from the local deli whose staff were in the room, serving everyone and clearing up afterwards. The whole shebang must have cost a small fortune but of course her sister could afford it now. Whoop-di-doo-da.

'Did you get some food? The veggie one's delicious,' said Cerys. 'Do eat. There's loads of it.'

'Ummmm.' Seren gulped down her wine like a proper alkie. You could always tell the ones with the problems by the speed of their drinking, wine like it was water, a gin and tonic as if it was lemonade. But she wasn't one of those mums with that problem. It was just today and this party that were doing her head in. 'It's so great you got people in to do everything, no cooking, no clearing up, not even glasses to wash. Brilliant. You hired them all, did you? So lucky. So easy having parties when you don't have to do anything. I'd be throwing them all the time.'

Seren laughed and smiled. Cerys didn't. She was unable to pretend that the words were sincere, that there was true love or good wishes in them.

'You can come down for a weekend. You're always welcome, you, Mark and the boys.'

Lies, lies, lies. But Cerys didn't want her sister spoiling her special afternoon. Hopefully she'd go soon, have to get back to her children, leaving Cerys to relax and enjoy time with the friends she was closer to than her family.

'Ha. You owe me a tenner Mark,' Seren called across the room to her husband, who ignored her.

Seren had bet him ten pounds that Cerys would say those words, after hearing her tell three friends in separate clusters that they must come and visit, within half an hour of them arriving.

'Easy on the wine,' he'd replied, his one beer finished, hands now being warmed by a bowl of hot food. 'You need to be careful with what you're thinking. You're becoming really bitter. Let her be happy.'

He'd walked away to chat with Dan, one of Cerys's friends from university. So Seren drank more and more. Watching. Wondering. Wishing.

'I am nervous about this you know, Seren. It's a big thing leaving everyone, moving out of London. I'm used to seeing my friends all the time and—'

'Oh please.'

She walked away to find her husband, needed to head home before she screamed *don't you dare, don't you fucking dare complain to me about this. I'd take it without a second thought so don't you dare, not ever, not near me, do you hear me? Don't you dare moan about what you've been given.* She buttoned it, as she always did with every acute feeling.

~

Mark drove as Seren sobbed. She wept and wailed as unhappy drunkards are prone to do, unable to stop once she'd started.

'We can visit in the summer. It's not that far off.'

She cried harder. How could he be so wrong about the reason his wife was upset? How could he not get her, not be thinking the same as her? What was their marriage, where were they, who were they? She was a bad person. She wished she could scoop her brains out and replace them with someone else's. Negative thoughts thrashed inside her head about every bloody thing in her life. She didn't know how to enjoy a normal day any more, dreaded waking up after not sleeping properly only to have to face another twenty-four hours so similar. She wanted to scream. She wanted to rip her hair out, claw the skin off her scalp, spoon the insides of her head out and throw the bloody mess over the walls and ground, splattering it everywhere until her body, flailing round, desperate for peace, found it by falling to the floor. Still. Quiet. Finished.

EIGHT

Cerys' possessions fitted in the Transit van she'd hired, along with a driver. The cost had barely dented the money that had been transferred into her bank account that month. She'd thought of being a passenger but that was bound to be awkward on such a long journey and she didn't want to chit chat. She wanted to read, picture herself in her new home, eat truffles, imagine lying in each day before she walked on the beach every morning, afternoon, evening, rather than setting an alarm to get up for work.

She'd mulled over asking Sam or Megan to go with her but decided it was important she arrived solo. This was a new adventure for her alone, hundreds of miles from Hackney, her home since she was twenty-three when everyone lived there because it was so cheap as it was a bit dodgy, guns and drugs and rave'n'roll parties under the railway arches.

The flat looked barren without her bits and bobs, which were all that were missing. She hadn't owned the furniture, white goods, bathroom fittings.

~

The floor to ceiling windows that fronted the kitchen-dining-living room were more stunning than they'd looked in the photos. The worktops were marble, not granite. The sea was closer than it had appeared in the pictures. Her sea, her view, her green grass, no moss, no weeds, a lawn that rolled down the hill to the lane on the other side of the fence, fronted by bushes which housed a gate that led to the path that led to the dunes, the beach, the water that was close enough she could smell it but far enough away that it would never threaten her property.

Behind her was a silver double-sized fridge like the ones in America-ca-ca, one shelf already full of food. *We thought you'd be tired after your journey and need some bits to get you started.* On the coffee table was a file containing leaflets: take-away menus, details of yoga classes, tennis lessons, library opening times and the days the cinema showed films in Theatr Mwldan, only a twenty-minute drive away in Cardigan. Plus if there were any problems that needed a plumber, an electrician, a builder, she was to call Cathy, remember her, she witnessed the contract signing, born in England but nice, very efficient. She'd be popping by soon to say hi and would always make sure Cerys was given top priority so she didn't have to worry about anything.

Mr Kendrick stood to her left.

'Please Cerys, call me Stephen. It's the third time we've met and we've had all those chats on the phone.'

Rhys, the accountant, was on her right, a little behind her. He was younger than she'd expected, his dark curly hair making him look like Bob Dylan on the cover of the *Blonde on Blonde* album but only an inch taller than her, short for a boy, a young man, so young he must still live with his parents. They were her unkempt bodyguards, no good in a physical fight but not to be messed with when it came to facts and figures. Her wealth guards, her trusting guards, her property and income managers.

'We'll leave you to it shall we? You must be tired after your journey and it's a lot to take in.'

'Yes. Thank you. Honestly, I can't thank you enough. I—'

So teary these days. So embarrassing.

'Hey.' Stephen rubbed her back, him the kind father. She sank towards him, accepting his comfort. 'No need to thank us. It's our job, isn't it Rhys? And you've made it an easy one. Thomas would be so happy he's left it all to you. He'd really like that. You'd have got on well, the pair of you.' They all smiled, quiet as they walked to the door, a clear path through her boxes that had arrived the day before. 'Any problems, you know where we are.'

She nodded and waved goodbye then ran upstairs to watch them from one of the front bedrooms, curious about how they acted when she wasn't with them. They were already in their cars. Rhys reversed out onto the road in his black Fiesta and Stephen turned his Toyota round, the same make as her car but grey rather than bright orange.

'It's good to have a bright colour on these roads in winter. Young lads drive too fast. All the better to see you with my dear. And it matches your kayak!'

They'd all laughed.

He indicated, even though it was only the drive he was leaving, cautious to the last. He didn't pull out. A cyclist in a red top went past, head down, helmet on, speeding by as fast as a car that kept to the speed limit. Stephen looked right then left then right again, and exited onto the road.

Cerys opened the box labelled 'bathroom'. She took out a bottle of Molton Brown hand wash and matching hand lotion, a new grey towel, thick, never used before, soft rather than hard and stringy like all her old ones that she'd given to the charity shop. She put them in the downstairs bathroom and washed her hands to kill the train journey germs. The smell reminded her of the time she'd gone to the Wolseley for Sam's birthday brunch. That's how tasteful her life was now, as good as the Wolseley, and she had the money to keep buying that brand so it was her constant, rather than whichever soap was on offer at the supermarket. Molton Brown was her new normal rather than kept for best, like when she'd been gifted a bottle for Christmas and made it last all year. Or Aesop. She could even afford Aesop – though would they deliver to Wales? So expensive. *People are using food banks, Cerys; Aesop is a step too far.*

She checked that the bedrooms were as real and gorgeous as she'd thought when they popped in to look at each one on Stephen's tour, bright and white with muted shades of grey and green on the Farrow and Ball painted built-in wardrobe doors. The brushed steel light fittings made a satisfying clunk when you turned them on, expensive, unlikely to break after a couple of years like her old plastic ones. She flung herself onto the king-sized bed in the master suite that sat over the living room, looking out to the sea, the view catching the evening sun as it set on the water. There was a walk-in wardrobe that was as big as a single bedroom; her clothes wouldn't fill a quarter of the drawers and hangers. The ensuite, a room she'd always dreamed of, contained a modern white free-standing bath, a freestanding sink like you saw in posh people's houses in magazines, and a shower big enough to fit two people. There were words in German etched onto the tap and sink that proved they were high quality, expensive. And clean. All of it so clean, shiny, perfect.

Cerys recorded a video of the room, finishing with the view but she didn't click send, not yet. That would make her an insensitive show-off. Her friends could see it when they visited or if they asked her for a photo. She took her socks off to appreciate the thickness of the carpet, which felt as soft as the cashmere socks Seren had given her on her last birthday, *the most expensive they had, pure luxury, the absolute best, do you like them?* She'd needed to know that Cerys understood and appreciated how much money Seren had spent on her.

Cerys opened and closed all the kitchen cupboards. They were full of dishes, plates, serving bowls, glasses and cups, leaving little room for the new crockery she'd brought with her. She took one of their glasses, one of *her* glasses and filled it with cold water on tap from the fridge, squealing at the brutal noise the ice dispenser made. She sat on the U-shaped sofa to flick through the plastic folders in the file which made her feel even more like she was on holiday. She was tempted to walk down to the beach to explore her new surroundings, but the light was fading. She might get lost. And who wants to come back to a dark, empty house they aren't that familiar with? Not alone anyway, that would be too scary. Plus she didn't want to leave the house. It might disappear. Meaning she'd gone mad, imagined it all, and actually another family lived there. They'd call the police when she insisted on coming inside, shouting at them that she owned it thank you very much.

She would stay home on her first night. She was exhausted. Plus there were Marc du Bois pink champagne truffles in her bag which would go perfectly with the small bottle of prosecco she'd spied in the fridge. The kindness of Mr Kendrick. Stephen. And as she drank, she'd work out where the cinema was, the nearest bookshop and supermarket. Stephen had said it was a fifty-mile round trip but they were nice roads, she could drive at a good speed, so nothing like the stress of driving twenty five miles each way in London.

She took the car key from the silver bowl on the dresser in the entrance, wedging the small case Rhys hadn't carried upstairs in front of the door to stop it shutting on her. When she pressed the button the lights flashed on and off as the car unlocked itself. She stepped up to sit inside and stroked the steering wheel. Everything about the fittings spoke luxury to her who'd always hired the smallest, cheapest cars. She pushed the start button, disconcerted by no turn of a key. The dashboard lit up like a spaceship. She only knew the engine was on by putting her foot on the accelerator, so quiet was the mix of electric and petrol. The gear stick was high on her left so she didn't have to bend down to move it, not that she'd need to move it much because once it was in D all she had to do was steer. She'd never driven an automatic before, but Stephen had said it was easy, though if she wanted a lesson the local instructor could take her out. They could organise that for her. Maybe it was a good idea. The car was so perfect she didn't want to stall or bump it and he could teach her how to park. She pushed the indicator up, loving the sound it made, deep and mature rather than all clickety clackety. When she turned the lights on they shone over the grey garage door. She pushed through to full headlights then full beam which lit up the whole house and the land on both sides. The screen to her left kicked into action. She would not touch it in case she ruined it. For once in her life she'd read the instructions first. It wasn't like she didn't have time to learn how to use it properly.

'Oh my god. My car, my car, my very own car. I bloody love you.'

She kissed the steering wheel. It was real. It was beautiful and it was hers, like the building in front of her with its driveway big enough to easily turn the car round in. There was no need to ever get stressed when she was near home at the thought of finding a parking space and having to reverse into it. She looked at the empty passenger seat and grinned as if there was someone beside her to share the joy. But she was alone. She thought of her parents, briefly: too painful. They would not spoil the moment. She threw them out of her winning day and rested her head on the back of the seat as she tried to take it all in.

Sam had offered to come down with her at the last minute, it would be exciting, good to get out of London, she couldn't wait to see the place, but her enthusiasm made Cerys want to soak it all up on her own first. And it had felt cruel. You come with me then go back to work, to the bills, the stress, the tiredness, while I stay in Wales all sorted, not having to worry about anything ever again. Even though Sam wouldn't mind, wouldn't think like that, wasn't a jealous sort of person.

A coconut scent wafted under her nose from the cardboard tree hanging off the rear-view mirror, making her sneeze, making her feel like she was on holiday, smothered in suntan lotion. A good feeling. She turned round to look at the back seats. There wasn't a mark on them; it was as if they'd never been sat in. She reached over to open the glove compartment drawer. Inside it was an instruction manual. She flicked to the quick bit for the screen, wanting to turn it on properly. When she pressed the map button, a map appeared, clear and precise, meaning no more lifting her phone that was balanced half in and half out of the coin tray, to snatch a quick look at Google maps when she was at a red light, cursing if they changed to green too quickly.

She pressed the pre-set button and it offered one option. Home. A lady's voice spoke: 'You are home, your final destination.' Home. Where she was destined to be. You are home, Cerys. You are there. You are here. She was. Here was her home, her house, her place, her life. Her bottom lip curled down. She had a word with herself, determined not to cry at such luck. There'd been enough tears because of sadness in her life, she would not let joy be taken over by them too. Bastard tears begone. She was lucky. She was happy. Life was fabulous.

NINE

There was only one other person on the beach so early, watching a chocolate brown springer spaniel as he bounded through the shallows. The wind blew Cerys's hair over her face, making her nose itch. Every time she pushed it behind her ears it blinded her again. She walked backwards. The wind blew her hair behind her, problem solved. She breathed in deep, that smell, the air full of the salt from the sea which took her back to being little, the top of her head reaching her father's thigh, his hand so large, the safety as it held hers with his skin rough and tough compared to a child's soft palm. Seren was next to their mother, too young to remember the shapes which were all Cerys could see now. The side of her Dad in blue jeans and a fleece, their mother in khaki trousers rolled up to her calves, her blue fleece a brighter shade, more royal blue than the navy tone of her Dad's one. Brown hair on the both of them. And that was it. No individual odour, no sounds from their lips, not even a smile, a frown, a shout. Nothing but silhouettes. Tears ran down her cheeks, joining the tributaries of snot dripping out of her nose. She told herself they were caused by the wind rather than memories.

Cerys wiped her cheeks and the top of her mouth with the edge of her sleeve then closed her eyes. She pointed her face at the sun. Welcome to Wales, the land of your fathers. Her mum and dad had given their children Welsh names because that's where her dad's dad was from. It was a cause of great pride. He'd have moved the family there in an instant if only he could find a vacancy for the type of work he did and maybe he would one day, you never knew, but whatever happened him and Mum would retire there. Or they would have done if it weren't for their lives ending early. In their ignorant meantime they visited every summer and Easter. Who needed fancy holidays abroad, and bugs and aeroplanes? He'd have been proud, her Dad, so happy that his eldest now lived permanently in the land of dragons.

Just turned thirteen, she'd read his favourite Arthur and Merlin book. It made her believe magic could be real. In her mind she stood in a long flowing dress with wide cuffs that hung gracefully from her arms, flowers woven through waist-length wavy hair, Merlin in love with her as she walked through the grounds of the castle. Everyone was in love with him but he was in love with her. The sun shone. It was never cold and wet in those Welsh imaginings. Sometimes Lancelot fell in love with her too. He was more exciting, more fun by the sound of it. When the family were awake early in the campsite and the mist hung over the grass like a layer of icing sugar on a cake, she believed the myth was true, that it had the same amount of truth as the bible and God. There was no reason she could see for one to be believed over the other.

'Over the bridge and who's first to spot the dragon,' their Dad would call every time they crossed the River Severn, as they zoomed over the border between England and Wales. The dragon was a good thing, not scary. She loved it. And so did Seren, even though she'd pretend to not be bothered. Her mood depended on how tired she was, how much traffic there'd been, how much rain was dripping down the windows meaning packed lunches in the boot of the car as they were forced to walk round yet another stone circle.

Cerys had always felt like Wales was where she belonged. She used to tell her school friends with absolute certainty that she'd live there one day. A part of her blood carried the Welshness of her grandparents and all the family before them on both sides, or was that make-believe nonsense? No matter. It felt right and when something felt that right it couldn't be wrong. She was standing on Welsh soil now. She'd live there and one day she'd die there. She had made a good choice. Every day she could choose to walk on a beautiful beach. Even if it only stopped raining for an hour she was close enough that she could nip out and enjoy it, no big deal. On other days, when the sun was out longer, she'd travel up and down the coast visiting castles with their cute cafes and gift shops, or other beaches that only locals knew how to find. She'd enjoy the journey, the comfort of windscreen wipers that worked properly when the rain fell and a windscreen that didn't get misted up, confused by hot to cold to wet to dry all within an hour. She'd get to know the land, the coast, the mountains. There was nowhere more beautiful in the world. Deep breath. Ha. She sounded like her mother.

'Morning. You've not got a dog?'

'No.'

'Frank. Frank!' the lady called.

She could get a dog. Maybe. No. That would make exploring more complicated and what if it did a poo on her expensive sofa? Seren had looked after her friend's dog once and woken up to diarrhoea all over the kitchen floor, then it had bounded out of the room, up the stairs, over her bed with its new duvet cover, stinky liquid shit everywhere. It had taken her hours to clear up the mess and the stains never fully went away. The damn thing wasn't even hers.

'He's gorgeous.'

'You're on holiday? Lucky with the weather. This is the second day in a row without rain.'

The lady pulled the elasticated waistband of her navy trousers up higher over her rotund belly. Her accent was English. One of those posh English people who lived in Wales but never sounded like they were from there. Or was she one of the *my grandparents bought a cottage here sixty years ago* people, vying to reach the lowest denominator with the scruffiness of the house – it has an outside loo, no electricity, dirt on the floor and soot on the walls from the fire which was the only source of heat. Here before the other people, others not as good as them with no right to think they belonged, like those who'd owned a holiday cottage since before it was popular, a certain smugness, a certain sense of Welshness.

'Actually I've just moved here. I can't quite believe it. I feel so lucky, so excited.'

The lady raised her eyebrows and momentarily engorged her stomach further with the deep breath she'd taken.

'Whereabouts? Cardigan? Aberporth? Aberaeron?'

'No. Here.' Cerys turned and pointed to her house on the hill. 'That's my one. It used to belong to Thomas Morgan. You might have known him. Are you local?'

Cerys kicked herself. *Are you local.* So rude, such a touristy thing to say. And she was a local now or within a few months she would be. The lady was too busy with her dog to answer or perhaps the wind meant she hadn't heard the question. She'd knelt down to kiss her pet's face even though it was wet and sandy. Cerys didn't understand the appeal when the creature wasn't dry.

'Help me up, would you.' The lady leaned heavily on Cerys's arm. As she pushed herself up to standing she squeezed her hand. 'You take care dear, lots of care, you hear me. Come on Frank. There's a good boy. Time to go home. Come on darling.'

Bemused, confused, Cerys watched the lady hobble towards the path that turned into a ramp that led to the town. Was that a warning or just a phrase like *have a good day*? Her head hurt. She needed coffee. Too little sleep meant she'd read too much into the sentence, of course it did. She turned to face the sea and raised her hands in the air, daring the wind to blow her over but instead it blew under the bottom of her hoodie, pumping her up with cold air. Freezing now. She needed proper clothes in order to enjoy the scenery. She'd kit herself out and that would help her fit in; then she'd go to events in order to make herself a local. Her stomach rumbled, leading to a hollow burp.

Food. She needed food. Food and a decent coffee. She turned to walk towards the path, the old lady faster than she looked, totally gone.

A family was setting up a windbreaker to mark their spot, best get out while the sky was dry. Next to them, a man was leaning on the rocks, watching her. Or his face was pointed towards her, but she couldn't tell if his eyes were open or closed like hers had just been. He could be studying the shore, the sea, the waves. He pulled a wetsuit out of a blue Ikea bag and balanced on one leg to put it on. Not watching her. The narcissism, Cerys. He looked up as he wobbled on one foot, directly into her eyes. Even though it was a public space she felt like she'd intruded on an intimate moment, was embarrassed to be caught staring at him as he dressed. She hurried up the path, purposefully not looking right or left in case visitors thought that weird lady was way too much into their business. When she reached the ramp she couldn't resist. She peeked over her shoulder. The man was bounding through the shallows like the dog had been. He jumped onto his board and paddled over the waves to the deeper water until all you could see was the bobbing of the red bits of his wetsuit. If the wind felt freezing imagine the temperature of the water. How could he bear it? The ground beneath her turned to rippled concrete. She tutted at the bicycle that had been thrown in the bushes; even in Wales lazy buggers fly-tipped their rubbish.

~

There was a cosy corner behind the counter, a fire for winter with two armchairs and a table in front of it. Outside offered shade for summer, huge parasols on the three tables big enough to ward off both sun and rain. She didn't tell the waitress she'd just moved to the area. She'd become a regular first, wait for them to ask her about herself which they were bound to do, one day. People did. Friendly people. She'd leave big tips every time she visited so they liked her, looked forward to serving her and chatted with her about this, that and the other, looks like the sun might make an appearance today, Madam.

As it was her first morning, all normal rules of life were thrown out of the window. She deserved a treat, so she ordered a scone with jam and clotted cream, plus a cappuccino, followed by a second one.

'Not my normal breakfast,' she joked.

The waitress smiled, not caring. Another table was impatient to give her their order, a family of five, cute, only one of the kids whining. Cerys didn't mean to sound so desperate for a chat. She checked her phone but there was no signal which meant she had to take note of the food she was eating and enjoy the moment. She studied the menu to see what she'd choose next time. Home-made soup would be good for lunch as long as it wasn't pea flavour. And their smoothies looked delicious. They were so nutritious, better than creamy coffees. She'd have one each and every day, her heart and organs grateful. In the summertime. The cafe was shut from 1 November to 31 March. How did they make a living in those months? Did they all still live there? She hoped so; it would be too bleak a place without people, too dark and grey and silent.

After using the toilet, Cerys explored. Cute houses. Old people. Pretty flora. A gorgeous church at the top of the hill. Ancient graves. A cobbled alley. Only one fresh burial. Iain Jenkins, aged eighty three. A good age. You couldn't complain about that one.

Her hands itched where the soap had dried them. She retraced her steps and turned into the road where, ahead of the Spar, there was a shop full of cushions and creams, lotions and potions. A perfect aesthetic, as Sam would say.

The bell tinkled when she went inside. The fragrance from a diffuser reminded her of Sam's garden. A young lady smiled at Cerys. Her beige overalls matched the hessian cloth bags, the tissue paper on the counter, the brown and green glass bottles on the shelves.

Cerys checked in her bag that she had her new debit card. Rhys had said not to bother with a credit one.

'What's the need? Really, what need is there for you to have one, considering your monthly income. You don't want to go getting into debt now, do you?'

He was right. Of course she didn't.

She took a step up into the second part of the shop and was greeted by an older lady in the same overalls as the young girl. She was standing in front of a white ceramic trough that had two taps hanging over it. Behind her was a dark wooden counter with drawers underneath it like in an old-fashioned apothecary's, the type everyone threw out in the fifties when they fitted shops out in plastics and now spent a fortune desperately sourcing on eBay so it suited their vintage look. Cerys bet the lady had a soothing voice that matched her flowing movements.

'Sorry, am I allowed in this bit?'

'Of course.'

She spoke slowly. Was she stoned? Or on diazepam. Perhaps she'd taken too high a dose that morning. Cerys scanned the shelves. There didn't seem to be any products for sale.

'Can I help you?' the lady asked.

'I'm after some hand cream.'

'Wonderful. Would you like to come over and try some?'

Cerys felt her eyelids droop after barely any sleep, a full stomach, the lady's gentle tone which was stronger than the caffeine in her cappuccinos. There were rows of brown bottles with pumps on a shelf just above the sink that you couldn't see from where Cerys had been standing.

'They're all organic and we use Welsh ingredients where possible. I'm sensing nothing too sweet for you. Shall we try the citrus blend? Or, if you'd like to relax, there's the lavender which is just gorgeous, perfect for night-time. You can keep it on your bedside table.'

Cerys's knees buckled. The silky voice made her feel as though she was floating, and when the tap was turned on, the water ran gently over the open spout then fell into the sink like a waterfall. Hypnotising.

The hand cream was a bit sticky but she'd support this lovely lady with her local business, buy some for each of her four bathrooms. Plural. Who'd have thought six months ago that today she'd have four bathrooms, three upstairs and one shower room which sat off the utility room, so you could jump straight under the hot water after a day at the beach, meaning no sand was brought into the house. The shelves by the door were already full of neatly stacked towels. There was a cupboard for surf boards, pegs for coats and wetsuits, shelves at floor level for shoes, all with a drip tray underneath them to catch any water, mud, stones, sand.

After Cerys tried each type of hand wash, the lady passed her a pure white flannel to dry her hands with. She called them flannels where Cerys would have said face cloth. Then she pointed to a hessian box by Cerys's side where the used ones went. Cerys felt cocooned in softness and luxury. She would repay the good feeling.

'I'll take two of each of the large lavender and citrus hand washes please, so four in total, and three of the large hand creams. They're so gorgeous. Your shop's beautiful.'

The lady's eyes lit up, Cerys was sure of it, and even though she was tempted to say yes to having them all individually wrapped in tissue paper with a sticker to seal the paper, she said, 'There's no need, for the sake of the planet.' But yes to a hessian bag to carry them in, carefully, all that glass, the danger of it smashing.

Usually when she was on holiday, Cerys would buy one bar of soap from a similar shop, not the beautiful big bottles that cost twenty-something pounds each, which was way too much of an extravagance. A single soap was affordable, her own slice of luxury to remind her of the time off work, being somewhere different. Today, buying seven bottles, she felt a rush at the decadence rather than guilt at the extravagance. It was a good thing. She was supporting an independent business, a local one. She'd always do that from now on. She'd become a regular customer, their saviour on quiet days at the end of the season when most tourists had gone home. They'd see her out of the window and think *oh good, here comes Cerys.*

'Your shop's gorgeous. I love shops like this.'

She flicked through the leaflets in the wicker basket on the counter: a surf school, coasteering, kayaking days out – half day or full, dawn and sunset – coastal walks, massages and Reiki therapy. Cerys took two of each for her visitors.

~

The bottles clinked together as the bag swung by her side, the wind and the bulkiness of the contents making it bang it against her calf. Cerys lifted the bag up, wrapping her hands through the handles as she held it in front of her chest like a baby in a papoose. She felt a little smug that she was getting to know her way round the village after only one morning. She smiled as she reached her road and decided she was feeling brave enough to go for a drive that afternoon, then faltered where the tarmac turned to the gravel in front of her house. A man was standing with his back to Cerys, looking through the study window. She was about to call hello when he banged hard on the front door.

'Come on. I know you're in there. Open up.' Bang, bang, bang. 'You can't keep ignoring me.'

Cerys stepped back onto the road and started walking towards the shops as if that was where she intended to go. Should she call Stephen? She couldn't be so pathetic. If she was in London she wouldn't be scared, so there was no need to think because she was in Wales someone was going to hurt her for no reason. She turned round and walked purposefully onto her driveway, her phone in her hand, fingers gripping it tightly in case she needed help but the angry person had gone.

'Hello. Hello, can I help you?' she called. Only her feet crunched on the gravel. 'Hello!' No reply. She put her key in the lock.

'Who are you?' a man's voice asked.

Cerys's heart flipped as she turned round to face him. Would anyone hear her scream? Detached houses meant a person was too far from their neighbours, so different to an inner city.

'Are you his new carer?' he asked.

'Excuse me?'

'Thomas.'

'Oh. I'm so sorry.' She put her hand to her chest, over her heart, a natural cliche. The boy stared at her, not asking why she was upset. He scratched his stubble, red hairs mixed with brown.

'I'm too late.'

'I—'

'He's dead, is he?'

'I'm so sorry. Were you close to him?' The boy walked away. 'Were you Thomas's friend? A relative?' She put her bag down and ran after him. 'I'm so sorry you found out like this, that you couldn't make it to the funeral.' He pulled a bike out of the bushes. 'Would you like a coffee? Or something stronger for the shock?' He cycled away. 'Please. Are you okay?' He turned in the road and cycled back into the drive.

'What do you care?'

She didn't know how to answer that. Such a strange question.

'I'll call Stephen, Mr Kendrick. He'll be able to help you.'

'Ha. So you got all this did you? It's yours now?' He flicked his head at the house.

'I was in the church. It was all by chance. I'm so sorry if it should have been... Look, I'll call Stephen and he can sort everything out. Tell me your name and—'

'Course you will. That's what you rich people do, isn't it, call your lawyers to give bad news rather than doing it yourselves, absolving yourself from any guilt. Look at you with your posh shopping and *oh dear I'm so sorry* bullshit. I don't know how you sleep at night. Shame on you.'

He shot away before she had a chance to defend herself.

TEN

Cerys jumped to the side as a car skidded into the drive, making the gravel scatter when it braked. A van rather than a car, a silver box-shaped Vauxhall, smaller than a Transit. The driver tied her shoulder-length blond hair in a ponytail.

'Sorry. Didn't meant to scare you. Did Stephen not tell you I was coming? I'm Cathy. We met before, at his office.'

'Yes. Oh my god, yes. Sorry. So sorry, I'm terrible with faces. Have you changed your hair?'

'I guess it's a bit blonder since then.'

Relief made Cerys grin, so grateful there was someone to go inside the house with her in case another baddie had broken in. She went to hug her visitor who stepped back. Embarrassed, she hurried past Cathy to open the front door.

'I won't keep you long. I've just come to go through some basics then I'll leave you in peace.'

Cathy clocked the hessian bag. Cerys was embarrassed that she'd bought so many expensive soaps rather than essentials, not what most people could afford. She put it down on the sofa, out of sight. At least she had milk and a box of Yorkshire teabags, the best brand according to her tea-drinking friends. So that was lucky.

'Tea? Juice? Water?'

'Tea please. Just milk. No sugar.' Cathy checked the room, glad to see it was no different to when she'd cleaned it two days earlier, apart from the bag of expensive smelling goodies. 'How are you settling in?'

'Great. It's stunning. So beautiful. I can't believe it. I'm so lucky.' When Cathy didn't reply she filled the void. 'I'm sorry not to have any biscuits. I'm going to the supermarket later. I can't wait to drive the car. It's so gorgeous.'

'No problem. I'm meant to be off the sugar, although I've got chocolate eclairs in the van. They keep me going but don't tell my daughter. She thinks I haven't had any for twenty-two days so far.'

Cerys laughed, winked and tapped the side of her nose. Cathy didn't join in. There was nothing funny about a confession. She sipped her tea, leaving the cup on the table as she told Cerys about the boiler, the remote controls for the television and sound system, the washing machine, the tumble dryer.

'My number's in the file so if anything does go wrong, not that it should because it's so well looked after, but if anything does, or you're not sure how to get the fire going on a cold evening or the boiler's playing up, not that it should, just give me a call and I'll come round or one of my staff will. There's three of us you can expect to see: me, my daughter Louise who looks like me but taller, and her boyfriend Gethin.'

'Great. Will do. Thank you.'

Cerys wished there was a natural flow to the conversation. She smiled uncertainly when their eyes met. Part of her wanted the woman out of her house, not liking the tough energy she brought to her living room. Which was odd. Because she wasn't cross or angry. She was just standing next to the table finishing her drink.

'The doors were sticking last night. Would you mind having a look at them before you go?'

'Which ones?'

'The bi-folds.'

'That's odd.'

Cerys stood beside Cathy as she checked them. She scanned the garden for a sign of the stranger who'd been shouting through her letter box but there was only the grass, no bushes to hide behind. The doors locked and unlocked easily. No-one had forced them open. While Cathy double checked that they slid smoothly on the runners, Cerys went into the utility room. It was empty, and the back door was closed and locked too. She pushed the shoe rack in front of it; no harm in being extra cautious.

'They seem to be working fine. Do you want to have a go?'

'No. Don't worry. It must have caught in the wind or something.' They went back to an awkward silence. 'Did you know Thomas, the man who lived here before me?'

'No.'

Cerys had hoped for a hint of who her benefactor was. Nothing in the house gave anything away. There wasn't an attic to explore, the garage was empty apart from gardening tools and some paint pots all stacked neatly on shelves that had been built especially for their different sizes. Cathy's clipped reply made Cerys not mention the boy on the bike.

'Right. I'd best be off. Thanks for the tea and you've got my number if you need me.'

After reversing onto the main road Cathy accelerated too fast for Cerys's cautious liking. She was about to shut the door when she saw a bike go in the same direction as Cathy's car. A red top. Followed by another bike going more slowly, orange top this time, then two teenagers on scooters. Hundreds of cyclists on Welsh roads in the holidays, families enjoying days out together, friends who were fitness fanatics loving the challenge of the mountains. Not necessarily angry strangers.

~

She bought a fancy coffee machine because she could afford it, couldn't bear to drink a mediocre cup each morning, and didn't want to have to walk to the cafe when it was blowing a gale. The salesman told her it wasn't often a person rather than a company ordered one but it wasn't unheard of, though she was only their second client in Wales. Most of their personal deliveries were London bound.

'Fancy loft apartments near Spitalfields is it?' Cerys quipped. He laughed along with her. Kerching.

She remembered the best cup of coffee she'd ever tasted from the cafe in Bath that Vicky had taken her to. It had been tucked away in the cobbled back streets, the sort of place you wouldn't stumble upon. Only those in the know knew about it, all brightly coloured drawings and writing on chalk boards that took up all the space on the walls. There were only five tables, two large ones you had to share with others unless you were a party of eight, ten at a pinch, all of you sitting on benches, and a small counter staffed by three busy waiters but the coffee, the coffee was so good that Cerys had two cappuccinos even though they only sat down for half an hour. Clifton coffee. That was the name of it. She'd asked the waiter and never forgotten the brand because it made her laugh that it was from Bristol not Bath, from the bit of Bristol where Vicky lived.

'Do you know it? Do they sell it at that deli near you, the posh one?'

Vicky shook her head, had never heard of it. She didn't recognise the packets of beans behind the counter, was unable to picture them in the deli she favoured.

Cerys googled Clifton coffee on the MacBook she'd bought before moving; wise advice from Seren.

'The mobile reception will be shit, get the latest iPhone and a MacBook – they're what will keep you going in the depths of winter, help you keep you in touch with everyone.'

She'd been right. Cerys would call her soon to see how she was doing.

The coffee company offered so many varieties of beans she didn't know which to choose, not a clue. She messaged Vicky. The answer was Frankie's. Cerys called the coffee company and placed an order for the blend that Frankie's cafe in Bath bought.

And that was that. The power of the internet meant she was on fire, brave, embracing all challenges. Now for the supermarket.

~

Never had a driver been so cautious. She drove at twenty miles per hour round bends, over bridges, under low hanging branches through glorious tree tunnels, through the car parking ticket barrier, breathing in and squeezing her shoulders up as if that would make her smaller, less likely to scrape the edges of the car. It was a pleasure to drive, or it would be once she learnt to relax. So simple only having to steer and brake rather than change gear all the time.

Cerys over-filled her trolley with more food than she needed: bottles of fresh juice and bags of expensive crisps in flavours she didn't like but guests might enjoy. She bought enough to fill her bespoke cupboards: packets of the branded biscuits, champagne, wines, the branded pasta and rice rather than the supermarket's own, the branded flour and sugar, one of everything in case she had an urge and needed them for cooking. She even put one of every type of spice and herb in her trolley, half of which she didn't know how to cook with. The rush of the shop, of spending money where it didn't matter what anything cost. She ignored the look from the cashier as she typed in her pin number. Five hundred and twenty-three pounds, nineteen pence.

'Would you like a receipt?'

'Yes please,' said the crazy rich lady.

ELEVEN

Seren thought about booking a visit to the doctor to get some pills. Apparently all you needed to do was sit in the chair at the side of his desk, say *I'm feeling a bit down* or *life's a bit tricky at the moment* and bish bash bosh he'd write a prescription without even checking that a chat might have been enough to help you, without delving into what was making you feel out of sorts at that moment. And it was a moment for her, not a lifetime thing, she was sure of it. No. She wouldn't go. She didn't need medicine. It wasn't that complicated a problem. Pills weren't a badge of honour, not for her, not like that other mum.

That mum. The one at the boys' primary school who always went on about the different things that were wrong with her children, that she thought were wrong but the doctors couldn't see it. Until she went to some private Harley Street man, wore him down with repeated appointments, flattered his ego, flashed her cheque book as she insisted *Something. Is. Wrong.* Easy money.

'Why yes madam, I do believe there is a problem with your darlings.'

She was finally, momentarily, satisfied.

The next year both her children *needed* brain scans. Of course they did. Of course nothing was found. The year after that she told everyone they were suffering from depression, they had issues.

'Too right they do,' Seren ranted to Mark. 'Living with that woman would drive anyone crazy. Apparently her husband's close to losing it too. Jenny's brother knows him from football, said he's never seen a man so unhappy. She's actually driving him crazy. Perhaps it's for the inheritance. His parents are super wealthy.'

'What's for tea again?'

~

At the mums' quiz night Seren had to sit beside her. She drank too much, too fast.

'He wouldn't prescribe something if they didn't need it. I knew there was something wrong. A mother's instinct. It just goes to show. I knew it. Always get a second opinion.'

'Two hundred, three hundred,' Seren slurred, laughing as she rubbed her right hand over her left palm like she was counting out money. Two other mums giggled. Munchausen by Proxy mama frowned. Seren bit her tongue to stop herself from sneering, *You do my head in. You're an idiot. Dangerous. You're the one harming your children. If it wasn't for you they wouldn't even be sick.*

Sober, she ran. Ran the woman out of her head. The mum needed her kids to have things wrong with them, for their family's life to be full of drama, because her actual life was so lacking. What better way to get attention than through the sickness of your children? It was the surest way to sympathy. It made her blood boil, like the NHS hadn't enough real sick people to deal with. People were actually ill, look at Shauna, so sad, just so sad, and Annie who had cancer, not yet forty, three kids under the age of eight. They're the ones who deserved help and sympathy.

Seren stood behind her in the queue for the nativity.

'It's just something I have to deal with in life. I mean I'm strong, it's the kids who have the illnesses, bless them. It's them I feel sorry for. I just have to learn to deal with it, support them as best I can.'

The longer people knew the mum the more cynical they became, so she turned into one of those people who had new friends every five years, saw old friends seldom. Busy, sorry, busy. No-one could be doing with her nonsense when their own lives were encumbered by real tragedies. On her more sympathetic days Seren decided the sad thing was the mother really did need help. She obviously had a real problem.

Seren wasn't unsympathetic to people who really did have issues. She believed it was the quiet ones who needed looking after the most, not the ones who told everyone how they were feeling all the time. Those who craved the adulation of strangers as if they were a film star or a big name in television, they got hooked on it, you could tell, their *I'm so low* posts getting way more likes than their *look at the pancakes I made this morning* photo. The sad person or the bad person got the most clicks so that's the character they stuck with rather than actually going off and living their life. It was all about the clickbait, baby.

She wanted to scream across the room, the bus, the pool as her kids were at their swimming lessons: 'Get on with it and stop your self-indulgent moaning. Work building stone walls in Wales for ten hours a day, eat three meals, no snacking, no social fucking media.' More physical work would be good for the Western world, leaving people so exhausted they had no energy to stay awake worrying, comparing, over-thinking. Including her. She shouldn't read the comments that wound her up so much it felt like her head would explode. But she had a right to think like that. She knew actual badness. She'd suffered real trauma.

She had.

Her and Cerys.

And they'd never made a big fuss about it.

Once the coffins were buried side by side they'd moved on because they had to. They both worked hard, needing good exam results in order to earn a decent living that would pay their rent, put food on the table. No parents were there to catch them if they fell but there was no need to go on about the tragedy of it because really, what was there to say? They never sat and wept, thinking what if, though Seren sometimes wondered if her personality would have been different if she'd had two people cocoon her in unconditional love as she grew from a child into an adult. Which was pointless. She couldn't change history. It had happened. It was shit. Things happened. You had to move on and not let them define you because if you did, then that was on you. Your life, your choices. Don't go blaming anyone else, you bastards.

Idiot of a woman, that woman, that mum. When Seren pictured her two dead parents, the coffins side by side, her and Cerys adrift, no more guidance, as that woman went on and on about her make-believe headache she thought was a brain tumour, she had to walk away even if it was rude. She headed to the car before she said what she really felt, before she barked with utter venom that would never be forgotten, *shut the fuck up you stupid motherfucker. Do you know how much I hate you?*

Lauren had laughed when Seren had been going on about *that woman* for nearly an hour.

'What?'

'Why do you see her?'

'What do you mean?'

'She's obviously bad for your mental health. If she winds you up that much, don't have anything to do with her.'

Seren's turn to laugh. That made sense. Don't see her, don't go on a night out when she knew that woman would be there. Hallelujah for the advice from one of her oldest friends.

She felt relieved. Sometimes guilty, but mostly relieved.

The relief at no longer being wound up by the fact that people really were ill, people had genuine, uncontrollable, horrid shit happening to them. And she could tell which direction that lady's family's future would take. The only way was up. Up to the next drama, up to heaven. Seren never told a soul but she'd have bet ten thousand pounds that the mum's ultimate achievement would be if one of her family tried to kill themselves. That would be her trump card. And who could blame them, having to live with the matriarch twisting their thoughts, manipulating their minds, anyone would be desperate to get her out of their head by whatever means possible.

Seren didn't want that to happen. She felt sorry for the children and the husband but she knew that with every year that passed, that woman would be looking for more dramatic ways to get sympathy and attention. When she heard about the husband on the grapevine, Zara's voice was cynical as if she too didn't believe it. Who needed five attempts, if you meant it you did it in one. Seren knew that for a fact. Look at her mother's cousin's brother-in-law's Uncle Simon, followed by his Aunty Louisa then a Great Aunt Jean who was older, no less tragic.

It was wrong.

So wrong.

Of that mum.

Her with all the pills for each of them that she got from her private doctor. Too many pills, keeping the pharmaceutical companies in business. Sell those pills, let the shareholders dance among the dividends. Seren had read about drug companies making up illnesses to be cured by drugs they'd created in order to sell them through the psychiatrists, all the parties happy as long as they made their millions. It made her want to scream. Everything was the wrong way round.

Everything was crazy.

She was going crazy.

Maybe.

Baby.

Run.

It was a blip. A mere blip caused by grief, unfairness, fuck this, fuck that, fuck you motherfucker. She ran faster for longer, her fitness levels increasing. Life was full of blips, everyone had them. That's what made some weeks, months, years, some years so good, some so painful. But the point of the difficult moments was they made you appreciate the good times.

People needed to deal with the bad as well as the good, to understand there were days and weeks when they would feel like shit and that was fine, that was okay, roll with it. They would get through it, then something good would happen and they'd feel happy. What they didn't need was a bunch of pills. Why not prescribe Smarties? That'd be good. Prescribe placebos to everyone except those whose eyes showed their need. It was the eyes that gave away the true state of mind, not the mouth. Not the words the friend had told her she needed to say in order to get the prescription.

Seren would not go to the doctor. She'd get through this by herself. She'd run rather than be that pilled-up person. But if she didn't tell anyone how she was feeling, if she stayed schtum, did that mean she was one of those people who really did need help? Was she a mad one? The anger, the thought of punching someone created such satisfaction, the glass she'd thrown, the plates she'd smashed then cleared up saying they'd slipped when wet from the dishwasher. Really, she'd held them above her head and thrown them to the ground with such force that some of the fragments had cut her leg, but she'd hidden that from Mark. She'd relished the pain because she deserved it, because she'd broken the precious things on purpose and now they'd have to spend their hard-earned money buying new ones.

She sprinted the last two hundred metres down the straight road with the big houses before you got to the cul-de-sac with semi-detached ones, not quite as pretty. Sweat ran down her face. Good. The proof she'd run hard, gone far enough. She smiled at the pain in her calf. She'd pushed through it, kept going and now she was glad. Pain was good. It showed she could hurt, showed she had feelings and pushing through it meant she was in control of them. She'd run rather than go crying to the doctor. There was no need to waste their time or hers. She had this.

And fuck Cerys. Fuck her fucking sister. Seren shook her head, wanting the jealousy gone. Too much negativity. She couldn't tell Mark because he'd think she was mad, bitter, twisted, and he'd be right. She didn't mean to be. She didn't want to be that person.

TWELVE

Cerys ran her hands over the brushed velvet sofa in time with the breeze that was blowing the grass backwards and forwards. The clouds flew past so fast she felt a little dizzy, tipsy after two and a half glasses of Prosecco. Deep breath. A strawberry and white chocolate truffle. Another truffle. Deep breath, Cerys.

Once the sun had set, lost behind the sea, it was like the world was watching her rather than her spying on it. She didn't like that feeling. She didn't like that there weren't any blinds or curtains on the huge floor to ceiling bi-folds. Without a cover to hide behind she felt like the girl in a horror movie where the baddies were watching her through the patio windows. Cerys moved her hands closer to her nose, comfort from the scent of lavender: her choice, her luxury, eight brands of hand lotion from five different shops that she'd discovered in different villages – or would you call them towns? – hamlets in the vicinity. Just her, her car, her debit card.

'No need for credit, no need for you to incur debt, not any more,' Rhys had said as he handed it to her along with a pin number, a login name and a password for online banking. 'It's easier this way. Keep your old account by all means but this way everything's neat, tidy and separate, all the better for me to help you with any problems, not that there'll be any of course, but better safe than sorry.'

He had an old-sounding soul in his young body but the kindness of those boys, him and Stephen, it made her want to weep. How lucky she was to have such people looking after her. That must be what it felt like to have parents. They'd worry about you, call to check you were okay, send you a recipe you might like or tell you about a television programme they watched the other night that was really good. *Are you okay for money, how's things, is everything alright, how about we meet up to go shopping, let me buy you a few treats then take you out for dinner.* That's what Sam's mum and dad did. Even though she was forty-seven, they'd insist on buying her a new top or something for her flat before treating her to dinner at a restaurant and they'd all have a big hug at the end of the evening. How lovely. What a beautiful thing to happen.

'You must never take that for granted. It's so wonderful you've got such loving parents. Don't assume or think it's a given because it's not, you know. Lots of people, they'd give anything to have that.'

'I know. I don't.'

In that moment Sam wouldn't but two weeks later Cerys's words would be forgotten as Sam moaned that her Mum had texted yet again asking how her day was or what was she having for her tea.

Cerys cried at the thought of such love. Christ. She was so over-emotional these days. They'd loosened something. Stephen and Rhys via Thomas Morgan's kindness and generosity. And Gwen's death. Ever since that phone call, Cerys's head had felt wobbly, even though nothing but good had happened to her. The good that made her forget the bad for too many moments as she signed papers, shopped, planned, shopped for more. She'd go to call Gwen then remember she wasn't in her house. She was lying in a coffin, her lips coated in pink lipstick. Cerys's heart winced as if it was under attack. She forgot to breathe as she remembered it was real. She missed Gwen. She hadn't realised grief would hurt so much when she was an adult. And it felt as if no-one understood her pain because it wasn't her mother, not even her mother-in-law. It was her sister's mother-in-law, so who was Cerys to hijack their grief? Only one day of compassionate leave from work for the funeral rather than the three that were allocated for a close relative.

She was used to getting on with things, dealing with problems, not making a fuss about pain, only breaking down once she was inside her flat, never in front of others. Lie. Very occasionally after too much to drink she'd lose it in front of an old friend who'd hug her, who knew about the past, who understood that words couldn't make it better. A tight hug in secret was the only thing that eased the throbbing. She rubbed her eyes and blew her nose. It was usually Seren who cried, loved, hated. Cerys would watch her knees, awkward. She was the calm, quiet, keep-your-cards-close-to-your-chest one.

But Gwen dying kept pulling Cerys out of her safe bubble. Gwen's house would have been a two-hour drive from where Cerys now lived, along wide, empty, scenic roads rather than grim never-ending grey motorways. If Gwen was still alive Cerys could have visited her every week, twice a week even, treated her to cream teas and a fancy meal on her birthday in the hotel she loved. She'd send her flowers and treats by special delivery because why not, it was about time she was spoilt. And she'd have collected her, brought her up to the house, made the spare bedroom with the ensuite Gwen's room.

'Oh Cerys,' her usually booming voice subdued by the shock, her accent gentle. 'It's beautiful.' She used to breathe in hard and quick, almost a gasp, when she really liked something, so lots of those would pepper her awe. 'Look at it. I mean look at it. Oh my God Cerys, look at the view, the gardens, the sea, the sofas, the kitchen.' Run those hands along that cool marble.

'Wait until you see upstairs. Come on. Let me show you your room.'

Gwen would fling herself onto her bed with total joy.

'An ensuite. An ensuite like in a hotel. Oh my God, Cerys, I bloody love it.'

~

86

After checking for a third time that the doors were locked, Cerys moved away from them. The further back she was the less a person could see of her. She dimmed the lights but still felt exposed. How could Thomas not have wanted to block out the dark once it surrounded him? She had a word with herself. This was Wales not America. People didn't own guns they'd bought in supermarkets, thrown in a shopping trolley with their burgers and salad, that they'd use to blast through the window smashing the glass to get to the rich lady. Plus it was too remote for that sort of deed. There was a low crime rate, much lower than in London, she'd googled when she was eating her dinner. Cerys needed to have more trust in her surroundings, have faith in the place, the peace, the people. Stephen didn't even lock his door, it was so safe. He'd emphasised that when she'd been sitting opposite him, grinning while he listed the numerous virtues of West Wales as the ink dried on the contract.

She pressed some buttons on the remote. The television still wouldn't go to a channel that was in English, all that appeared were Welsh-speaking soap operas and interviews with farmers. She couldn't find the instructions in the file or the drawers of the dresser the television sat on. She messaged Cathy, emphasising it wasn't important, no need for her to rush over, maybe next week, Monday perhaps if it wasn't an inconvenience, thank you, thank you, have a good evening.

Her mind flittered back to the view. She scrolled through her photos of a week's worth of walks by the beach, a glass of Prosecco on the balcony of the sailing club, her sitting on the rocks as there was no need to rush home. The dolphins. The mum shouting *look Lottie, look at them playing.* Cerys had looked too, sitting on the rocks next to the family, warm in her new fleece, hands cosy in the zip-up pockets. Three dolphins played, catching, chasing, hiding, seeking, all *here I am again, surprise, surprise.* Then another two appeared behind them. Every person in the cove watched, quiet, appreciative of their luck at seeing such freedom and beauty. The sun lit them from behind, drifted down from red to pink to yellow.

'I wish we could live here forever. Why not? Why can't we?' Lottie said.

Cerys nearly shouted out *I do*, all excited that she had something someone else wanted. But she held back. The thought was more powerful for the quiet. I do. More satisfying than a marriage vow. I do. In sickness and in health, until death do us part, me and Wales, now and forever.

~

No-one replied to her messages inviting them to come and stay. They'd all be out having fun, enjoying a curry, a drink, the cinema. She checked her phone again. Duh. They'd be at Michael's boyfriend's fortieth. Of course they were. No wonder they hadn't answered. They were disco dancing, enjoying a wild night, unable to even get her messages on the basement dance floor where there was no reception. She checked Instagram to see what they were wearing, whose house they'd met up at beforehand but everyone posted less now the novelty had worn off. None of them had added new photos.

Cerys clicked on a link to new trainers but Confirm Order didn't excite her. That morning a top had arrived that she'd only thought was okay, not loved, which used to be a prerequisite of her buying anything. When she tried it on she didn't like it but couldn't be bothered to send it back, then felt guilty because it was a waste. Forty-nine pounds including postage, when people were going hungry, unable to afford any new clothes. She hated herself, made a vow not to buy things again just for the sake of it. She never used to before Thomas's gift, so she'd go back to being that person. It was people she was after, not possessions.

Cerys wanted someone to comment on a film with, to share the sunset with, to pour drinks for, to fill up their plate with delicious food, insisting they take some of the cake home with them because she'd bought far too much and couldn't eat it all, it would only go off, keep the Tupperware, honestly, I've got loads, you have it, honestly, no problem.

She sent a photo of the sunset to Seren, and then, even though it felt false –

Be lovely to see you all soon. There were dolphins in the bay.
The boys would love it.

The messages were read straight away. Her sister was in on a Friday night, watching the world through her phone rather than out enjoying it. Of course she was, with two kids and babysitters so expensive.

Cerys scrolled through her contacts. She wrote down a list of all the people she'd like to come and visit, in the orange Moleskin notepad that she'd bought to match the car. If she could arrange it so that every weekend or every other weekend, let's not be greedy, a friend came to stay, then the four days of the week when she was alone would be easier. And she mustn't moan. Christ. Not to anyone. To complain would be wrong. How dare she complain when such luck had been thrown into her lap, letting her get on with life without a single worry?

She turned to a new page and wrote a To Do list: Yoga, massage, gym, walking group, French classes (maybe online?), cookery classes, photography classes, books to buy, local charities (volunteering?), cinema times, Cardiff for day? Weekend home? She crossed out the word home and replaced it with London.

Her phone pinged.

Sounds great – lucky you. Work mad busy, am utterly exhausted
– how about May half term? We can come for week if that works
for you.

Cerys was sure she'd told Seren about the three day rule, though maybe not after her sister had acted so prickly when she realised Cerys really was moving. She didn't open the message, didn't want to get into it now. She'd leave it as if she hadn't read it then reply in the morning.

After double checking all the doors were locked she went upstairs with a bottle of water, her laptop, her phone, two spare chargers already in her bedside drawer, everything she needed in her bedroom in case she became trapped and had to call for help because she'd heard an intruder. She purposely didn't look out of the windows.

~

The living room bi-folds were still closed, the front and back door still locked, no signs of tampering. She replied to Seren:

> Brilliant, but aargh – so sorry. It can't be more than 3 nights, not allowed.

> But it's SUCH a long drive!!!!! I thought you owned it? Who are they to say how long your family can stay for?

Cerys replied with the *what can I do* emoji, knowing that would wind Seren up more but words weren't working and the more she explained, the worse it sounded.

> What about a B&B for a night on the way here and back? Nice 5 day break then?

> Too expensive. Need 2 rooms now boys are older. Can't afford it.

Cerys should offer to pay. She knew how it must look, her not saying don't worry, I've got it. But she couldn't. It was a rule. They'd been very clear about that and Cerys didn't want to risk going against their kindness. She checked her balance, plenty of money. Rhys wouldn't know. But she would, plus she didn't want to lie to him after all he'd done to help her. If she offered to pay fifty pounds towards one of the rooms, it would make her sound even tighter. She filled up her water glass. Her old bank account. That still had money in it, money she didn't need any more. Simple. She'd transfer Seren the money for the B&Bs and that would make her sister happy.

> I can help with the B&Bs. Would £400 be enough for you all? Or £450? Send bank details – I'll transfer, no problem. And

when you get here no money needed – my guests, my treat, no money to spend at all at this end.

She added a thumbs up emoji.

Half an hour later she got the reply she'd hoped for.

Really?

Absolutely

That'd be wonderful. Thank you.

Brilliant. So exciting. Hurray! Can't wait to see you all.

She meant it. Absence had made her heart grow fonder. She couldn't believe how excited she was to see her sister and the boys, Mark being more of a background person, easy to get on with so no need to worry about him. And it would be fine. Better than that. It would be fabulous, she'd make sure of it. Once they arrived everyone would be in a good mood because they were on holiday. The house was big enough that the boys wouldn't be in her way and there was the beach, the huge garden, her own room for sanctuary if she needed it. She'd buy a trampoline; fun for her as well as her nephews. She'd stock up on all their favourite foods and put a toy for each of the boys on their beds, making her the most brilliant aunt ever. Seren and Mark could have a day out together, like a date, time alone. Cerys would cook on the first night then take them all out for dinner the next two evenings, no cooking, no dishes. Brunch too if they fancied it. It would be easy, relaxed, fun. Three days was the perfect amount of time before getting on each other's nerves; clever Thomas for making that a stipulation.

~

One more glass then she'd go to bed. She wouldn't buy the big bottles of booze again, only the small ones that were a good portion for one person. One small bottle of fizz a week and she'd start to eat healthily, get super fit so she felt fabulous instead of sitting inside gorging on truffles and ice cream.

Can't work TV out, sorry to be SUCH a pain. Can you show me how to do it whenever suits you? No rush.

Plus want to get blinds for big windows. Advice welcome. So kind. Thank you.

The third glass made everyone so kind. She messaged Stephen.

Loving it here so much. Thank you SO much for all your help. You're SO kind. I'm so lucky.

And everyone in London:

Miss you all SO much. Love you more than the world.

Come down SOON you will LOVE it, not as much as I love you – HA! Miss you. Wish I could hug you. Can you tell xx

And say happy birthday to Michael for yesterday!!!!! Love him so much, the darling xx

Hope you had a dance for me. Send photos. So quiet here.

But beautiful.

How many texts?!! Ha! A bit tipsy. Love you all. Kisses.

Love you.

~

She was in bed reading when the doorbell rang. Cerys pulled a dark green hoodie over her pyjamas and went downstairs.

'The TV.'

The girl had long blond hair. There was a white Fiesta parked behind her, next to Cerys's car, someone sitting in the passenger seat, head down. Two mountain bikes were attached to the back of the boot.

'Mum sent me. I'm to show you how to use the television.'

'Right. Great. Sorry. Laura is it?'

'Louise.'

'That's it. Oh my god, I can't believe you're here on a Sunday. I'm so sorry.'

'You said you needed help with it.'

'Yeah, but it wasn't an emergency. It's so early, I—'

'I can go if you'd rather.'

'No. I mean, whatever works best for you. If you've got time that would be great seeing as you're here but if it's a pain... I'm so sorry. I hope you didn't get up early especially for me. I feel terrible. I—'

'It's fine. We'd be passing anyway, off on a ride. It's no biggie.'

Cerys pretended to understand all the instructions even though Louise went through them too fast for her to follow. She'd rather have on, off, up, down, plus volume buttons, but this one had green, red, orange and blue buttons that you had to press in a certain order. It was all so confusing.

'Is there an instruction booklet?'

She'd rather have a piece of paper in her hands that she could hold and flick through, double checking she was pressing them in the correct order.

'I don't think so. There might be one online. Would you like me to see if I can get you a hard copy?'

'Really? That'd be brilliant. Thank you. But I don't want to be a pain.'

'It's fine, no biggie. If they've got one they've got one and if not...' she shrugged her shoulders. 'I guess I could come over again.'

'No need. That was really helpful. I think I've got it, thank you. I really appreciate it.' She wouldn't ask again. That would make her too needy and Cerys wanted the girl to like her. 'You must be fit, mountain biking round here.'

'We're training for a triathlon.'

'No way! Wow. Super-fit then.'

'I suppose. You should always keep fit. I don't understand people who don't. I mean, there aren't any down sides to it are there? Even if you don't enjoy it, to know that you can run, swim, ride a distance, it might save your life one day or someone else you need to get help for. You never know what situation you might be in, do you? My mum always says you never know when you might need to outrun someone.'

As Louise reversed out of the drive, her passenger kept his or her head down. Cerys couldn't tell if it was a boy or girl because their hair was shoulder length and that hadn't helped with deciphering the sex of someone since the sixties. Louise said something, was shouting by the looks of it. Her passenger turned to the left, checked there was nothing coming down the road. He was a boy with a neat beard to go with his shaggy hair. Oh to be in a cute young couple, mountain biking in Lycra. Wise too. Louise was right about the exercise. Cerys needed to get fit like they were. There were no excuses, look at all the time she had. And it was a fair point about being able to run, to get away, to know how to punch baddies who stare through windows in movies. Strength, agility, flexibility. She'd look for self-defence classes, become a ka-ra-te nin-ja-ja-ja.

THIRTEEN

Cerys planned a routine: Tuesdays and Wednesdays yoga. She'd only drink a smoothie before driving to the classes. Rhiannon, the instructor, had a voice that made her feel like she was having a treat rather than doing an hour and a half's workout, so gentle and calm that Cerys floated out of class, her relaxation button pressed.

On Mondays and Fridays she walked to the beach then ran along it and back up the hill, following the coastal path. Unless it had been raining, then she stuck to going up and down the sand because the clifftop was too slippy and the last thing she wanted was a twisted ankle or broken bone. She did not like the mud. She did not like the edges. They made her feel like she was going to fall, disappear over the side. She didn't like walking or running in the rain, the uneven surfaces more dangerous. Cerys only liked to be out on dry land, blue or grey skies, not black clouds, no heavens full of thunder.

Thursdays and Saturdays were for online squat and lunge workouts. She could feel her muscles start to tighten by week three. The workouts took up the mornings which meant afternoons were for treats like reading, a nap because the run had exhausted her, eyelids drooping as she approached a new chapter. The decadence of being able to snooze rather than work. Blissful.

How did she once fit in fifty hours work a week at her day job? No wonder Seren was jealous. Cerys might have been too if it was the other way round, though she did long for another soul to talk to. An old friend, not a new person in the queue at Spar who couldn't quite remember her name or where she was from.

She'd become shyer since she'd moved, her confidence had lessened. It was hard pushing yourself onto people at her age. And she wasn't used to it after living in the same postcode for so many decades, having friends within a bus ride or walking distance. So rare in London. Something they tried not to take for granted but had all become used to.

She wasn't working in Wales so there was no chance of meeting people that way. And she was too old to be out clubbing with one friend, meeting a new set by the end of the night. It's not as if she was a student, where you met tons of people all the time. She missed her university friends, and their friends of friends, her big circle for chats and chilling. She missed laughing and them knowing each other's histories, no need for explanations about certain behaviours, reactions to triggers, are their parents alive or dead, her poor sister, his cousin, did you hear about Tim's uncle, dead before he hit the floor, an artery snapped, he wouldn't have felt anything so at least there was that. They'd all agreed you'd rather not suffer, though such a shock for those left alive. Christ. It made you think. It was the ones left alive who were in pain, not the dead one. They were gone. For them the feelings were over.

Her friendship group knew just about everything that had happened in each other's lives which made the job of looking after one another easier and having fun less complicated. Unconditional love and support, that's what they had.

On nights where she missed them so much she thought of heading to London straight away, never mind the time, Cerys would comfort her lonely self with a smoothie for dinner followed by a whole box of truffles from the shop in the village where they were laid out behind a glass container, tongs used to pick up the ones customers pointed to. They cost nearly one pound per chocolate, but she could afford it. She'd gorge on crumbly chocolate fudge from the shop she'd been to in Bath, near the cathedral. It turned out they delivered, of course they did. She bought in bulk, the only way to justify the cost of the postage, then she'd eat all that the man in the van had delivered. If it wasn't for the exercise she'd be squishing her tummy into new clothes that were too small for her, no doubt about it.

~

The old man winked at her nineteen pounds and seventeen pence bill. Cerys smiled to hide her shame. It was greedy, excessive. It proved she had no control over herself and now there was a witness.

'I'm buying some for the wife. It's her birthday tomorrow.' He chose five chocolates, their price after being weighed, four pounds and eighty-nine pence. 'You know the secret of course.'

'Sorry?'

'Drink water after them, then you'll be okay. I prefer the Galaxy so I can get a lot more for my money; a bar a day I get through, unlike the wife with these fancy ones, but the sugar, that's what gives you the diabetes. This friend of Barry's, he told me, and his daughter's a nurse so he should know because she would know, well she said to him if you drink lots of water after eating sweets it flushes the sugar straight through you so the diabetes won't be a problem. The doctor will be none the wiser and not able to tell you off about it.' He tipped his head back as he laughed. 'How about that then?'

'That's a great tip. Thank you.'

'I know.' He tapped the side of his nose with his finger like it was their secret. 'It works, I tell you. I'm eighty-nine, ninety in June and you wouldn't think it, would you?'

His nose was bulbous and his cheeks a mass of broken red veins from too much of something, but he was ninety, nearly twice her age, so good on him. What were the chances of her making it that far?

'You look amazing. And thanks again about the water. I'll start doing that.'

She'd been going to say the chocolates weren't for her but why pretend? She'd fill a litre bottle full of water and drink it while she ate them, because there was no way she was disciplined enough to eat just one, for the taste of it, or two at a time leaving the rest for another day. When it came to sugar, she had to eat everything.

The bell on the door tinkled as Cerys pulled it open for the old man. He tapped his cane slowly towards it and, once he was level with her, stopped to catch his breath. She glanced out of the door, saw a man standing on the road, holding a bike, wearing a red top. He looked right at her, she was sure of it. He had a beard, a neat one like an office worker rather than a hairy biker. She tried to slide in front of the old man but couldn't without being rude. She willed him to hurry up.

'Water, that's the secret to a long life. Drink enough water and you can get away with anything.'

Once he was through the door she searched up and down the road, careful for cars because once you were down the steps there was no pavement. But she was too slow. The boy and the bike had disappeared. She couldn't get his face out of her head. His aura, if there was such a thing.

'Christ on a bike.' The old man leaned heavily on his cane. She supported his elbow to stop him from falling.

'You saw him too?'

'Getting old is no fun. No fun at all. I bloody hate it, I tell you.'

He had looked like Christ. The old man was right. Christ on a bike. The phrase her dad used to say if he was frustrated, jaw clenched, close to tipping over into angry.

~

Cerys kept seeing the boy's face. To her he was a boy rather than a man. A youth, though that word made him sound like a criminal ready for a court appearance after a minor misdemeanour. His skin had been fresh compared to her and her friends' after all the parties, smokes, drinks, the sunbathing, a mash-up of hard living that had taken its toll. The boy's skin was clear and tight, his cheekbones sharp, eyes bright rather than bloodshot. That's what she imagined when she zoomed in for his close up.

Why was he watching her? What was he after? Perhaps he knew she was rich and planned to rob her. After she'd given him what was in her account, would he return each month wanting more? He might know she was given a regular large sum of pocket money. The new lady in the big house who doesn't have to work for a living. That'd be it. That's what he was after. She'd tell Stephen about him, *any worries, just let me know.* Christ on a bike was a worry. He kept popping up, scaring her, his expression judgmental, she was sure of it.

Had he appeared because of something she'd done, because she was living in Thomas's house? Maybe he was the boy who'd been knocking on the door, his stubble turned to a full beard in the weeks since she'd last seen him. She had something that was his. Something that was in the house perhaps. Maybe he was Thomas's son or nephew, a boy who'd cared for him in his dying days, who Thomas had said he'd leave everything to then along came this woman, this *no-one knows who she is* absolute stranger who didn't deserve anything. She hadn't cleaned up after Thomas or cooked for him, changed his sheets each morning. Cerys moved the thought quickly on. She didn't like the picture her imagination was painting. They'd been in love, or were good friends, young and old, and now the young boy felt betrayed by the older gentleman.

That meant she was a thief, the baddie, and the boy was the hero. She'd done a bad thing taking the spoils from Thomas's long life, all his years of hard work. Greedy girl. Seren thought so. She'd said Cerys shouldn't take the money; she didn't even know Thomas so why should she get an inheritance? It had been a choice. Cerys had been offered this or that, sign or don't sign, like Adam and Eve in the garden of Eden. Would you like a new life or are you happy with your current life which, if you take the new life, will become your old life? She hadn't hesitated. She'd bitten the apple, gobbled it up in seconds. *Sign here.* Done. *And sign here.* All done. *Sign here and here, then there and you're finished.* Champagne all round. Sorted.

What if Thomas had been a baddie and that was why he needed someone to pray for his soul? He'd done a deal with the devil to get a load of money and in order to not go to hell when he died, someone had to pray for him, absolve him of his sins. Along she'd come. Cerys Jones, Lauriston Road, Hackney. If that was true, it meant the devil now owned her soul and the man following her on the bicycle, he was there to make sure she didn't run off, checking out the new human his boss now owned, making sure she knew he was watching.

Or maybe it was the opposite and he was Jesus, sent by God who'd heard the devil was playing tricks on those little humans again. What if bicycle boy was actually Jesus, checking up on her to see if she was good or bad when it came to the gift she'd accepted, the temptations that such wealth afforded? Would she be generous or greedy, selfless or selfish? Testing. They were testing her. And they'd made it complicated by throwing in the you cannot share rule. Stephen had. So Stephen was god's right-hand man or the devil's. The other door in his office, it led to a staircase, up or down, which way was it? He was the devil. Mfanwy and Rhys were two of his demons. Cerys was an easily manipulated human, a toy for them to play with, an experiment. Another one bites the dust, they laughed when she left the building, clutching her copy of the contract, going straight to the bank to check the balance of her account like Rhys had told her to. Classic. She'd acted like all humans do. Self. Self. Self. And the big man was judging her. Did her accepting the money, wishing for it, playing the lottery, always wanting more, more than she had, did that mean something had to be given in order to be received? If you win, someone else loses. She'd caused Thomas's death through all her wanting. Had he done the same? Thomas and others before him. Were there others? There'd be records, names on bills, the council would have a list of everyone who'd lived in the house before her. That was the way to do it. She'd check to see if it was true or her imagination playing silly buggers.

Silly buggers, silly her. She'd gone into bicycle boy's father's house, said a prayer for a dead man she'd never met and it turned out Seren was right, there was more to it than met the eye. It was a test. All of it was a test by God and Jesus and she was failing because all she'd done was think of herself ever since it had happened.

She'd bought presents only for herself which was what they'd told her she was allowed to do but what if she didn't actually have to do that? What if she could help her friends, her family, the homeless? Stephen had told her she had to follow the rules but her doing that was still a choice. She didn't have to do what they said. What was the worst that would happen if she veered from their path of righteousness which was actually a path of wrongness that God was testing her with, his son Jesus down on earth, watching, adjudicating. Imagine if everyone followed the rules all the time. What sort of society would that be? One run by powerful bastards, always getting their way by telling the people to follow the rules for the good of themselves even though the top dogs didn't follow them. That meant they had obedient servants rather than a free-thinking society, good for them, bad for the poor people, the middle ones, most of the population. The rich-rich looked down, guffawing. *Look at them all. Hahaha.* Bastards.

The rules she adhered to, how convenient it was that she'd accepted them, no questions asked. Was she following them to the letter because they happened to suit her? *Oh dear, I can't share, would if I could, you know how it goes, sorry, my lawyer told me not to.* People followed rules that worked for them, grumbled at ones that didn't, the ones that made them poorer, inconvenienced them, hurt their lives in some way. Stephen telling her she couldn't share meant she had no decisions to make, no conundrums, no long nights of the soul peering into her conscience, working out what to give everyone. Such a cop-out. Until now. Now she was starting to see more clearly. She was onto them, onto Christ and his daddy. Damn it and damn them. She had a mind, a strong one. She could make her own choices thank you very much. It was up to her how she behaved, what she did, what she spent the money on and the excuses she'd previously given herself, they stopped right now. She was a good person. She would rebel, a little bit at first then loads if she felt like it. That'd show them.

And God would be pleased with his child. So far, she'd failed his tests. *A place in heaven, you've got to be kidding*, God would say, bearded son by his side, holding his bike as he smirked at the cheek of the selfish woman. *Look at what we gave you, all the chances you had to do good, to help people, to make others happier and look at what you did. Nothing but shopping. How much expensive hand cream does a person need, really?*

If she kept behaving like she had so far, she'd forgo her place in heaven. Her coffin would sit peacefully in the bright white church she loved so very much but after that. Whoosh. Straight down, down, down through the earth, no serenity for the bad one.

She'd change. Things would be different. And she knew exactly what she'd buy first, a present for her hard working sister, a quick win for the Missy. Her phone pinged pulling her out of the rabbit hole. Cathy.

Sorry. No curtains or blinds allowed. Nothing in the house can change. They should have told you that.

Then another one.

Anything else just text me.

The darkness peered in, the moon shone a spotlight on her. God could see what she was up to, and his friend, his enemy, the devil. Though surely they could spy through anything: concrete, tin, bricks, mud, hay. If they wanted they could whip up a tornado to blow the house down like the big bad wolf, a big bad wolf man, Christ with his beard. He was the wolf man sent to watch her, to follow her to the chocolate shop, peer at her through windows. She ran upstairs and sat on her bed facing the door. Nothing could sneak up on her that way.

FOURTEEN

The sun warmed the gravestone. Cerys replaced the flowers in front of it with fresh freesias. Their scent blended with the sea air.

'Peace be with you, Thomas.'

Aged eighty-seven. Had he been a follower of the rules or a wild and generous one? He couldn't have been kinder with his hard-earned money than passing it all on to a stranger. Assuming it was his choice, assuming it was hard earned. She hadn't asked Stephen how Thomas gained his wealth. What if he'd also prayed over a dead body in the church so it was easy come easy go, and that's why he got to be buried in the beautiful graveyard, like she would one day.

The handle groaned, same as last time. No coffin today. Thank god for small mercies. No visitors. Yet. The local news had predicted five days of blue skies which meant the beach would soon be busy. Wales busy, not *Where's Wally* busy. So hurray for that. *Diolch yn fawr.*

The white walls reminded her of a house on a Greek island rather than a church in West Wales. If it wasn't for the grey on the outside and the slate altar that was in front of her, she'd think she was back in Kefalonia. She sat in a pew and prayed for guidance to the god she didn't believe in. A test. A joke. Sort of. The need for a sign that she'd done the right thing accepting the wealth. It was wrong to take and not give. That's what you were taught when you were little. No-one should be a greedy, selfish person. Her head hurt above her left eye from the over-thinking.

'Oh my god it's gorgeous. Come in here, John. It's so cute. Come and see it.'

His mumble must have been a no because the lady left the church instead of venturing further inside. To the beach. They'd be going to the beach to grab a good spot which was what Cerys needed to do. She needed to clear her head, reach the space behind her rocks before someone else nabbed it.

~

From the top of the hill Cerys spied four clusters on the sand and a fifth near the bottom of the path, tiny families rather than groups of ten or twelve. It was a good beach. Here beachy beach beach. Better than a dog, easier to look after. The cafe's shutters were locked until ten o'clock, but the toilets were open. Her spot was still empty. She'd risk a wee before getting settled.

The breeze was warm, continental, like the Thorntons chocolates she used to love but had to stop eating because she'd gorge on ten at a time. She had no control, that was her problem in front of vanilla, Viennese, lemon and strawberry truffles. She took a deep breath in, determined to make it a good day: sunshine, a book, tasty food, bodyboarding, a long shower at the end of it and a deep sleep from hours of fresh air. No-one could ask for more. So what was her problem, why was her jaw clenched rather than relaxed and mellow?

That man. He was her problem. Her heart fluttered, a mix of scared and *what are you doing on my rocks, you bastard.* She mustn't call the son of God a bastard. His dad might flash a lightning bolt down on her for dissing his only boy. She checked for allies in her peripheral vision but the only adults near were focused solely on slathering sun cream over their children's faces.

'Don't miss the back of their necks Stuart. Get your hat on Sophie, I won't tell you again. If you don't we're going home, I mean it. And no ice-cream.'

They wouldn't notice if Cerys disappeared in mysterious circumstances. If she went missing and the police had to interview everyone who'd been on the beach that morning, no-one would remember her. She was unimportant to anyone's life but her own. Friends might be sad when she was gone, momentarily, then they'd carry on in the same way they had after she'd moved to Wales. So what did any of it matter? She had nothing to lose by going right up to him, that man with his closed eyes, head tipped towards the sunshine, all serene. Bloody Jesus. It was time to confront him. Never mind actions speaking louder than words, she'd use actions *and* words. A double whammy, straight in there, no messing.

He didn't run away as she approached him. When close enough that she'd invaded his space, he opened his eyes and smiled as if he'd been expecting her.

'Why are you here?' she asked.

'Pardon me?'

'Are you American?'

'No.'

'Are you Jesus?'

'Excuse me?'

'Why are you following me? Are you Christ the Lord our saviour?'

'Is that who you think I am?'

His bemusement infuriated her.

'I asked first. Are you?'

'I don't think so. Is that who you're looking for?' He leaned back on his elbows, crossed one tanned leg over the other. His toenails were neatly clipped. The skin on his feet looked soft, as if he looked after them, had pedicures.

'You don't *think* so. Don't you know who you are?'

'Does anyone really know who they are? Some people say other people know them better than they know themselves. Has anyone ever said that to you? And who are you, lady? Who are you to be asking me if I am Jesus?'

106

Cerys shuffled away, too tired for his nonsense. He caught up with her, walked beside her, parallel to the shore.

'I'm not saying that to be annoying. I mean really, who does know who they are?' He filled her silence. 'Who are you? And whatever your name is, are you actually that person? What does a name mean? Whatever it is that comes to mind as you reply, are you her, who you'd like to be, or are you behaving how you think you should? Do you pretend a bit? Are you the product of your circumstances? Would you have become someone different if your life had been less tragic? It's all twists and turns isn't it, like some mad game and of course, it's what's on the outside that shows up but the inside of you, could it be that it doesn't match your exterior?' He paused for breath, a huge deep one expanding his skinny ribs. 'That's what I think. About myself I guess. What about you? Maybe you too rebelled against familial circumstances, what was meant to be your pre-determined destiny, so you became someone else entirely from the person God intended you to be or who your parents hoped you'd morph into. You're a chameleon, always changing because you're someone who can't be told, can't be ordered to do this, that or the other. You won't listen to anyone else, not ever. Can you even hear me?'

'Are you on drugs? Stoned? You sound like you've been smoking too much weed or taken too much acid, but you're too young for that aren't you? It's not what people do nowadays. Is it speed? On and on and on. Wasted while spouting nonsense. It's so obvious.'

'Ouch man.' He tapped his heart with his fist, three sets of two beats, bu-dum, bu-dum, bu-dum. 'That's pretty harsh, if you don't mind me saying. Not a nice way to talk to your Jesus.'

Cerys stopped walking. What was she doing being so rude to a stranger, someone who obviously had mental health issues, a druggie, high at ten in the morning? So many men had beards and moustaches these days. They all looked the same because the hair covered up their features and she was rubbish with faces. A boy on a beach taking in the sun, that's all he was. And he was right, she was the one who'd started it.

'I'm sorry to have bothered you. You can go now.'

'Are you Jesus?'

'What?'

'Look at the train of thought you've put into my mind, deep in my brain,' he pointed to the side of his head. 'Jesus asked questions, simple ones, that made people think and look at themselves, those around them, the lives they were living. That's what you've just done. Always questioning your choices… Is that why you're Jesus or why you're looking for him?' He looked round the beach and called out to a man holding three ice creams. 'Look at the skill he has. You Sir, are you Jesus?' He pointed at a woman who was balancing two bodyboards on her back while carrying a toddler in her arms as she walked down the path towards them. 'You're Jesus. Are you? Or his mother. Are you Mary?' He knelt on the ground as she reached them, bowed his head as he made the sign of the cross. 'Blessed be the mother of god for she is wondrous.'

The mum hurried past them onto the sand, away, away, turning her head twice to check the madman wasn't following them. Cerys went in the opposite direction. When she looked back the bearded man was walking towards the rocks. When she looked down from the top of the cliff he was lying on the rocks sunbathing. At the start of the path was a bike on the grass, unlocked, the owner not scared it would be stolen. She was tempted to take it, hide it so he couldn't follow her, assuming it was the bike she kept seeing. She picked it up then quickly let go so it fell onto the grass. She didn't know if it was his. She checked from the top of the path. Chatty man was in the sea, his surfboard in front of him as he jumped the waves, hair tied up in a bun meaning he no longer looked like Jesus. No longer Christ on a bike. Just a boy on a surfboard.

FIFTEEN

Cerys sat opposite Rhys as he filed her receipts. All she had to do was put them in a zip lock bag, no need for her to worry about them being in any sort of order. There was nothing for her to keep track of. He organised everything. Such a kind boy. That's what she told herself as she refused to look directly into his eyes in case he saw her soul or read her thoughts. Therein lay the danger. He mustn't know that she was onto him.

Stephen's voice boomed hello to the receptionist, a boy called Christopher. St Christopher is what that name always made her think of, a silver pendant on a silver chain around her mother's neck, a present from her grandmother when she'd had her first holy communion, meant to protect her when she travelled. The irony. He must have been asleep that day.

A breeze blew through the open door, making her ears itch where her hair tickled them. Stephen closed it. Rhys was in front of her, the boss man behind. She was trapped between her demons.

'Cerys. So lovely to see you. I didn't know you'd be here today.'

Liar. She turned to smile at him. 'So nice to see you too.'

'Are you in a rush? Fancy a bit of lunch? Rhys, are you free or hard at it?'

Rhys shook his head as he pointed at the computer.

'Alas no, perchance to dream.'

Stephen laughed. Cerys smiled. She knew why Rhys spoke like that. He was an old soul in a young body. An old demon or perhaps an angel, she wasn't sure which. Yet. Who was good, who was bad? In theory Stephen was the devil if the bicycle boy was her Jesus and that meant Rhys was a baddie, his right-hand man.

~

They got a seat near the back of the cafe and both ordered chicken and sweetcorn with mayonnaise on ciabatta, diet Coke to drink.

'They say it makes you crave real sugar,' said Stephen, 'but I love the taste of a cold can on a hot day. You're the same?'

She nodded. And was brave enough to test him.

'I'm thinking of going to Cardiff for a day's shopping. Stay the night then come home again.'

'Lovely.'

'That's okay then, if I do that?'

'Of course,' Stephen laughed. 'Why wouldn't it be?'

'All the rules, I get confused sometimes. Sorry.'

'No need to apologise.' Chuckle, chuckle. He took three gulps from his drink. The ice clinked against the glass as he put it back on the table. 'Don't look so worried. You're not a prisoner!'

She laughed with him, relieved she wasn't in trouble, cross with her stupid imagination for making herself think she would be. She'd got herself worked up over nothing, imagining all sorts about people who'd been nothing but kind to her. Silly woman.

He hummed as he chewed, eyes to the left, the door, the handful of crisps on the plate next to his sandwich. He didn't realise she was hatching a plan to break the rules and rebel. Or was he bluffing, pretending, going along with her trip because he actually knew what she was really planning. The devil would be a good liar, of course he would be. A demon would be able to read her mind, know every thought in her brain. He could be inside her head right now, damaging her freedom.

'Have you booked somewhere to stay?'

She shook her head. Cardiff was a name on road signs they used to pass on the way to Tenby for their summer holidays when she was little.

'Here.' He got a biro out of his jacket pocket and wrote on a serviette. 'This place is gorgeous. It's just outside the city centre so you don't have to drive round the one way system and they offer free cars in and out so you don't have to worry about buses, bags and the like. It's on our side of the city so all your driving will be on the nice roads. No stress, no bother.'

Cerys softened. She liked how he cared that she was too nervous to drive on busy city roads she didn't know well, offering her a solution without making it obvious she had a problem. Like a nice dad would do. He was kind. She was foolish, had let her imagination run riot because she had too much time on her hands. His thoughtfulness made her heart yearn for someone to look after her, but she mustn't cling onto Stephen. He had his own children, a first grandchild on the way. She had to accept she didn't have a dad, or a mum. And that was fine. Really. Fine. She'd survived years without them, then been blessed when Gwen had arrived on the scene, so much love, more than the previous two in one. Cerys had been so lucky to have Gwen in her life and now she was gone Cerys mustn't turn too desperate for another parental figure. She swallowed some Coke to drown a sob. She didn't need him or the dead ones. She didn't need his hotel where they'd have cameras set up in the room to spy on her, to check what she'd bought, monitor her movements. She'd book a different place and not tell Stephen because it wasn't his business.

'Do you believe in God?'

'Oh yes. You?'

'I'm not sure. Do you believe in Jesus?'

'In what sense?'

'Do you think he exists?'

'You mean existed?'

'I don't know. This sounds silly but I keep seeing a man around the place, near me, near the house, at the beach, and he looks like Jesus. The only difference to olden day pictures is he's got a bicycle and wears a red top all the time rather than a kaftan, not the same top but the same colour. I don't know why because it makes him easier to spot. He's not a very good spy or maybe he's cocky because he's got God on his side. Ha. I sound mad.'

'No, not at all. If you say you see him, you see him. Call me next time if you're worried, and I'll tell the others to keep an eye out too. Don't fret. We've got your back. We've all got your back. We're your A team, remember.'

He grinned then took a big bite of his sandwich, conversation over. Cerys was relieved he believed her, supposed it was good he hadn't made a big deal of it. That said something, that it wasn't a big deal, it was simply her turning it into something it wasn't. She shook her head, neck muscles tight. It would do her good to get away, spend some time in a city.

~

The boutique hotel was in the centre of Cardiff. She found a different car park to the one Stephen had suggested, outside the city, still on their side, as he'd say. She jumped in an Uber to take her to the hotel.

No-one from London had been free to join her even though the suite was paid for, her treat. It was too short notice. Of course it was. They'd have loved to see her, really they would, especially Sam, Ellen and Jim but she was going to be there Wednesday to Thursday and it was already Monday. They couldn't get time off work, the train was so expensive unless seats were booked months in advance and they had things on, for sure they did. People in London weren't free on a whim like Cerys was.

The hotel foyer was full of funky seventies decor, orange, lime green, plastic. Her room had a living room that opened into a bedroom, a bathroom as big as her old bedroom in Hackney, too large for one. She'd only brought a washbag, no changes of clothes, not even pants. That meant she had a purpose, to fill her suitcase with new purchases. After a cappuccino and glass of water in the foyer, Cerys stepped out onto the busy streets.

~

There's only so much a person can buy before they feel the need for nothing. Cerys shrugged as she let go of cushions and hand-crafted stone mugs. She passed a rack of dresses, not inclined to flick through them. What was the point of clothes when she had nowhere to go? There were no parties on the horizon, no dinners at restaurants, zero long lazy Sunday lunches booked on the Southbank. There was little need for a pedicure or manicure now she could afford them.

Part of her was tempted to buy things she wasn't that bothered about owning because physical things were proof that some of her spending money had gone, money that was burning holes through the pockets of her expensive trousers, full price, easily come by but what was the point of another pair. Who would the purchase satisfy? Clearly not her. The shopkeepers, yes. The delivery drivers, maybe. Or the opposite because they were tired, fed up from having to deliver three hundred parcels each day or you're fired. Her accountant, definitely.

'The more receipts Rhys needs to type into a spreadsheet the better it is to keep him out of trouble,' Stephen joked. 'You go for it. Enjoy yourself.'

She wasn't sure she liked having every spend monitored quite so closely. It made her self-conscious even though Rhys didn't judge her. He didn't show any emotion.

The scent of lavender provided a solution. When in doubt, buy soap. Cleanliness was next to godliness. Soap was a necessity. The voice of the assistant was so mesmerising and so focused on Cerys that it was as if she was all that mattered

113

in the pure-smelling world. The bustling store faded into the background as Cerys ran her hands under the tap. She tested hand wash, exfoliators, hand balm rather than hand cream. Why not add in some shampoo and conditioner, a tub of body balm, hand and body care fundamentals Madam. The way the lady described the products, it was as if they were the basics that everyone needed in their life, especially Cerys. She deserved them. The assistant's attention didn't leave her customer. Two hundred and seventy pounds later she suggested, 'Why don't you leave the bags here rather than carry them round the store when they're so heavy. We can look after everything for you.'

Cerys tried not to like how money made people treat her.

'That would be wonderful. So kind. Thank you.'

Confident with a first receipt tucked into the zip pocket of her purse, she headed to the bag department. There, in the centre of the Mulberry display, was a tagged Bayswater in the oxblood colour she'd promised she'd buy herself if she ever won the lottery. It was the old style she preferred rather than the new one with gaps in the side that she didn't understand because rain would get in or a pickpocket might slip their hand down it while the owner was waiting to cross the road, phone stolen, purse, or worse, the keys to their house, their car, their life. The old style was the one she'd always craved. It was fate. Her heart fluttered as if she was about to grab it and run out of the store. STOP THIEF, they'd shout at her. Cerys bit the edge of her lip. She could buy it with her debit card. She could buy four of them and still have three grand left over, her balance had built up so quickly. She could buy one for herself no problem. And one for Seren. They'd never know. How could they if she bought them in two batches, two receipts but she'd only hand in one. It wasn't like they'd be checking through her wardrobes and if they did happen to query it she'd say both bags were for her, she liked them so much she bought them in different colours. That's what rich people do, models and movie stars, but they wouldn't ask because she was down in Cardiff, away from their knowing. There were no witnesses plus she'd pay to have Seren's delivered straight to her house from the store.

When the assistant realised Cerys was actually going to buy rather than just looking thank you, she gave the customer her undivided attention.

'If I buy this one today, can I use it straight away?'

'Of course Madam.'

'I've wanted one for ages. It's so hard to find the older style in stock.' She stroked the back of it, inhaled the smell of the leather. 'You don't happen to have the purse that goes with it?'

The assistant unlocked the drawers beneath the counter. They had three styles of the oxblood purse for Cerys to choose from but only one in the earth grey shade she'd chosen for Seren, which was fine because it was a treat and anyone who unexpectedly received it in the post would squeal with joy, never mind the style of the purse bought to go with it. The assistant wrapped, boxed and addressed the parcel, assuring Cerys it was guaranteed, signed for, next day delivery. As Cerys transferred the contents from her old handbag into her new one with the matching purse and key ring, the assistant smiled at the man behind her. She didn't usually like beards but the brightness of his eyes as he watched the lady's joy... There was something sweet about him, mesmerising.

~

Cerys sipped her prosecco, just the one, she didn't want to become a lonely old drinking-too-much lady. Her new handbag was tucked tightly by her side, her elbow constantly touching it, making sure it wasn't stolen right from under her. She stroked it like a little puppy as she watched couples, families, friends and wished she had someone beside her to laugh with as they excitedly listed all the things they'd just bought. She would have treated them to gifts, shared the lotions, paid for lunch, dinner, coffee, everything, even a haircut if they'd wanted it. She checked her phone. No new messages.

~

After she'd parked in the driveway Cerys checked her phone for the fifth time that day.

OH MY GOD OH MY GOD OH MY GOD!!!!!!!!!!!!

THANK YOU THANK YOU THANK YOU!!!!!!!!!!

I can't believe it – I'd never be able to afford one my whole life!!! Screaming with joy here!!!!!!!!

It's SO beautiful. The most beautiful thing I've ever seen. THANK YOU SO MUCH.

The messages made Cerys smile more than the bags she unloaded from the boot. What was the point of so much money if she couldn't share it, make others happy? That's what she'd do from now on. She'd send friends gifts they wouldn't buy for themselves: cashmere throws, expensive cushions, candles that cost the maximum fifty pounds, tea and biscuits as a what-the-hell-Wednesday treat from Fortnum and Mason. It was all suddenly so simple. There were huge amounts of joy to be had from passing on Thomas's kindness. She'd give people unexpected moments of happiness and God would be happy she was doing that. He'd give her a big tick, good girl.

Her phone pinged.

Can you pop by tomorrow? One more form needs to be signed. It's never-ending! My fault you missed it last time. Sorry! So sorry! Thanks so much. Mfanwy.

SIXTEEN

Cerys climbed the stairs to Stephen's office. She'd ignored three more messages from Mfanwy and had two missed calls from Stephen. They sent Cathy round to check she was feeling alright; they were worried about her. Cathy, who'd insisted on arranging a time there and then for Cerys to visit Rhys then Stephen, please.

'Plus they said to bring the latest receipts as Rhys is going on holiday on Friday, so he wants to get ahead of himself with this month's paperwork. How was Cardiff?'

'Lovely. Lovely thanks, such a great city.'

~

Rhys flicked through the white slips of paper.

'Fabulous. Anything else? Your coffee machine?'

'That was in last month's.'

'Of course it was. Ha. Too many hours in front of the computer. What am I like? Just as well I'm having a week off eh. So this is definitely everything?' She nodded. 'Right. There we go then. Off to see Stephen now is it? You couldn't give him this for me? Save me a walk in the rain seeing as you're going there anyway.'

He picked up one of two identical brown envelopes from his desk and held it out to Cerys.

~

She was greeted with an unsure smile from Mfanwy rather than her usual warm beam. It reminded Cerys of the face the headmaster's assistant had pulled when she'd been sent to see him after the Geography teacher caught her smoking at the bus stop while wearing her school uniform, ruining the school's reputation. She was let off because of the parents, the lack of parents, a warning this time but don't do it again young lady.

No warm sun shone through the window. Rain, rain go away, come back another day. The town was coated in a heavy greyness.

'He's ready for you. Go straight in.'

'Thanks. You well?'

'Not bad. I... Yeah, not bad thanks. You? You take care.' Mfanwy bowed her head to write on a luminous green post-it note.

'Are you sure you're okay? You seem—'

'Cerys,' Stephen boomed. 'Welcome back. How was your trip? Fabulous, I imagine. Fabulous. Just some paperwork to sort out. Don't look so worried.' He peered at her over the top of a new pair of black plastic reading glasses that were perched on the end of his nose. He squinted as if he still couldn't see her properly, concentrating hard rather than smiling. 'How was Cardiff? Did you have fun? How was the hotel?'

'It was great, thanks.' She handed him the envelope from Rhys. He opened it and frowned, disappointment in his eyes as he read the pink sheet of paper. 'I ended up not staying in the hotel you recommended. It was booked up.' Why the lie? She could stay where she liked. What was she doing? 'I found another really nice one though, a bit more central. It's such a lovely city, I never realised.'

'Isn't it? I must go again. To my shame it's been years since I've visited but that's often the way, isn't it? You keep meaning to do things, then time passes or circumstances send you off somewhere else and you forget what you'd promised yourself, or others for that matter. Easy to do though, breaking a promise.

We all make mistakes, don't we? Have you been to St David's? Now that's a cracker of a place. It's the smallest city in the UK. Did you know that? Beautiful, just beautiful, with the most wonderful fudge shop and a gorgeous tiny book shop. You should make that your next trip. I would if I was you,' he smiled.

'I think we stopped there for the day when I was little.' She shifted in her seat, hands gripping her new bag.

'Now then Cerys. Have you something you want to tell me?'

Stephen rested his hands on the desk, palms up, arms relaxed as if he was about to meditate. His face looked so serene he might as well have closed his eyes. She held tight onto her bag, the soft leather a luxurious comfort. It couldn't be about Seren's bag. He couldn't have found out already. No. She was being ridiculous. She put her bag between her feet, self-conscious that its newness seemed loud, brash, obvious.

'No, I don't think so.'

'Sure?'

'Is it that I didn't stay at the hotel you suggested?'

'Ha,' he tipped his head back. 'No, that's no bother. To be honest, I might try your one if I head down there with Glenys. It's our wedding anniversary in October. You'd recommend it would you?' She nodded again, unsure where the conversation was going. 'No, not the hotel. Is there anything else you'd like to talk to me about?'

She pictured Cathy at the front door, no time to come in, hands on her hips as she checked the state of the drive.

'They've been worried about you. I'm just checking everything's okay. Can you call them please. They need to see you asap. And do you want to arrange a day to take the kayak out? Louise and Gethin can go with you, show you how to use it until you get your confidence up.'

She'd plucked some weeds from one of the borders before she got back into her van, reversing onto the road without so much as a wave or a smile goodbye. In theory Cerys was her boss but it felt the other way round, like Cerys wanted to please her whenever they met. Bingo. The bi-folds at night time.

'The curtains. Is that it? Or blinds, I don't mind which. Did Cathy tell you? I want to order them for the living room windows, the bi-fold doors. I feel a bit exposed at night you see. I know it sounds silly, but I keep thinking that when I've got the lights on people can see into the house. Too many movies I guess, but I'd rather cover them at night, make it cosy. Cathy never got back to me properly, but it looks like she was waiting for an answer from you. I asked her to double check, you see.'

'Ah. No. She never mentioned it.'

'Oh. I assumed she'd asked you. That's a shame but never mind I suppose, I'm here now. So it's okay is it? I can order some?'

'I'm afraid not. Nothing can be changed in the house you see. I thought that was clear in the paperwork.'

'I thought that meant building work, as in don't extend it or knock something down. I didn't think it meant soft furnishings.'

'It's all in the interpretation of the meaning isn't it? Apologies if you misconstrued the words which mean you mustn't do anything that causes a change to the building. And curtains or blinds that haven't been put up already, I'm afraid that would mean drilling into the walls, breaking through the pristine plaster and the thing is Cerys, we don't want the place damaged, not at all. Or rather Thomas didn't. But cushions, your new coffee machine, a new dressing table, all the things you've been buying, fine and dandy, absolutely no problem. Just no drilling I'm afraid.' He shuffled the papers on his desk and picked up the pink sheet of paper. 'Now then. This is what I actually wanted to talk to you about.'

Cerys looked at the sheet he handed her. It was a photocopy of two receipts for two Mulberry bags and purses, including the delivery charge for one to south-east London, signed for next day delivery. Her brain wasn't used to thinking quickly after so many weeks off work. She was too slow to make up an excuse though what was the point of a denial. They had the proof. She was cornered.

'It's one of the rules you see, an important one.' He'd never sounded so sombre before. 'Do you want to tell me about it?'

She plucked at a loose thread on her trousers. 'It was a present for my sister. One of them was, the grey one. The other one was for me.'

She lifted her bag up to show him. Stephen raised his eyebrows and widened his eyes, disappointed, shocked but not shocked, more *what a shame, I expected better of you.*

'Her birthday is it?'

'No.'

His brow furrowed to create crevices on his forehead.

'She works really hard you see, full time in such a stressful job, cramming seven days worth of hours into five plus she's got two kids and a massive mortgage. She never buys herself anything, honestly. We always used to joke how if one of us won the lottery we'd buy ourselves a real Mulberry bag and I saw this one, the one I'd always wanted and I thought of her not having one but me buying one for myself and it was just... It felt wrong, tight, so selfish. I mean I can afford it can't I? Next month's money was about to come in and I still had well over a month's left in my account and I knew it would make her happy, so happy. Honestly, she was over the moon. You should see the messages she sent me. I'll show you.' Cerys searched in her bag for her phone. 'She was ecstatic. She doesn't get many treats you see, no surprises, so I thought it would be a good thing.'

She scrolled through her messages to find Seren's thank yous but Stephen wouldn't take her phone. She let it rest on her lap. As she stared at the edge of his desk, she prayed for leniency. She'd sounded like she was begging. Why was she pleading for forgiveness from this man? Was he God, the Archangel Gabriel? Or a baddie? It was hard to know which side Mr Kendrick was on.

'But it was against the rules, Cerys.' He didn't look cross. He wasn't shouting. She lowered her chin in shame. 'Those rules are there for a reason, to make things simple for you. It's good to have boundaries, they're important in life. You do understand?'

'Yes. I'm sorry. I'm really sorry.'

'You won't do it again?'

'No.' She shook her head. 'Absolutely not. Cross my heart and hope to die. I promise.'

She waited to hear what her punishment would be, a month's money lost, the car given to someone more worthy...

'Enough said then,' he smiled. 'Let's draw a line under it shall we, move on? No more treats for anyone else though Cerys, I mean it.' He wagged his finger at her. 'It's meant to be your gift, solely for you. That's what—'

'Thomas would have wanted.'

'Right. Exactly that. You've just got to follow a few simple rules and look at all you get to enjoy, courtesy of Mr Thomas Morgan.'

Stephen opened one of the cardboard files on his desk and started to flick through the sheets inside it. She was dismissed. She could go now.

'How come he was so wealthy, if you don't mind me asking?' He started to make notes on a pad of yellow lined paper. Cerys stayed seated. 'Stephen. Stephen.' He looked up. 'I wondered, what did Thomas do to get so much money. Was he a banker, a farmer, an investor...?'

'He inherited it.'

Ah. Lucky. It was so easy for those who received.

'Family wealth then. I've a friend who's had that.'

Stephen peered at his notes, crossed a line out, went back to double check the file. She opened the door.

'Actually, it was in the same way you did.'

Cerys hesitated. Exactly like her? Or from his mum, dad, an old childless uncle, a great aunt in Aberystwyth.

'What do you mean? He prayed for someone?'

Stephen nodded and smiled like it was no big deal.

'I thought you'd have realised. Sorry, I should have said. Not that it matters. Mind you, I thought I'd told you. Honestly, my memory.' Stephen knocked on the side of his head with his fist. 'Some bits of getting older are no fun, Cerys, no fun at all. It makes life difficult, there's no denying it.' He looked more puzzled than Cerys felt. 'I thought you'd have seen, that you'd have realised. It's nice though isn't it, a good thing, and the same thing that you'll be doing, years from now. Passing on the luck, changing a person's life through kindness, giving them the chance for everything to be wonderful.'

It was nice. He was right. More than nice. Phenomenal.

'You must keep that a secret though. There's no need for anyone else to know. That's one of the—'

'Rules.'

'Ha. Yes, that's right. You've got it.'

'Where was he from?'

'Thomas? Birmingham I believe. He used to come here for the walking, once he'd gone part-time, half retired, I think. It was his favourite hobby, that and drawing.'

'Did he have any family? Was he married?'

'No. I don't think so, may have been divorced. I don't know. He was quiet, a bit of a loner. He never mentioned anyone when we were sorting out the paperwork.'

Like her. Cerys didn't want Stephen to think she had no friends, that she was alone and vulnerable like Thomas had been.

'That's so sad. To live here and not be able to share it, three nights a week maximum, don't worry, no rule breaking.' She laughed. 'I've got friends coming down from London soon, lots of them are coming on different weekends. It's going to be a busy summer.' She needed Stephen to know she had people who would miss her. If she disappeared in the middle of some devil versus the Lord thing, people would wonder where she'd gone. They'd call the police, try to find her. 'I'm so excited to see them.

But first of all my sister and her family are visiting next week for half term, then different friends on different weekends. The weeks are going to fly by.'

'Fabulous. Wonderful. It's a big house, be nice to see it full of life, and it makes sense having people to stay when you're so near the beach with all that space, all those bathrooms. Ha! Hopefully you'll get better weather than today, mind. Excellent. We did say you could have people to stay didn't we? We did encourage that Cerys.'

They had. When they were showing her the spare rooms, they'd said the house was perfect for friends to visit from London and, although they'd said she couldn't give gifts that cost over fifty pounds, they'd emphasised she could take people to dinner, treat them to ice cream. They'd encouraged that, given her ideas for ways to share that were different to buying people physical things. Her mind had obviously gone on a big loop-di-loop from having too much time on her hands, on her own. Too much thinking time was never good for a person. Stephen and Rhys had been honest whenever she'd asked them something, more so than a lot of people were in life. Look at Stephen telling her Thomas had inherited everything in the same way that she had. He could have lied. He could have said Thomas had won it on the horses and she would have believed him because what did she know. As she turned on the windscreen wipers, she realised he hadn't told her when Thomas had inherited it, how long the old man had enjoyed the luxury.

~

Mfanwy knocked on Stephen's door. She handed him a letter, a tissue in her hands because she'd known she'd cry, of course she would. That was one of the reasons she had to get away. The ups and downs along with the secret-keeping made her too emotional.

'What's all this then?' Stephen knew. He wasn't stupid. But for her sake he pretended he hadn't known it was coming. 'Oh, Mfanwy.' He looked up from the letter. 'We'll miss you. I'll miss you. It's been so lovely working with you, efficient and smiley to boot, who could ask for more. You're sure we can't persuade you otherwise?'

Mfanwy properly cried. 'I'm sorry. I'm so sorry.'

'Hey. Don't worry. Dry your tears. Come on, petal. There's nothing for you to be sorry about.'

'It's too sad, you see. The death. And too upsetting. The rows. The fallouts. Always a fallout from the will, isn't there, except for that one time, and now when I meet the new ones it's like I know what's ahead of them and I want to warn them but I can't, can I? It's against the rules.' She blew her nose. She wiped under her eyes.

He'd wondered when they took her on. Rhys had warned him she'd got upset when they found a dead rabbit by the side of the road, so God knows what she'd do if a human went on them. And it turned out to be humans. Plural. Stephen had had doubts about how she'd deal with all this, and he'd been right. It was too much for such an empathetic cariad. He should have trusted his gut. He'd be more careful next time, ask more prudent questions in the interview, hire someone tougher.

SEVENTEEN

There were handwritten labels on the three homemade meals that had been delivered to her door: shepherd's pie, lasagne, and beef casserole, plus sides of dauphinoise potatoes, tenderstem broccoli and salad. Bliss. Bliss to be hungry and not have to cook. Bliss to be a host with such delicious dinners on offer, all bases covered. Her guests were bound to like one of the choices. Cerys checked the freezer. Five tubs of Mario's ice cream: Brecon honey, chocoholic, coffee ripple, clotted cream vanilla, and coconut. There had to be a flavour everyone would enjoy from that selection. Happy days. Such happy days. So exciting to have people come to stay. And in the cupboard next to the fridge there was a tub of expensive waffle wafers plus a box of twenty Cadbury's flakes to go with them, for the boys, because that's what she'd have been excited by when she was young. She'd even bought one of those ice cream scoops like you got in the ice cream beach huts where the girl or the boy at their summer job pressed a button and a curved line of silver metal freed the ice cream from its grasp. They'd flick the scoop over and press down on the top of the cone so it didn't fall off as soon as the customer licked it.

She should have bought chocolate sprinkles. And hundreds and thousands. Then her house would have been like a proper ice cream parlour. They could have poured them onto a plate and rolled the ice cream round, coating it in sugary gorgeousness. Spray cream, chocolate sauce, caramel sauce, in case they wanted to make a knickerbocker glory in those tall glasses. Long spoons with a teaspoon sized end that helped you scrape every morsel from the bottom. She'd buy the glasses for next time, something new to surprise her nephews with on their second visit.

A car tooted in the driveway. It was too late to go to the shops now and that was fine. It would be fine. Everything would work out how she'd hoped and prayed it would. She and Seren hadn't spent a night under the same roof since she was eighteen but it would be okay, of course it would. Her stomach churned. She waved at their car as she headed towards the door that Max, the youngest, had jumped out of.

'Wow. Is this where you live? Really? It's like a hotel. Or a spaceship house.'

She gathered him in her arms for a hug even though she wouldn't usually. It was so good to squeeze and touch someone, such a relief to have company. He squirmed out of her grasp and ran inside.

'Mum. Mum! Come and see this. It's amazing.'

~

They gawped through the living room bi-folds, unable to believe the view, the size of her land – and it was land rather than a garden – or the enormousness of the trampoline that had been fitted into the ground so there'd be no worries about one of the boys flying off the edges and breaking their bones. Cerys rushed them upstairs, excited to see their faces when they saw the gifts she'd placed beside their beds.

'Yes. No sharing,' called James, bending his arm into his waist, hand in a fist shape like he was a winner. His mum had told them they might have to share a room, who knew, and whatever happened, be polite about it. Their whooping when they saw the bodyboards, snorkels, wet suits and flippers by each of their beds, still in the plastic, labels hanging off them. Cerys had checked. Rhys told her she was allowed to buy them even though they cost more than fifty pounds because they were for the house, to be used by whichever guests came rather than taken home to south-east London. She didn't tell the boys that though. As far as they were concerned they were their presents that they owned, the deal being they left them in Wales for the holidays.

'What do you say?' said Seren, smiling, laughing, relaxed.

'Thank you, Aunty Cerys.'

They were good nephews. It would be okay. She did love them.

'And this is your room. It's got an ensuite. I hope you like it.'

On the bed sat new bath towels with matching hand towels folded neatly on top of them, bathrobes that she'd bought for all future guests, two pairs of white fluffy slippers beneath them, a box of handmade truffles on each pillow, twenty four of them with no need for sharing. Lilies in a vase by the window, Seren's favourite for their smell, their core taken out so there was no chance of a stain on the white carpets. A tray sat next to the flowers with still and fizzy water bottles on it, two glasses upside down beside them just like in a posh hotel. Finally, three books sat on either side of the bed, from the local bookshop who'd been so helpful when Cerys had told them the sort of fiction Mark and Seren liked to read. They'd known exactly what she should buy for them.

'You can take the books home. And the truffles. I've got more downstairs in the fridge so save those for home if you'd rather. But keep them in the fridge so they don't go off. Some have fresh cream in them.'

Cerys needed them to feel pampered and cared for so they'd want to visit again in the summer holidays which were seven weeks from now, she'd checked on the boys' school website.

'Bloody hell,' said Mark. 'Cerys. Seriously. This place, it's absolutely amazing. Thank you. And good on you.'

She beamed back at him. Seren smiled but didn't say anything.

~

They headed to the beach before dinner. The boys searched for sea glass, not thinking it was stupid or babyish like Cerys had worried they might. Instead they got competitive, seeing who could find the most pieces, green, brown, white, look out for orange, it's the rarest, nearly impossible to find. While the lasagne cooked the boys bounced on the trampoline. Cerys popped posh crisps into a bowl while Mark cracked open the vintage champagne. They toasted Wales and Cerys's luck, her inheritance.

'*Iechyd da*,' said Mark. 'To your wonderful Welsh life, my darling.'

'Cheers. Thank you.'

'Ooh, that's sharp, a bit dry for me. Do you have any prosecco?' asked Seren.

'Oh. Sorry. Shit. No. I've got a different make in the fridge. Or white wine, red if you'd prefer it?'

'Don't worry. It's fine. This will do.'

Seren ignored Mark's glare.

After dinner they ate all but two of the truffles and kept drinking until eleven thirty, when Mark and Seren's eyes closed as they curled into the corners of the biggest sofa they'd ever sat on. Parents were always tired. Cerys wished she'd made her after dinner coffee a decaf one but she'd been so excited to have company, she'd hoped they'd be up until the early hours like at a sleepover.

Mark yawned. 'God, I'm falling asleep here. This is so comfy. It's like one of the ones you see on Grand Designs but nicer.'

'You have to have the space for it don't you?' Seren stroked the velveteen. 'It wouldn't fit in a normal person's house, only in a rich person's mansion. Look at you, all bling bling.'

Cerys listened to the boiler fire up, the water rush through the pipes as her guests got ready for bed. It was the first time she'd heard other people move about in her house. She stopped clearing up when they spoke, trying to catch the tone of their voices. She imagined them saying how gorgeous the location was, and the house itself, how beautifully the bathroom had been fitted, how expensive the sheets felt. You could tell the quality as you ran your hands along them. What a good host she was, generous. She needed to be sure they'd come again. That was the main thing.

Dishwasher empty, surfaces wiped, floor swept, flowers back in the centre of the table. Everything looking perfect for the morning. A picture-perfect start for the ideal day she'd planned for her family.

EIGHTEEN

Bastard booze caused all sort of problems. Amazing alliteration meaning higher marks in English. Crappy Christians looking down on her once she'd left their fold. Dear old Dedalus, Joyce's complex character causing her to drop a grade in her A-level English. E. E. E. That letter flummoxed her. E for... She couldn't think of a good word for that one.

Cerys stumbled from the toilet to the living room. Too drunk. Too pissed or pished as one might say, yah yah baby. But she had to drink more, needed to keep drinking to numb the feelings, because look at Seren giving her the evils all day. Cerys couldn't pretend it was okay any more. What could she do? She couldn't change the past. She would have shared it all with her sister if Seren had signed the book. But she hadn't. So that was that. It was one of the rules. You couldn't break them.

'You should have bought a place in London, Cerys. Everyone your age could afford to buy. Flats were so cheap then. Why didn't you?'

Cerys shrugged. They'd had this conversation too many times before.

'Why bring that up?'

'Never mind.'

'No. Go on.' Bolstered by the booze, another alliteration, though Cerys knew she shouldn't feed this particular fire.

'Because if you had you could be renting it out now and getting money for nothing really.'

'But I don't need more money.'

Mark went to get another beer from the fridge, a sure sign that he didn't like what was about to be said, didn't want to hear it, would rather not be near it. Seren shrugged, all *whatever* at her older sister.

'What? Go on. Say what you're thinking.' Cerys knew she wouldn't like the answer but couldn't stop herself from asking.

'What's the weather like tomorrow?' said Mark. 'If it's sunny we could go body boarding again. The boys had a cracking time, as did I. I'm thinking we could book them surf lessons in the summer. They'd love that.'

'Seren,' said Cerys.

'I'm just saying if you'd bought a flat, seeing as you say you can't share any of this, well, you could have rented it out or maybe given it to your nephews one day, left it to them in your will or something. Only when you're dead of course, when you wouldn't need it anyway.'

Seren drained her wine glass. The words had sounded less ruthless when she'd argued the points in her head.

'You're the one who chose to have children. You're the one who's responsible for them, not me.'

'You could give a shit about them.'

'Seren! That's a shocking thing to say. Don't be that person.'

Mark broke their promise to not put each other down in front of anyone else, not ever. They had to be on the same side in public. They snapped at one another. Him having a go at her. Her having a go at him. Snap, snap, snap, Mrs Crocodile, my my, what big teeth you have. Cerys couldn't cope with their negativity. She needed to be alone to have a little cry because what else could she do when her most thoughtful gifts weren't good enough.

'I'm going to bed. Help yourselves to anything.'

Not quite anything. Not her house, the thing she knew Seren wanted most of all after so many barbed comments, so much sniping, too many bitter remarks. Her sister had sucked the joy out of every treat Cerys bought or offered them that day.

Mark got more and more embarrassed as the sun hid below the horizon. He apologised to Cerys on the walk to the restaurant, their cardigans and hoodies wrapped around them, against the sea breeze. It was never warm like abroad, that was the thing with holidays in the UK, not like in Italy, Greece, Portugal, where you were warm enough in a T-shirt and shorts or a summer dress in the evening.

'She's not been the same since Gwen died. It's really eating her up. Some people rage against the grief. Give her time. It'll get better.'

Cerys wasn't sure if it was her or himself he was trying to convince.

'It must be hard for you too. I mean, she was your mum. How are you doing?'

'I'm fine, okay, you know. It's Seren I'm worried about. It's really upset her. She's been acting all... you know. You can see. It's the stress with the grief, I think, but it'll pass, one day. It's such a confusing time. No-one can understand why mum did that with the house. She always said she wanted to help us all, that she would if she could, so to get so little...' He shrugged. 'It's a strange one, hard for everyone to get their heads around. She was so lovely.' He sighed heavily. 'Anyway, the thing is don't take what Seren says to heart. She's not herself. And she's the same at home, always sniping at me and the boys. It's nothing personal.'

Cerys didn't like it when adults made excuses for bad behaviour, continuous really bad behaviour. Everyone had problems but you had to get on with things, make the most out of life. Less of your whingeing. And. AND, she wanted to shout and scream, I was closer to Gwen than she was. I saw her on her own and she told me she thought of me as her daughter, and I loved her. I really, really loved her and miss her and wish she was here today, every day. Her death hurts even more than our parents' did so don't you dare excuse Seren when she's behaving like such a cow. It is not okay. It is unacceptable behaviour.

Seren got away with the emotions when they were young too: the sadness, the anger, the upset. Then one day there were no more extremes. It was like she'd woken up different. She became utterly focused on not letting what had happened mess up her life. Onwards, onwards and bloody-upwards. Until now. Except this time. Up until Gwen's death, if that was the cause of this mischief, though Cerys had her doubts. She kept her suspicions to herself because she'd be thought of as a meanie for being so cynical. She had to be kind. Look at all she had. She must give Seren the benefit of the doubt, believe her brother-in-law, accept that Gwen's sudden death was what had damaged her sister.

Cerys cried quietly in her room. She shouldn't have drunk so much. But Seren wanting her to own a flat, to have things to gift her nephews. Was Cerys right to think that was weird, a little bit awful? Her head hurt. It would be worse in the morning and her stomach would be upset by all the rich food. At least she had her own bathroom so there'd be no embarrassment about the smells. She replayed Gwen telling her she loved her like a daughter. She'd told Sam about it but never Mark and Seren, not her family because it had sounded creepy, too weird and desperate. Poor Cerys with no-one else to love her, clinging onto Mark's mum, bless her. But she'd taken Gwen's words to heart and adored the sentiment behind them. Her and Gwen had a big hug in the hall before she left to get the train back to London, the last time she'd seen her. The hug was meant to say what Cerys couldn't. Love you too Gwen, the most in the world.

That was the problem with a sudden death. You didn't get to tell the person how you felt. Cerys hoped the squeeze at the end of the hug had let Gwen know. She found it so hard to say that four letter word but the hug, that was meant to show Gwen the absolute strength of the love Cerys felt for her.

She blew her nose, went for a wee, washed and exfoliated her face before coating it and her neck in serum and night time moisturiser. That felt better. She drank all of her water bottle even though she wasn't that thirsty then went downstairs to fill it up again. They'd left the hall, kitchen and living room lights on, lucky she needed a refill. She pushed the bottle into the dispenser on the fridge. It became cool to the touch as the liquid rose. When she went to the light switch nearest her she saw them on the sofa, kissing. Not kissing. Tussling. She froze, not wanting to gain their attention. That wasn't right. That wasn't who they were, what their relationship had become, surely.

'Get off,' he grunted, pushing Seren back with both hands. 'Christ. I can't take much more of this. What's happened to you? Sort yourself out for all our sakes. And stop drinking so much. It doesn't suit you. I'm going to sleep in Max's room.'

'Like I give a shit,' Seren sneered at her husband as he walked away, sad rather than cross, which made her even angrier. 'Like I give a fucking shit about you bunch of fuckers, ruining my life. I used to have fun you know. I used to enjoy myself.'

Cerys didn't want to go to bed leaving her sister in that state. What if she turned a hob on and left it burning, started a fire or spilt a drink? There was an open bottle of red on the coffee table that would leave a huge stain if it spilled onto the sheepskin rug underneath it. That's what the problem was. Red wine. It always made Seren antsy when she drank it after white wine let alone champagne, white wine and a gin and tonic while they were waiting for their table at the restaurant.

'You're still up. I was just getting some water.' Cerys waved her bottle in the air, her proof, her alibi. Seren's eyes were half closed. Her mouth drooped as she swayed backwards and forwards. 'Let's get you to bed. Do you need the toilet?'

Seren shook her head. Cerys tensed at the stress of having to guide her, a hand under her sister's arm. Upstairs, she gently pushed her onto the bed then turned her on her side so she was in the recovery position. Seren started to cry.

'I wish I had a mum and dad like other people do.'

'I know,' said Cerys. 'Me too.'

She went downstairs to get a big bowl which she lay on top of a beach towel so any sick would splatter onto the brightly coloured cotton rather than the carpet. She wished she could find some words to comfort her little sister but years of protecting herself from the pain meant she had nothing to give. On the landing she listened out for Mark but it was all quiet in the boys' rooms. Cerys hadn't thought to make up another bed. She would next time, if a couple or a family came to stay, in case there was a chance of an argument or they just slept better in different rooms because of snoring, drinking, breathing.

~

The boys ate their breakfast in silence, sensing the tension. Their dad looked sad when usually he joked around, all cheerful on holiday even if it was raining.

'Still better than being in the office. Oh yeah!'

A terrible guilt overcame Cerys, the sort where tears seep out of your eyes even though you aren't the one who is suffering. It was empathetic, no doubt about it, hopefully. She hoped it wasn't selfish. The tears needed to be for another person not for her who had everything.

She found her sister curled up in bed, staring at the curtains, an empty bowl by her side. Cerys stood by the edge of the bed, not too close to the dormant body. She didn't want to risk them accidentally touching.

'Go away.'

'I'm sorry,' Cerys said, even though it wasn't her who'd done a bad thing. It was just a thing that had happened.

'Go away.'

She made herself touch the duvet that was on top of Seren's foot, just for a second, trying to convey love and how much she wanted to make it all better. Seren flinched, pulled her foot back.

'Go away. I don't want to talk to you.'

136

Cerys left the room because she didn't know what to do, didn't understand her sister's pain. How could she? She wasn't her. She could not advise. She could say 'there there' but what use were those words when they didn't change anything. They didn't make it better. They didn't make the bad feelings go away. Her sister's confused fury and upset, sadness and frustration, was a reminder that a bad thing had happened and while that would never change, it had changed everything ahead of them forever. If it hadn't happened their lives would have been different, like Christ on a bike said. Seren had been younger. She'd missed more than Cerys, had fewer memories, barely any, not even the smell of them, just a silhouette on the beach, their backs covered in fleeces, hair flying as they walked into the wind, away from their children.

That made Cerys terribly sad. Her heart ached. Why since all this had started did her heart hurt so much more than it used to? At least now she could afford private medicine to find out. Ha-ha. But that didn't matter, not here, not like in America where you died early unless you were a millionaire. No. Stop. Do not get distracted.

Cerys lay on her bed, curled up like her sister had been, wishing she could take the pain away from her, wishing Seren could see that when she hurt Cerys hurt too and, even though they weren't close, there was a bond. Cerys felt for her, she really did, she desperately wanted to make it all better. But that wasn't possible. Not in the way Seren wanted because Cerys couldn't give away the money that was sitting in her bank account. It wasn't allowed. There were strict rules. She had to adhere to them.

Money was the root of all evil. Who said that? It didn't have to be, not if you were generous with it, if you shared and weren't too greedy. But if you kept a fortune for yourself... What if you had no choice but to do that? When you weren't allowed to share the cash it caused nothing but anguish, torment, jealousy, bitterness, all the negative emotions instead of joy, excitement, pleasure, freedom. It felt the opposite of freedom. Cerys couldn't do what she liked. She couldn't even pick out a pair of curtains to hang in her living room. What sort of life was that? Was it what she wanted? She could say no to it all, turn her back on the car, the house, the monthly income, hand the keys back to Stephen and the debit card to Rhys. She had a Mulberry bag, a coffee machine, enough money in her bank account that she could transfer it to her old one and it would pay for a deposit to rent a new flat back in Hackney, not to buy, without all this she still couldn't afford to do that, but she had enough to cover herself while she found a job, returned to where she'd started. Which hadn't been so bad. She'd been happy. She'd been near her friends who she missed so much now she wasn't geographically close to them.

The dream had soured and she was unhappy. So soon. She hadn't expected that. She'd thought the winter might get to her rather than a sister visiting in the summertime making it all feel rotten. But she mustn't blame Seren. It wasn't all her fault, what Cerys felt. The negativity wasn't all because of Seren wanting it more than she now did. Which was strange. So hard to get her head around. Cerys had dreamt of winning the lottery for so long, but those daydreams had been less complicated. There were no conditions attached, no rules, no need to watch over her shoulder.

Her. Me. My. Me-oh-my-oh. She'd made all the thoughts about herself. Christ was right to judge her. She was selfish and naughty for swearing though sometimes it felt so good. Some days the only words that worked were the bloody bitchy bastard ones.

NINETEEN

Cerys needed sugar. They all did. It released chemicals. That's what nutritionists and scientists said so it wasn't a myth that it made a person feel better. She sneaked out of the house to buy truffles for the adults and mixed bags of sweets for the boys, the biggest ones they sold, enough to last the day and their car journey home, plus comics and the most expensive hand wash with a matching hand cream for Seren then back to the newsagents where she grabbed five magazines for her sister to flick through.

~

Seren watched Cerys hurry down the drive towards the village. She listened for the others, checked out of the window, the three of them playing football in the garden. She nipped into her sister's bedroom and pulled a copy of the contract from under the mattress, the same place Cerys had hidden private things when she was a teenager. Seren flicked through the seventeen pages searching for numbers. There it was. Which explained the fancy coffee machine and two Mulberry bags. Five thousand pounds a month not fifteen hundred. Bitch. Fucking bitch for lying to her. Plenty to share between the two of them. Both their lives could have been changed for good, forever.

~

The man in the red cagoule had his back to Cerys. The street was busy with families walking up and down, suddenly stopping to look in shop windows. A group of ramblers tried to decide which chairs to sit in outside the cafe. Their eyes looked skywards: *was that rain, drizzle, did you feel that, was it spitting?* She had lots of potential witnesses.

'Hey! Excuse me. What are you doing?'

'Sorry?'

She'd look stupid for asking but what the hell, nothing to lose, no-one she knew was about and who cared if she made a fool of herself in front of strangers. He was the same man, she was sure of it. Or was he? His hair looked slightly different, darker perhaps but his eyes were blue like the beach boy's had been. No. He wasn't that man. She didn't think. His beard was a different shape. It could have grown. How fast do beards grow? So terrible with faces. She needed to take a photo to catch the shade of the eyes, the angle of the cheek bones.

'Are you Jesus?'

'Excuse me?'

'I said, are you Jesus?'

'Is that who you're looking for?'

His smile infuriated her.

'Stop it with that nonsense. Why are you following me?'

'I'm not.'

'Liar. I've seen you so many times, riding past my house, there when I was at the beach, hanging round here all the time. I keep seeing you way too much for it to be a coincidence. I'll call the police on you. Or I'll let certain people know that you've been hassling me then you'll be sorry.'

'Certain people? Are you threatening me? Are you a gangster, Mafiosa, an FBI mole with a new identity who's hiding in deepest darkest Wales?'

She refused to let him scare her with his mad talk. Cerys spoke firmly like Seren did when she'd had enough of the boys and they'd better behave or she'd really lose it. They'd sense the rage in her voice, know not to even think about pushing her further.

'You need to go. Now. Leave me alone.'

He checked behind her then whispered. 'What if I'm the answer to your prayers, here to protect you. What if I am similar to Jesus in some ways, which means you need to listen to me. Please. Not enough people listened to him. You need to be one of the people who believes what he's saying, when he's alive like.'

He didn't smile. He wasn't joking. He was mad. Was he a freak, a drug-addled hippie, or a full-on believer in the Lord? It was all too much on top of everything.

'No. No thank you very much. No offence but I'm not a believer and I'm afraid I never will be.'

'Why afraid? Do you wish you did believe in case there really is a heaven? Is that where you want to go? I've often thought hell sounds more interesting apart from the pain, I wouldn't fancy that. It's funny isn't it? How it affects humans so much, how it's been thought about and pondered upon trillions of times a day for hundreds of years. You don't see a dog or a cat or a guinea pig worrying about what'll happen after they die, where their spirit will end up if there even is such a thing as your insides floating off. I guess they're too busy concentrating on living. They keep saying we should do that. All the wellness people tell us to focus on the now, focus on what you can control, just look at the present, which is easy to say if you've got a roof over your head, enough money for food and bills. I always want to throw that back at them but can't be bothered because they're so out of it, out of this world, they'd never get it. Have you ever had to sleep outside because you've no money to sleep inside? It's not a good feeling.'

If there was life after death, would Cerys's mother and father be waiting for her there, wherever there was, up or down though that seemed too simplistic, as did purgatory. Was that still a thing or had they taken it out of the system? Bad PR and all that, about time because it was nothing but cruel. All those poor babies who hadn't been baptised. They hadn't committed a sin. As if. That was some cruel cunt who'd made that one up. Cerys winced. She didn't say the C word. She hated the C word so why had she said it now, albeit in her head, but still it was as if it was real and the venom attached to it, the fury. That was not her, not who she wanted to be. She was not the angry one.

Sorry Lord.

His lips were still moving but she couldn't hear a word he said. Cerys hoped there was nothing afterwards. She already lived in a heaven on earth with all the possessions money could buy so what need had she of a perfect after-life. And if she did die and go to her parents, then what? What would she say to them? It had been so long, their bond too short. It worked better with them in pairs, them together up there, both dead, her and Seren down on earth, instead of a cosy family foursome. And if she was honest, Cerys and Seren were separate souls, far apart on the planet. Neither of them would be in the other's eternally ever after mind. Her sister had her own family. Apart from the odd weekend lunch because she felt she had to and the annual offer of Christmas dinner that Cerys had declined for the last three years, both of them relieved at her choice. It was less tense when she was with friends. She had more fun enjoying a decadent Christmas Day lie-in followed by a morning bath, a walk and a roast plus prosecco that carried her and friends from a fun afternoon to a cosy evening. Then she'd head home to her quiet flat, her own bed, a Boxing Day where she ate truffles while watching movies in her pyjamas.

'And then where would we be? All the religions of course, so many I mean, which would you choose...'

There he was, still blathering on like a speed freak. They reached the crossroads. She spoke over him.

'This is where we go our different ways. Have a good day.'

Be polite. Always be nice. You never know, they might be your boss one day. On the journey down you could bump into those you'd met on your way up. Treat everyone well. If he was a baddie he might remember and look kindly on her rather than hurt her some night in the future. Jesus man hooked a foot over his bike and sped off without a goodbye. Christ on a bike. Rude. Ignorant. Idiot. He turned his head.

'Nice to see you, Cerys!'

'What did you call me?' She didn't care if people stared. 'How did you know my name? How do you know me?' she screamed after him.

He held his hand up to acknowledge that he'd heard her but kept on cycling down the road, speeding up rather than slowing down. She'd get in her car. She'd drive around and she would find him. When she turned to run back to the house, Rhys was a foot behind her. Stopped before she'd started.

'Ooh, fudge is it? What flavour this time?' He pointed at the bag in her hand, the logo a navy font on brown paper. The front of his shirt was hanging out of his trousers. Always so scruffy. Was it on purpose? Good hair though, thick black curls like Robert Powell in the Easter film that she'd watched when she was a child. Maybe Rhys was Jesus. No. Rhys's thick locks were too dark for him to be her man. Bicycle boy's hair was brown not black, more honeycomb than dark chocolate truffle. Rhys was her young Bob Dylan. Or he could be Moses, a friend who turned into an enemy of the Lord's son. His hair had been dark and luscious in the film. That would be good, if she got Rhys to turn on his master, switched him over to her side.

'Baileys and chocolate. Would you like some?'

'You're a creature of habit then,' he laughed. Another old phrase from young lips. Perhaps it was a Welsh thing, copying older generations words, mimicking their mannerisms.

'Why do you say that? How do you know?'

'Your receipts. There's always lots of fudge and truffles.' She did not like that he knew what she ate, her comfort eating. It wasn't right that he knew all of her business. 'Is everything alright? You seem a bit—'

'Fine thank you.' She didn't feel like eating the fudge now which was good as there was already too much sugar in her veins from the truffles she'd scoffed the night before. She'd give it all to Seren. 'Do you know that man?'

'Which man?'

'The one on the bicycle.' She nodded down the road but could only see cars now, driving slowly, on the lookout for parking spaces. 'You must have seen me talk to him.'

'Sorry. No. I didn't see anyone.'

'But you must have. He was just there. He knew my name.'

Rhys twisted his lips, perplexed.

'Are you sure?'

'Of course I'm sure. He said nice to see you, Cerys. You must have seen him. He was just there.'

'No. Sorry. I didn't see anyone.'

She glared at him. Liar, liar.

~

Seren could tell the white sheet she'd slept on was expensive by the crispness and softness, a clash of feelings that didn't come cheap. It was a new sheet that had never been slept on before, with sharp creases not yet ironed out. It smelt as if it had been trapped for too long under a plastic wrapping. If Cerys really cared about her guests, she'd have washed their new bedding. The sheets on Cerys's bed were washed and ironed, a hint of lavender. Imagine having the time, the energy, to iron your bedding.

'Someone does it for me,' Cerys had said. 'I hate ironing, always have done.'

Of course. And why wouldn't you send out the washing if you could afford it. Fair enough. Seren would too, definitely.

Skin blotchy, eyes red, the pain that had been brought to the surface was still messing up her head. No-one understood. Not her husband or her sons, not her friends, not her sister. And that was one of the hardest parts. It made her so angry. It made her sad. She didn't want to be weak. She didn't want to be upset in bed while the sun shone outside when they were on holiday and meant to be feeling all good, happy, look at the beach, the pretty cafes, the delicious menu, the creamy ice cream. That made her cry even more. It was so pointless. All of it. What was life for if you felt shit all of the time even when you had a whole week off work and were on holiday? There had to be another way. There had to be a way to feel better or even better than that, to not feel. That would be best of all, to feel nothing. That's what people took pills for.

'I want to go home,' she said to Mark when he came to check on her.

'Tomorrow.'

'No. Now.'

'One more night. That's all we've got. You can do that, for the boys. They're having a great time. They love it here.'

'I'll go crazy if I have to stay a moment longer.'

'For fuck's sake.' Seren tensed. She was the victim. Why was he getting angry with her? 'It's not always all about you, you know. My mum died five months ago and we've been at home ever since where you've done nothing but go on and on and on about how unfair life is now that Cerys has all of this, whereas before then you'd go on and on and on about how unfair it was that she didn't have things. I mean, make your mind up. There's no pleasing you. And look at what she's done – inviting us to stay, buying us all those presents, paying for all the food, champagne each evening, loads of ice creams for the kids. She hasn't let me put my hand in my pocket once, you know. You couldn't ask for a better host. She even got the trampoline installed for the boys. Why can't you enjoy it? We're off work, the sun is shining. We're having a luxury long weekend away totally for free, with a beautiful hotel to stay in on each leg of the journey that she also paid for yet still you're moaning.' He raised his hands in the air like God might have an explanation as to why his wife was like that. Then he started shaking his head. 'I don't understand. Why can't you be grateful and enjoy it, because honest to God Seren, if this doesn't make you happy, nothing will.' He paused at the door. 'You need to have a good, long think about things, you know, about who you are, who you want to be, about what you want your life to be like. I mean it. For all our sakes. Because I can't keep doing this.'

He left the room before she had a chance to reply. She got the message, that he didn't think he could keep living like this, with her, them together. Fine. Fine by her. Motherfucker.

Seren rolled onto her back and surveyed the guest room, not a mark on its white walls, the ensuite visible through the open bathroom door, fittings made by that German brand she'd read about in Home and Country and could only drool over and dream of.

She would have told Mark more about how she was feeling if he'd stayed to listen. She wanted to try and explain why she felt like she did but he'd gone off to bounce on the trampoline with his boys. Laughter seeped through the open window, taunting her. Bastard. Another bad person to add to her list of not nice people, those who didn't try to understand her or her feelings, how she couldn't control them and why everything that had happened was eating away at her.

He was right about one thing though. She did want what Cerys had, if not all of it then she'd be happy with half. That would be fairest. She'd been at the church too so it was only right that she owned a portion of the house rather than just being a guest in it. That would be good. She would feel calm and content, that's what her aura would be once justice had been done. She'd said RIP in the church and in the name of the Father and the Son and the Holy Spirit Amen, and if she hadn't had to rush off to placate her grieving husband she'd now be getting two and a half grand a month, would be generous to everyone, telling the boys they could pick whichever trainers they liked rather than the cheapest ones. She'd be friends with her sister, insist that Cerys lived in the house because she didn't own a home. They'd all be happy. Seren would be satisfied, joyous that she could now choose to work part-time, having more money in the bank while less exhausted. She replayed the church scene, stoking her own fury. If Mark hadn't been all needy in the car at the beach at that moment in time, their whole future would have been different. Stupid. Stupid. Bastard.

She shoved her head into the pillow.

That wasn't fair. It was her fault, not his. He was merely a bystander. It had been up to her to sign the stupid book. Look at the idiom that turned out to be true, actions speak louder than words. You made things change by acting rather than thinking, doing rather than day dreaming. She should act. She would change. She'd shake off her angry shackles and carry through one of the plans she'd hatched in the middle of the night when she couldn't sleep, when the thoughts were tunnelling into and out of her brain like hyper-active worms, not hurting her but definitely damaging her, like those long tape-worm things that people twirled round a pencil to get out of their body, being careful not to break them because if the worm snapped, the half that was left in you would go manky and septic. It would poison your blood, destroy your brain. She was the worm, destroying herself. She had to pull the badness out of her head. She picked the skin off her ears to rip away the layers of madness. She imagined all the what ifs followed by a eureka. It was gone. She was free.

She would face forwards, say yes to every opportunity that came her way. If she'd done that earlier she'd have written in the book. Saying yes meant life would change. If Seren did that, the bad feelings would stop eating away at her. Instead, her and everyone else's lives would be better and she'd create a surge of happiness in all those who surrounded her. Her life would change in a good way, like Cerys's had.

~

147

They stopped talking when she entered the room. Four of them on the sofa, her family.

'I'm sorry. I'm really, really sorry I was such a cow. I didn't mean to spoil things for everyone. All better now and no wine for me tonight, not for a long while, I promise,' she grimaced. 'Do you fancy going to the beach? It looks like the sun's out again.'

Mark gave her a huge hug when the boys were getting changed into their swimming costumes.

'Sorry for being such a bitch.'

'No worries.' He kissed the top of her head. 'I love you.'

'Love you too. I really miss your mum, you know. It's messed me right up.'

He held her tightly and stroked her back as she cried.

'I know. Me too.'

Cerys triple checked that her purse was in her bag. She'd treat them all to whatever they fancied all day long and buy more truffles on the way back from the beach, seeing as they'd finished the last lot, including lots of the vanilla ones, Seren's favourites, lots for her to take home with her. Gifts were the answer. That's how she could make people happy.

TWENTY

Rhys raised his eyebrow at the clear plastic zip folder which was bulging with white, pink and yellow receipts.

'My sister and her family came to stay.'

Cerys wasn't sure why she always felt like she had to explain herself. He worked for her rather than the other way round. She was the one who paid his wages, or a chunk of them at least.

'Lovely. Did you have a nice time? You've included everything?'

'I think so. Mainly. All the big things.'

He put the folder down.

'I know I've said it before and it might sound silly but even the little things, a pint of milk, a can of coke, they all add up so it's best to always get a receipt. Even for, I don't know, a packet of sweets that cost fifty pence. Just get the receipt, pop it in the bag and bob's your uncle, job done.'

'Right, sorry.' It didn't seem worth the effort or the waste of paper for such a small amount of money. 'Is it for the taxes? Is that why you need them?'

'Sort of, yes. It's complicated with the money being in a trust and all that. No need to bore you with the details. It just tends to make life easier in the long run.'

'It's quiet now they've gone. Such a big house... Lovely though. Perfect really.'

When she'd been alone in the house, Cerys had rehearsed what she might say, had imagined Stephen and Rhys's reactions. *I'm thinking of leaving.* Boom. Would they be shocked, sad, indifferent?

Her phone vibrated in her bag. While Rhys was checking the computer, she peeked at it.

Sam.

A missed call.

A message.

Fancy a visit this weekend? Short notice I know but weather where you are looks gorgeous and I've taken a week off work – new boss doing my head in.

Then another:

No worries if not. Such short notice!!!! No pressure. xx

YES! Perfect. Come on down. Definitely. Definitely. Just out. Will call later. xx

She would stay. For now. Have some fun with it.

~

Sam shrieked as Cerys turned into the drive.

'Fuck me, lady! Look at this place. Bloody hell. Is it really all yours?' Cerys nodded, embarrassed by the opulence. Her friend walked behind the sofa, stroking the velvet cushions. She opened and closed the kitchen cupboards.

'Sorry. I'm such a nosy cow. I love kitchens and this is so gorgeous. You classy lady, eh?'

She stood in front of the bi-fold doors taking in the view, deep breath.

'Wow.' Stunned. 'I mean, wow.' She turned to Cerys. 'Whoo-hoo! I feel like I'm on a film set. Crack open the champers then. Let's have the best weekend ever.'

~

Cerys was glad she'd made strong coffee after dinner. They stayed up until three in the morning chatting, laughing, as Sam filled her in on how everyone was doing in London. They

150

wondered where the years had gone. Sam reassured Cerys everyone missed her and they were planning to come down, all of them, it was just a bit awkward to get to, you had to admit that. Cerys nodded because fair enough, it was a good point, but they would be visiting one day?

'Absolutely. Are you coming back to London for a visit at all? Jim's planning a party. It's going to be a big one. Everyone'll be there and they'd all love to see you.'

'Yeah. Sure.'

'Excellent. When?' Cerys hesitated. 'What? Is something wrong?'

'No, nothing, nothing bad.' She took a deep breath in. Her shoulders rose and fell like the waves outside the window. 'I'm thinking of coming back permanently.'

'No way? Why? Fuck. Seriously? Why? Christ. Let me do a wee then we need more wine because this, my dear, is a big one.'

One bottle later.

'If you're not happy. I mean really, really not happy, then don't stay.'

'People will think I'm stupid.'

'What people?'

'Everyone. Seren.'

'Pfff. What's she got to do with it? This isn't about her. It's about you. It's your life you're talking about.'

'I shouldn't have given up my flat. I should have waited to see how it went first.'

'I believe I did suggest that to you.'

'I know. I know, I should have listened. Though they said not to. I couldn't. It's one of the rules.'

'Okay. Look, let's be honest. This place is fucking amazing so leaving it and the money you're getting, well...' She shrugged. 'Best not rush the decision. It's like starting a new job, isn't it? You've always got to give it at least six months to get in the swing of it, get to know which colleagues are an actual laugh, which are wankers. And for the first few months you're always thinking *what have I done, I can't do this, I don't understand it, I should have stayed in my old job*, but that's so rarely the case once you give it more time. Why don't you do the same with this? I mean, what is it you don't like? The shitty state of the house, the awful view, the embarrassing cinquecento in the driveway because for that, I do understand your pain.'

'Ha.'

'Okay, seriously. What can you do to make it better? Look at that first before rushing back to dirty, smelly old London with fried chicken wings on the pavement and all the shitty pollution.' Cerys knew Sam was right. To give up so soon was a cop-out. 'How about while I'm here we go and try some new things, see what you can do to make it less lonely. Let's go meet some local people. Good god woman, somebody's bound to like you.'

~

As Cerys brushed her teeth she felt normal, like she was a person who could have fun and had friends, was happy, who looked forward to things. She loved Sam. She loved all her friends so much. Life was about balance. And doing things. Actions speaking louder than words. That's what Seren had said in the card she'd sent Cerys to say thank you for having them to stay and treating them so much, they couldn't wait to visit again. If Cerys wanted to be happier like Seren now was, she had to take action, change her life and make it so. What programme was that from, that catch phrase? Make it so. She was sure it was a comedy or perhaps a sci-fi thing...

Her moaning was laughable, outrageous. She'd been hiding away in her big house waiting for things to fall into her lap like the inheritance had done, expecting new friends to appear when she'd made no effort to find them. You had to put out the energy you wanted back. As of tomorrow she would change, with Sam boosting her on. Thank god for her visiting. Cerys would send her flowers when she was on the train home, the best bunch from M&S that came closest to the fifty pound limit.

~

After yoga, when Cerys was in the loo, Sam chatted to three ladies.

'No, I'm just visiting. My friend Cerys is the one lucky enough to live here. Have you met her? Here she is. Cerys this is Juno, Ceri, and Frankie. I love the name Juno. You don't hear it often do you? Is it after the Sean O'Casey play?

In the cafe opposite the Spar, Sam made Cerys take photos of the book club poster and the craft club one.

'You never know you might get into knitting, and look, there's a pottery club. Oh my god that would be so cool, and you've got the time to do it. Pleeease sign up for that one. You never know, you might be a natural. Make me a pot for Christmas, darn it.'

They tried to get on a kayaking trip but everywhere was booked up.

'I've got one.'

'What?'

'A kayak. It's stored in a shed in a place called Aberporth.'

'Whaaat? Have you not been out in it?'

'No, not yet.'

'Cerys! What's happened to you? In London you were the one who was always doing things. Come on. Let's go and see it now. Maybe we can have a go in it today. So exciting!'

~

Louise and the boy from the car were standing by a wooden hut that that was full of metal racks that were full of orange, red and yellow kayaks. He didn't try to run, didn't look worried that Cerys would recognise him. That meant he couldn't be her Christ on a bike. He must be a different boy. She tried to study him without it being obvious. His beard was more brown than red. His eyes she wasn't sure about. It could be him. Or not. There'd been more red in the other boy's moustache, possibly. Maybe. Louise hurriedly put her cigarette out as if she'd been caught by her mum. Sam looked to Cerys for an explanation when the girl said hello like she knew her.

'This is Louise. She works for Cathy, the lady who manages the house. She's her daughter. And, sorry I don't know your name?'

'Gethin. But you can call me Jezz.'

'Of course I can.' From Jezz to Jesus, bejesus, bejezzuz, begethin, begotten. There was that phrase. You scared the bejezzuz out of me. Stop scaring the bejesus out of me you bastard.

'Sorry?'

She needed to be more careful about what she said inside and out loud; too much time on her own made her forget when she had company.

'You look like a Jezz, that's all. Actually a bit like Jesus,' she laughed.

'Ha,' said Sam, too loud, trying to push past the awkwardness. 'We're here to see Cerys's kayak. Do you know which one it is?'

They led them to the second rack. It was the third kayak up from the bottom, bright orange like in the photo, its plastic edges scraped and battered, two paddles strapped on top.

'Have you been sea kayaking before?' he asked.

Not since she was little, her and Seren each with a parent in a double kayak until she'd insisted she was old enough to go out in her own one, Seren back in the tent that day because she had a cold and the mum in the pitch next to them was happy to look after her while her family were off coasteering. Cerys was tipped over into the water by a wave from a too-close, too-fast speedboat, Mum and Dad to the rescue. They scooped her out of the water, huge hugs, it's okay, we'll always save you.

'I can take you out if you like,' he offered. 'Be with you all the way so you get used to it, to the coastline.'

'Yes,' said Sam. 'Perfect. Are you free today so I can come too?'

'Ah. Sorry, we're heading off in a minute. I've got work. How about Tuesday?'

Sam looked at Cerys who knew she had to say yes. That was the deal with this weekend, her seizing the moment to create a future. And if she fell in the water he'd save her. That was his job. He had to.

'I've got yoga on Tuesday.'

'You can miss it for one week. What time's the class at? What time were you thinking Jezz?'

'Let me check the tides.' He started scrolling through his phone. 'Two o'clockish? Two thirty latest?'

Yoga was at eleven. She didn't want to have to do two things in one day. It felt too busy.

'Cerys?'

She couldn't throw Sam's enthusiasm back in her face. That would be mean, ungrateful, and her friend was right. Cerys needed to put the effort in. That was the deal with a new start, you got out what you put into it.

'Perfect. Shall I meet you here?'

'Yeah. Have you got a wetsuit?

She shook her head. 'Sorry, no. I need to get one. Don't worry. We can go another time, it's no problem.'

'No bother. You can borrow one of those.'

He tipped his head to a green basket in the corner of the room that was full of black wetsuits, arms and legs entangled, a yellow hose lying next to them in a puddle of water.

'We really need to go,' said Louise. 'Sorry.'

'Lovely to meet you,' Sam called after them. 'So cute. Can you imagine being that young again? God, those were the days. All beautiful and able to wear anything you like. That's so great you're going kayaking, you know. Well done saying yes. So much more fun than being in the office. You've got to send me some photos. Deal?'

Cerys wanted to cry, to moan, *but I only want to go if you're with me.*

~

They ordered drinks at the pub that overlooked the sea. Sam shivered as she zipped up her hoodie.

'Such a beautiful sunset. Cheers darling. And thank you for having me. I've had the best time.'

'Thank you for coming. Honestly Sam, you've made me feel so much better which I know sounds like a load of wank because I'm beyond lucky but you have. I really appreciate it.'

They clinked glasses.

'To both of us being utterly fabulous.' Sam followed Cerys's gaze to a man in a red top standing at the end of the coastal path where it was still wide enough for people to meander past him. He watched them as he held onto his bicycle. 'Who's that?'

'Do you think he's looking at us?'

Sam checked him out again. 'Yeah. Definitely. Ooh, a new lover perhaps,' she said. 'Hey, I'm only joking. What's the matter?'

'I keep seeing him. Whenever I'm out, or most of the time. He's always there, watching me. I've even seen him near the house a few times.'

'Shit. Seriously?'

'I don't know what to do. Do you think I should tell Stephen?'

'Or the police.'

'I don't want to make a fuss though.'

'Said the woman found dead in a ditch. Sorry. Bad joke. Sorry. Have you asked him who he is, why he's there?'

'I tried a couple of times. He just goes on and on about life and death stuff. I think he's a nutter, a stoner or too much acid. But they can be dangerous can't they?' She took a sip from her drink. 'Do you think he looks like Jesus?'

'I guess so, if you're going for the whole Christian flowing locks version which we all know is bollocks so...' She shrugged and took a big gulp of wine. 'Right. You stay here and I'll pretend I'm going to the loo but instead I'll head down to talk to him.'

'No. Don't. Honestly, it might not even be him.'

'Soon find out.' She pointed to the inside of the bar and walked towards the entrance.

Cerys angled her chin to face the sea but her eyes looked to the left, watching the man watch her. His posture changed as Sam ran towards him. He turned his bike around. It got caught in some low bushes. He twisted the handlebars, desperate to pull it clear. More fearful than frightening as Sam closed in on him.

'Hey. Hey you. Can I check something please?' Always be polite before possible adversity. 'Excuse me. Can you wait a minute please?' she shouted cheerfully.

The man tugged hard on the bike. It came free. He stumbled into the path of a family who were heading home, the kids tired, buckets full of sand, pebbles and shells. They stopped to let him go in front. He pedalled up the path.

'Oi! Oi you little shit. Come back here. How dare you scare my friend. Don't you run away you bloody coward.'

The dad glared at Sam.

'Language please,' said the mum, pointing at her children.

'Sorry. Sorry kids. Don't do drugs.'

She winked at them and ran away before the mum could have a go at her. Cerys started to giggle. By the time Sam got back to the table she was full-on laughing as her friend downed her drink.

'What a fucking coward. Honestly.'

'I can't believe you chased him. Oh my god, I love you for doing that. That was so cool. I'm so glad you saw him. I thought I was going mad, that I was imagining it. No-one else has ever seen him. Oh thank God. I thought I was going crazy seeing this weird Christ on a bike Jesus man but he's real isn't he? He's totally real and now I've got a witness, should I ever need one. And you chased him rather than the other way round. That was brilliant.'

~

Sam re-filled their wine glasses and water glasses before they moved from the table to the sofas.

'I'm sorry but knowing you bought the bag for Seren, having a copy of the receipt. That's so creepy. Big no to that. If I was you I'd set up a different bank account, make sure they don't have the password. And who the fuck are they to say you can't have curtains in your own house. It's for safety isn't it? I mean that's not to say you're not safe. It's fine and you'll be fine but it's about how they'll make you feel, isn't it? Sorry Cerys but I'm not having this. You're not having this. We'll arrange an appointment tomorrow, it's too late now. We'll get someone from one of those blind companies to come round and ta-da! It'll all be sorted and what's Mr whatsisname going to do about it? I mean seriously. Fuck. That. It's your life not theirs. You need to take control, hon. You're the boss of all this. You need to take charge of your own life and then you'll start to enjoy it.'

~

Suitcase in the boot, seatbelts on, Cerys began the drive to the station. She'd given them two hours rather than the one and a bit Google maps told her it would take. They'd park up, have a coffee and a wee before Sam's train.

'That was the business. Thank you so much for having me. And the truffles, the soaps, such a treat. I'd never buy them for myself.' Cerys didn't see how Rhys would know that she'd given Sam two of the big bottles of hand wash and matching lotion that she'd bought the month before. He wasn't a mind reader. He didn't know everything. 'And once I've checked with work we'll get another week in the diary. Maybe September, once all the schools are back. I can't believe how beautiful it is, you know. Honestly, you're so lucky. It's stunning here and your house, my God. Wait till I tell everyone about it, they'll all be lining up to visit. I can't wait to come again and next time, we'll both go kayaking.'

'I'm so glad you came. I can't begin to tell you how much it means to me. Thank you.'

'I'm the one who should be thanking you. Seriously, you treated me like a queen and I bloody loved it.'

Coffee, cake, a hug, a wave. Empowered by her friend's confidence, in the spirit of trying new things, Cerys decided to drive home via the scenic route, over the hills and beyond the mountains.

TWENTY ONE

Full headlights on for the long tunnel. Too long. Dark. Darker. Darkness. Let there be light. Headlights off, back into the greenery. Beautiful. God's own country or was that somewhere else, the Cotswolds or Kent or somewhere? She checked the sat nav but it was dark like the tunnel had been. She carried on for a few miles then had another peek. Still a blank screen. She drove faster to see if the higher speed would boost the power. Pedal faster Cerys. Put your foot down. But that gave her nothing. She wouldn't look at it again until she was at the top of the hill. There was bound to be better reception there, like her phone when the WiFi was shitty, hold it high and suddenly a bar would light up, the message would be sent and that was that. Sorted.

At the peak of the crest there was *de nada*. She didn't know the way home without it, didn't have a map. Stupid Cerys. Always have a map, that's what her dad said. He'd have refused to rely on a sat nav if he'd been alive. She indicated and pulled into a viewing point which had space for four cars. When someone's laptop went blank at work they'd all call out 'have you tried switching it off and on again', and it would work. It always worked apart from the time Jason spilt coffee on his and the IT guy buttoned up his anger as he told him it couldn't be fixed, they weren't meant to eat or drink near their computers, none of them were. All eyes down, guilty, caught.

She could do the same with the car. She'd been driving for thirty minutes so had about an hour of her journey left, not too far except she didn't know where she was and there were bound to be lots of windy roads now she'd gone the scenic, most indirect way. It would be dark soon, then she'd really be in trouble. Cerys pressed different buttons but the screen gave her nothing.

'Come on, you bastard.'

She should be nice to the car because she did love it and what if it could actually hear her, because humans assumed a lot but didn't know everything.

'Come on. Please.' She stroked the steering wheel. 'There's not far to go and then you can have a sleep. I'm sorry I swore at you. I didn't mean it.'

She pressed the screen again, harder, more desperate, but there were no graphics, just a whirring noise as if the car was too tired to even think about taking her home. That was no good. No cars in front of her, a clear road behind. There was nothing for it. She turned the engine off, counted to twenty then turned it on again. The whole dashboard was blank.

'You've got to be kidding me.'

She'd turned it on too soon. That's what it was. Such an idiot. Gail in IT always said you had to wait at least five minutes before turning a laptop on again so that it had time to relax and get itself together. Cerys checked her phone. No signal. Of course there wasn't.

She reached into the top glove compartment and pulled out a Cadbury's chocolate eclair. Sucking the chocolate through the toffee soothed some of her annoyance. It was fine. Calm down, Cerys. She had nowhere to be, no job to rush home to. She wasn't going to be late for anything. But she was parked in a desolate stretch of road, the sort of place a murderer might bury a body and it would never be found, like in that footage from the olden days, the desperate parents of those poor children. It was so upsetting to watch the grainy film of the policemen digging and digging, the mum watching from next to the car. Even though Cerys had never met them, her heart hurt for their pain.

The car would start. It was so new it was bound to and she'd drive on, only stopping when she arrived at the next town. And there would be a town. Wales wasn't that big. It wasn't as if there was a 500 kilometre road ahead of her like in Australia. She'd keep going until she arrived somewhere, and she could afford a hotel or B&B for the night. She'd be safe until daylight in their best room because she didn't even need to think about the cost. As long as it had an ensuite she'd be fine, and there was bound to be a shop open where she could buy a toothbrush and when she got home she'd use her electric one for four minutes rather than the recommended two, sure to get the plaque off her teeth, each and every one of them. She'd find a toothbrush, of course she would. Green. Or pink maybe. And toothpaste, though the hotel might provide that. Every town and village had a Spar, that was the beauty of them. The bright green and red sign letting the world know they were open until eleven pm. There was comfort to be found in consistency.

Cerys pressed her foot on the brake and pushed the start button but the engine remained silent. She checked the screen in case it was the same as when she'd first driven the car. The engine had been so quiet she thought she'd stalled it every time she stopped at a red light but it was the electric part of it, spooky, watch out pedestrians. The dashboard was blank, zero neon messages. She pushed the start button twice. Dead as a dodo. Was that the phrase or was it dead as a doughnut? She couldn't remember. Her phone still had no signal. She'd been a fool to think that willing it to work would make it happen. She'd become too used to getting her own way, to having the things she wanted happen with a click of her fingers, just like that. A car sped behind her, half headlights on to say I'm here in the dusk that will soon be the night time.

'Shit.'

She should have waved her arms at him. Or her. She'd been so wrapped up in herself she'd missed the help that was nearing. In the rear-view mirror she saw a dot. Not a car, it was too small.

A motorbike. It was approaching fast enough but there was no sound, so too quiet for a bike. Their engines made her jump and panic at the aggressive acceleration, the backfiring exhaust. She would ask for help. Unless it was a ghost or spirit come to get her. The dot could be a baddie. She opened the door to face what was coming, keeping her bum on the seat, feet flexed ready to kick if it attacked her, hand on the door poised to shut it and seal herself inside, safe from any danger.

Cerys leaned forward and waved her arms at the bicycle rather than a motorbike, that was going too fast to stop. It sped past her.

'Shitting hell.'

She wished she smoked or vaped. This would be the moment she worked out a solution to her problem, sucking deeply in then blowing out her problems. She walked round the car, raised her phone in the air to offer it up to the communication gods but it wasn't happening. A squeak of brakes made her turn. The cyclist circled her like a shark, head down, covered in a black helmet, coat zipped up past their chin. Fight or flee. Flee where and in what, the car was useless. She'd fight the faceless rider. He kept circling, watching the road in front of his bike rather than her, not stopping to ask is everything okay which was what a normal person would do. She stepped back towards the open car door. He stopped, unhooked his cleats. Cerys's stomach twisted. A breath caught in her throat. The fear she meant to hide leaked onto her face. Fight. Be strong. Fight him.

'Who the hell are you?' she shouted.

He lowered the bandeau that had been covering half his face, protection from the wind. More stubble than bushy beard. Long hair tied behind him in a pony tail. 'Excuse me?'

'Who are you?' She did not add a polite please. She would order an answer not beg for one as she side stepped closer to the open car door. 'Why are you following me?'

'Do you need help? Are you lost? Broken down?'

'Ha! There you go. You have been following me. How would you know I was lost otherwise?' He laughed as if she was talking nonsense but Cerys was sure the madness was in his eyes. And she was an idiot because now he knew she was lost and alone. She'd given away her weakness. 'The breakdown man just texted that he'll be here in a few minutes. If you try anything, he'll get you.'

The cyclist held his hands up like he didn't want any trouble, confused by the weird lady. He zipped his jacket up tight under his chin, a black jacket over a black top. Not her Jesus.

'Easy. Peace man.'

Was he the boy she'd seen before? His eyes looked different and his shoulders were wider. Were they? It was so hard to tell who was who when they had such similar hair colour and growth that could have been cut, a beard turned to stubble on purpose to freak her out. Or maybe she was the mad one, the aggressive baddie. There were so many cyclists on the long country roads, too many young men with beards and shoulder length hair. What were the odds that she kept seeing the same one? It was she who was asking odd questions, not him, she who was attacking. He hooked his cleats onto his pedals and rode away.

'Where are you going?' she screamed after him. 'My car won't start. Come back and help me!'

The road in front of them lit up as a van pulled in behind her. She swivelled round to jump into her car.

'Alright, Cerys?' David shouted out of his window. 'Where to are you going?'

'Oh my god. Oh god. Thank you. Brilliant. Brilliant.' She raised her arms in the air, triumphant. 'I couldn't get the car to start. Oh god, that's so lucky. The sat nav stopped working and I didn't know where I was so I turned it off and on again then did the same with the whole car thinking that would make it work like when your laptop shuts down but nothing at all would go on after that. Not the sat nav or the engine. Nothing. Everything was caput. Oh my god, it's so good to see you.'

He laughed as he jumped out of his van. Bonnet open. A light hooked onto it that he angled so it shone on the engine which was so clean. His hands were covered in oil. A wire had come loose in the something-or-other. Quick to fix. He was heading home via Newport so she could follow his tail lights back. The luck, the relief. It wasn't until something was taken away from you that you realised how much you needed it, how you took it for granted. She was jubilant.

'That's so lucky you were passing. I can't believe it. A cyclist freaked me out. Ha. Did you see him?'

David shook his head as he clipped the bonnet back in place.

'There's loads on this road. All over the bloody place. But don't you worry, I'm here now. No need for you to worry about that lot.'

~

She'd been on the sofa for an hour, legs under a good Welsh blanket, the darkness outside blatantly returning her stare. What if. What if that man had been Jesus? What if she'd done the wrong thing in taking Thomas Morgan's money, buying expensive soaps, trinkets and truffles she didn't actually need when people in the world were starving. But it wasn't her fault. Stephen and Rhys, they said, they *insisted* that she mustn't share the money so that took it out of her control, meant it wasn't her guilt to own. It was Thomas's if it was anyone's. God had to understand that.

The way that man had looked at her across the road the other week, it was as if he knew things about her, thought she was a bad person. That couldn't be right. What did he know? She knew nothing about him, not even his name, just that he liked red jumpers and riding round the roads on his bicycle.

She wished a car would hit him hard so he was gone. Problem solved.

Why a problem?

She'd made him her problem. He hadn't said or done anything bad to her. The opposite. Every time they met he asked if she needed help. Maybe she did. Because look at her imagining what was going on in his head, putting words into his mouth from her over-active imagination. Perhaps she'd imagined who he was, which meant none of it was true. Imagination was not the reality.

Or was it, some of it?

What was real and what was she wrong about?

She was right about the bi-fold doors. They should be covered in curtains or blinds to stop people being able to see in. She would sit in her bedroom rather than the living room. At night. Once it was dark. She'd do that until she'd bought cosy curtains to hide her vulnerability. A woman alone in a big house in a strange town. Anyone could make themselves comfortable at the bottom of the land, her land, binoculars in their hands, spying. So she would sit in the bedroom. And she would be safe in her big house. She would be happy that way. Secure. Security. That's all anyone wanted.

She sat in the quiet. She listened. There was no noise, not even her breath because she was holding that, could hold it for over a minute, had always known it would be a great skill if hiding from a burglar. She stared at the air. She stared at the dots and the dashes in front of her. Cerys believed all people could see them, they just didn't look hard enough. She definitely could. She could see lots of little bits, like when television programmes finished for the night in the seventies and the screen would fill with black and white juddering dots. It was like that now except the dots were see-through. When she was fourteen she'd told her friends at a sleepover and they howled with laughter, too much hysterical cackling because it wasn't that funny. They'd taken the mickey out of her for weeks, months, so much so that she never told another soul in case they thought she was mad as well. Since that night she'd never told anyone anything that might make her seem different. So what to do about Mister Christ on a bike. What to do, what to do. She could visit Stephen. Maybe. He might think she was a crazy lady, which might not be allowed. Did you have to be of sound mind to keep the fortune? Was that another rule that must not be broken?

TWENTY TWO

Heaviness fell. It sank through her core to her thighs, calves, feet. Even her toes felt like they didn't have enough energy to carry her from the hallway to where she desperately needed to be, which was lying down, allowing the currents of grief to sweep through her body. Cerys had to get to bed. Once she was there she'd let it overwhelm her, go with the flow like people said you're meant to.

They needed to be careful about the advice they offered, those people. Because one mustn't go with all flows, certainly not the anger, the fury brought forth by a bad grief. Look at Seren. How she acted was no good to anyone, not even herself: the shouts at the length of the queue in the supermarket, the swearing when she was cut up by other drivers, the baiting of her sister. Cerys refused to engage with the passive aggressive quips. Refused. Declined. Didn't. Couldn't. Wouldn't. It wasn't in her to shout back. Her nature was to sink down when faced with a threat rather than rear up to challenge it.

She lowered herself into bed. She'd be okay as long as she was cocooned beneath the duvet that was white, watching the curtains that were grey, the sky beyond them blue, lime green grass fanned by the breeze. A shout from the road reminded her life carried on though for now she decided to ignore that fact and wallow in memories. Tears fell. Sadness engulfed her.

It was not fair that Gwen was dead. She was too young. And so kind. Really lovely to Cerys. She didn't have to be, they weren't related. She told Cerys at the drinks held the day before Seren and Mark's wedding, after she'd drunk two half pints of cider in the beer garden, her cheeks flushed, stomach about to turn queasy, 'I saw something sad in you and wanted to hug you as soon as I saw you. I wanted to look after you there and then. I don't know why. Perhaps it's the mum in me.'

Cerys knew why. It was the lost look strangers noticed she had about her, as if she was searching for someone. A replacement for them. Both gone. Her. Always on the lookout. From the inside out. She never told anyone but they felt it when they got close. That's why men steered clear after a few months. Too much need in those big brown eyes.

She was placed next to Gwen at the wedding dinner. After polite introductions to the rest of the table they spoke only to each other, laughed, touched an arm in sympathy at a sad remembrance, swapped numbers before the disco started.

'You must visit. Definitely come and visit. I mean it, I'm not just being polite you know. If I didn't like you I wouldn't be offering.'

So Cerys did, nervous as the train pulled into the station. But it was easy. They sent cards to one another which morphed into birthday and Christmas presents, both so good at knowing exactly what the other would love. Friends. More than friends. More like mother and daughter but without the complications of a shared history, so easier than that. Seren's eyes rolled upwards when she heard about one of the visits so Gwen and Cerys never again mentioned that they were in touch. It was their business, no-one else's. And now no-one understood how much Cerys missed her, apart from Sam. She got it.

'Oh you poor, poor thing. She was like a mum to you, wasn't she? I'm so sorry.'

Why was it always the lovely ones who died, leaving so many mean people alive? Cerys had a theory that good people were so kind and worried for others so much it damaged their hearts, wore them out like the soles on a favourite pair of shoes that had been trodden on for too many miles. And once the heart went, the other organs, all the other parts of the body that were connected to it, they broke down too until the kind person fell over. Dead. They dropped to the floor with tiredness from only a tenth of their body working and when they closed their eyes, the doctors couldn't get them to open again.

Another theory was that God wanted them in heaven. That's what the priest had told her and Seren that day. If only she could believe it, how simple life would be.

Her third theory was sod's law. You may as well be a bastard in life, especially if there wasn't a heaven or a hell, no punishment in the ever after. All those psychopaths who didn't care about others, they got away with their cruelty by sleeping soundly through the night. Their cells regenerated. They woke rejuvenated and refreshed every morning, unlike kind Gwen who'd phoned a different son each day to check they were happy, that her grandchildren were alright. She told Cerys how she worried about others. Cerys said, 'What about you? Are you okay? You look like you've lost weight.'

'Me? I'm fine and dandy.'

The thoughts hurt Cerys's insides but she couldn't stop herself from thinking them. She missed Gwen. And her friends, especially Sam. She preferred it when she had company. Even her sister and nephews were better than no-one.

~

A long night of sadness plus the stress of the broken-down car resulted in Sam's voice breaking into her head.

'Go for massages, facials, manicures, make-overs. Honestly, Cerys. You've worked so hard your whole life. Kick back and have some fun. You deserve it.'

She took the leaflet out of the folder. Thirty-five miles according to the route planner. Fifty-two minutes to reach Olwen in Aberaeron. Too long a drive for a treat she didn't need, not now the maudlin feelings had lessened. She mustn't waste money. A massage meant there'd be nothing to show for the pounds she transferred with a tap of the card. Unlike a bag, dress, fleece, her new running shoes. A physical thing was proof of the spend. She bought things because you can't buy feelings. She knew that. You can't buy feeling better. You might enjoy a short-term fix, but that was of no help to a long-term problem. Not that there was a problem. She was fine, fine and dandy, thank you very much.

Take care of the pennies and the pounds will look after themselves. She'd been raised to do that. So little money when they were children, hence camping instead of the Algarve. And there was even less after her parents had gone, the sisters a burden on whoever looked after them. Thank you. Say thank you. You must say thank you. We will. We did. We have, three times already. You're lucky they're having you to stay. If you use up all the hot water they won't offer again. We won't. We haven't. We didn't.

Cerys couldn't bear to waste a penny on nothing. Hand cream, body wash, soap that cost more than an evening meal, those products were used every day so it was fair to call them necessities. Glasses, plates, cups, the same. Even her Mulberry bag. She used it all the time rather than keep it in a cupboard, proof it was another necessity, no need to feel guilty about that one.

She put the leaflet back. No need for her parents to turn in their graves at money spent on nothing. She texted Sam.

Massage was bliss. Will treat you next time. Loves ya.

~

The wind threw the rain sideways. The sea was the same shade as the slate tiles on the roofs on the houses. Cerys would stay cosy inside rather than make herself go out like she had been doing, every day since Sam had visited. It would be a day of rest. One missed yoga class wouldn't matter. She felt calmer at the simplicity of her choice, not having to call in sick, no rent to worry about. Lucky lady.

As the coffee machine warmed up Cerys went to check for post but the mat was bare because everything was sent by email these days. She'd like to receive a letter but one must give in order to receive. She'd write postcards, send photos of the beach to tempt her friends down for a visit. Her phone pinged.

All good for 2.30. Seas calmer than the skies are making out.

She'd assumed it would be cancelled, that she wouldn't have to go out in such atrocious weather.

It looks rough from here. And I've not done it in years.

She added the emoji argh face.

Brightening up later. Your lucky day. Thumbs up.

And sure enough the clouds were pushed out of the way by a stubborn streak of blue sky. Damn it.

~

Gethin and Cerys carried the kayak to the edge of the water. Lou had to help her mum clean a cottage for a midweek changeover. They were busier than ever since Airbnb meant holidaymakers didn't have to book for a full week at a time. Such flexibility meant Cathy's business was booming.

The kayak kept banging against Cerys's thigh. She tried to contain her grumpiness at the pain by focusing on what she'd enjoy when the two hour trip was over: a hot bath followed by tasty food. Perhaps she'd order new pyjamas. She'd always wanted silk ones, and some loungewear for when she was hanging round the house, loose enough that she could do a yoga pose without having to get changed first. That was it. Something to look forward to, her evening sorted. She'd order pyjamas, cashmere socks, fleecy slippers to get cosy in when she was back from bumping over the sea in her bright orange kayak.

'You were right. It's really calm.'

Jezz doffed a pretend hat.

'Okay, in you get. I'll push you off then follow in mine.'

His kayak was bright yellow, no fear of it being camouflaged in the good Welsh sea that was the same colour as the good Welsh slate even when the sun shone on it. She studied his face, hair tied up in a man bun. He couldn't be her Jesus. He was friendly, never ran away from her, and if he was guilty of following her he wouldn't have offered to spend time close by. Sam said he looked nothing like the other guy. She'd laughed at how bad Cerys was with faces, always had been, always would be.

'Promise me you'll never point someone out in a police lineup, Missus.'

Jezz paddled beside her. 'Okay?' Cerys nodded. The sun settled on her face. It felt good to be out of the house and on the water. 'Let's go then. I promise you'll love it. There's nothing like seeing the coast from the water rather than the other way round.'

The only sound was the waves sloshing against the kayak, the odd screech from a gull, the chip-chop of the blades, satisfying as she made her way from the shore, faster than a swim, run or walk. Her arms were strong from downward dog poses, handstands and press ups, so much stronger than the last time, her first time alone in a kayak. She was warm in the wetsuit. Horrid to put on but worth it plus the shoes, sandy bits between her toes but at least the heat meant she'd keep going longer. She would do this again. It was freeing. She would buy her own kit, ask Jezz's advice about which brand was the best and which fit to get. He'd said the fit was important.

Cerys was glad the water was dark grey rather than turquoise like in exotic photos of abroad. If she could see to the bottom and a shark appeared underneath her she'd freak out. Though what if there was a shark or worse hidden by the shade? Her friend had gone kayaking in Florida, dirty water, loads of plants, and there had been alligators, huge ones. She'd never been so scared in her life, and this was a person who'd once bungee jumped off a bridge in New Zealand. But the alligators. They'd rocked the boat. She thought they were going to tip her into the water and she'd be rolled around until she was unconscious, saved for later, their dinnertime.

'There's no sharks or anything?' she asked.

'Only basking ones and they won't hurt you. See up there.' He stopped paddling, so did she. 'A peregrine. Beautiful.' Cerys wasn't used to boys liking nature. She liked the new man thing, that they weren't scared to be appreciative. 'Fancy checking out a cave? Nothing dark. When the water comes in it lifts you up like you're on a fairground ride.'

She didn't fancy that. But she also wanted to seem brave and up for fun. His confidence was cheering.

'Sure. Sounds good. Is this what you do for a living? Take people out kayaking.'

'Yeah, in the summer. Plus I help Cathy out, plus I clean caravans.'

'Wow. Busy then.'

'It's all bits and bobs of hours you know. You've got to take what you can round here, make as much as you can in the holiday season. This is my favourite thing, though.'

'I bet. And you're training for a triathlon.'

'That's just to keep fit. Everyone should keep fit. I always think it's healthy body healthy mind more than healthy mind healthy body.'

'Yeah. Right. Same.'

'What do you do?'

'Not at much as I should. I used to go to the gym in London. I've done a bit of running since I've moved here, nothing like you and Louise, and I've been to a couple of yoga classes plus I do the Nike app workouts.'

'They're great. It's important isn't it, to keep fit. You never know when you might need it, when you might need to run away.' He watched the cliff as if what he'd said was normal. Was

174

that a warning, a threat? Or nothing, her reading too much into it again. 'This is what I love, seeing the coast from the sea. Not enough people do that.'

She followed his gaze. Walkers watched them. A child waved, the motion of the kayak tilting him from side to side. Cerys wanted the parents to pull him back. Didn't they realise how dangerous it was? A coast could crumble without warning, pairs of feet slip down the cliff, upright bodies flipped over into tumble time. So she imagined because she hadn't seen them. She only heard them. Not words. A wail, a female wail. Her dad didn't have time to shout out before his head hit a rock and consciousness was taken from him. Which was a good thing. The noises from her mum made her sick to the core, a gip, a retch. Pull the child back. Edges are too dangerous.

'Okay?' Gethin rested his hand on the front of her kayak to try and lessen the rocking motion. 'People think you can't get seasick when you're outside rather than in a boat but you can, and more so as you get older.'

Old lady Cerys. Not that old.

'Shall we go on? I think it's better when I'm moving.'

They floated under some natural arches into a calm cove.

'They're out early today.'

Three dolphins a few feet in front of them, much bigger than she'd thought they would be close up. She knew they were beautiful but all she could think about was them toppling her kayak over, then what if a shark got her or one of the dolphins turned to attack mode? How many seconds did you have if you fell into the sea? It was probably minutes in a wetsuit and Jezz was there to save her. He'd call sea rescue or the RNLI, they'd pull her onto a boat or tell her to grab the ladder thrown down by a man in a helicopter. She'd be alright. She'd survive. Her main injury would be mortification at the drama she'd caused. All those people at the bottom of the cliff, a red and yellow helicopter landing on the sand, lots of adults crying, strangers wrapping their arms around the two young girls' shoulders, the poor, poor darlings. Did you see? Such a tragedy. Focus. She wasn't on a cliff, she was in the water.

'Are they dangerous? Sorry. It's just they're so big.'

He sighed, disappointed that she'd broken the spell. Cerys felt like she'd failed a test. She could get him back on side, tell him about her parents, in front of her one minute, gone the next.

'It's best we head back now. There's a storm coming.' He nodded towards the dark grey horizon.

~

She held out a fifty pound note. Jezz put both his hands up to block her generosity.

'No need thanks. I tell Stephen when I take you out and he pays me directly.'

'In that case, consider it your tip.'

'I can't. It's too much.'

'Please. I was really scared going out there, imagined all sorts of crazy things, beasts in the sea and all that but I had the best time. Honestly, take it. I'll feel bad if you don't.'

She helped him lift the kayaks into the storage racks. It was good to feel useful. She'd been an idiot to consider abandoning her luck when days could be spent on the ocean, walking over the hills. People would kill for that. Gethin grabbed his bike to walk up the road with her.

'You cycle everywhere do you?'

'Mainly.' He patted his bike like it was a good doggie.

'Lots of young people cycle round here, don't they?'

'I guess so,' he shrugged.

She wanted to be cross with his ambivalence to her important question but his aura was all peace and love, not that she believed in auras but if she did that's how she'd describe his.

'Did you take Thomas kayaking?'

'No. It was too cold for his hands. He had arthritis in them so you know, the cold and wet holding a paddle... Poor old guy.'

'What about in the summer?'

'He wasn't here last summer.' Gethin hooked his leg over the bike and started pedalling. 'Nice to see you. Have a good one.'

He was away before she could ask him why Thomas wasn't there this time last year. She watched him disappear round the corner, his back curved over his bike. Familiar. Like Jesus.

'Christ on a bike.'

Her phone pinged. Sam.

How was it? Photos please Mrs. Raining here. Again. Roll on summer. Loves ya xx

TWENTY THREE

Seren smashed the chicken breasts with the wooden hammer, flattening their flesh.

'Why did she get it? How come she got the luck and not me?'

'I thought you felt sorry for her.'

'What do you mean?'

'Because she isn't married, doesn't have children. You always made out like her life was missing things, *even though she never says it*, that's what you'd say when she left after a lunch, a bit smug to be honest. Why can't you just be happy for her?'

Mark didn't understand. He didn't understand his wife, he didn't understand her feelings.

'Jesus,' she screamed. An agonised shriek that made him jump, that went on past the moment the words stopped. Caterwauling replaced speech. Mark had never heard her make such a noise, not when she was giving birth to their babies, not even at the moment they tore through her. Seren's whole body jerked with the sound, joining the agony of the bad thoughts that couldn't escape her. Mark floundered. It felt as though if he went closer she'd bash him the same way she had the chicken, but if he stayed back she might hurt herself.

'Seren. Please.'

He was invisible to her. She was lost in the madness of a never-ending negativity. On and on she wailed. His eyes watered. The pain his wife was in, his inability to help, his dislike of her for letting such thoughts get the better of her when she had a house, the boys, him. He worked so hard. Why wasn't it enough? Why, since Gwen died, was there always more that she wanted? If she kept on like this she'd never be happy, none of them would.

'You don't get it.' She was quiet now, tired, curled into the corner of the sofa. 'It's not about wanting more. It's about her having so much for doing nothing. It's about you working sixty hours a week for so much less than she has.'

'I don't mind. I like my job.'

'I see how tired you are. I see how near to having a heart attack you are with your jaw clenched, your stomach churning from the stress. Don't tell me you enjoy it.'

'That's not all the days. I like the people, the satisfaction of completing things.'

'But if we won the lottery you'd stop. If you had the choice, if you didn't have to work you wouldn't. You'd enjoy hobbies, learn to do new things for the fun of it, no pressure.'

'You'll drive yourself crazy if you think like that. It's never going to happen.'

'It did to Cerys,' she snapped, the bitterness back.

Mark bowed his head, closed his eyes, took a deep breath before opening them. 'I don't know what you want me to say to that.'

Seren sipped the coffee he'd made her. It was just right. He knew how to make it just how she liked it, so why couldn't he understand what she felt about the Welsh thing? There was nothing he could say to make her feel better. He'd tried everything. She'd ignored everything, not on purpose, she just couldn't get her brain to think differently. Maybe she needed a doctor, pills. That's what people did when they couldn't face the life they'd created for themselves. An easy out. Take a pill, blur the brain, don't bother with reality.

'You don't get it.'

She sounded sullen, brattish.

'I do. And that's what worries me. If you think that keeping going like this means I'm going to end up agreeing with you one day, you're wrong, so please try and stop. Get help if you need to. I hate seeing you like this. I don't like the person you've become and it's not fair on the boys. Every day they're scared of what mood you'll be in, how angry you are. It's not a good thing. It's not right Seren. You have to let it go. You have to move on and stop it eating up inside of you. Please, honey.'

She knew he was right but couldn't admit it. She went to the toilet, locked the door and burst into tears. Swear to god she could bash her head against the wall like a mad person in a movie, to make the pain go from the inside of her head to the outside of it. If she was wounded, if there was blood everywhere, then he'd see how much it hurt.

~

Seren slipped the tablet into her mouth. Might as well feel serene. That's how Lily said they made you feel. Lily, the lover of pills. She got hers from the doctor and bought others on the internet; a pill for any problem, that was her catchphrase.

'You'll become serene Seren. I promise darling girl. Take it.'

Seren took one at home to see if it was true and sure enough, poof or rather whoosh, there was the clarity of thought with none of the panic. Gone was the clamped rage that had become her new norm. All was calm. All was well, like in the carol they used to sing in primary school at Christmas time.

The beautiful pills took away her twisted reality. No wonder people got hooked on them, said they couldn't survive without them. They made life so easy. Saved her. Saved her from saying things she didn't mean, losing friends, people thinking she was a horrible person when she wasn't. As if she'd do something awful. She only thought bad things. She'd never actually carry through with the actions. She kept the bad imaginings inside her head so they remained thoughts rather than words rather than deeds, because if she enacted them they'd put her in prison, which wasn't where she belonged. That would be the worst result of a crime, the opposite to what she dreamt of.

And they were only dreams – day dreams and night dreams to keep her sane, to make her think things would or could change one day if she wanted them to. She was in control. It was a choice. When she did nothing she was choosing to let it be, if she did something she was choosing to take action, make a change. But she wouldn't do anything apart from buy a lottery ticket and sit cross legged on the floor deep breathing as she visualised winning as if that would actually make her get all six lucky numbers.

~

She did not win.

Not yet.

She'd try again at the weekend. Better still, she'd go away for the weekend. Free food, free hand wash. That would be her, winning.

TWENTY FOUR

Cerys moved from the sofa to the stairs to listen out for the doorbell, curtain man due any minute. There was no crunch on the gravel from a van or car. She went to the kitchen to check there was enough tea and coffee even though she knew the cupboards were full of decadent choices. It comforted her to see them, to stroke the tins. No message on her phone that he was delayed. At midday she picked up the landline in the study to call the shop. A hand pushed through the open window making her scream.

'Sorry. Sorry. My little joke,' Cathy laughed. 'It's because I'm Cathy. Wuthering Heights, you see.' She sang the song, badly.

Cerys laughed as she was expected to with the friend not foe. She wanted to endear herself to this woman. You only joked with people you liked so if she tried hard she could become her friend. She needed a local one. When she opened the front door Cathy wouldn't come in.

'Everything okay?' Cerys asked.

Cathy curled one foot into the other, not like her. She usually straight talked, no messing.

'Did you arrange for Barry's Blinds to come and take measurements for the living area?' Cerys felt a blush rise. Was Cathy a spirit who knew everything that was going on everywhere? 'It's just that it's not allowed. I'm sorry but we did say. Or Stephen did. And he told me to tell you that Barry won't be coming. Sorry about that. You have a good day now.'

Cerys was too tired to list the reasons why she should have them. It was too weird that Stephen knew the blinds people had an appointment. That was way too in her business.

'How did you know?'

'Sorry?' Cathy checked her watch. 'Shit. Got to run. I'm meant to be in Aberaeron by twelve thirty.'

'How did you know he was coming today, the blinds man? Cathy!' She followed her to the van door Cathy had already opened. 'How come you knew about the appointment?'

'It's best you ask Stephen. I just popped by because he told me to.'

'Don't shoot the messenger, is it?'

Cathy was in her new van, dark green, electric from the way it had crept onto the drive, camouflaging her as she drove over the moors and the mountains. How come Cerys was the only one with bright orange metal that was visible from miles away, that warned the world she was approaching. She messaged Sam.

> That's bang out of order. Go and see Stephen. Demand to have them. It's not fair to not feel safe in your own home. Remember who's in control of this situation! Your house, your home!!!

If they didn't want her to have blinds, was it because they were the ones who spied on her through the windows each evening? She'd have to live upstairs from now on, as soon as it was dark. She had room. She could set up camp there. She'd eat her tea at the table then retreat to the bedroom rather than the sofa area. She hated the thought of being watched so closely. That wasn't the life she wanted.

~

Stephen wouldn't succumb to her pleading. He couldn't because of the rules, the contract, the signing. It was out of his hands. Out of her hands. Rules. Contract. Signed. Legal. Sorry.

'In that case, I'm thinking of leaving.'

'Ah. Righty-ho then.' Why wasn't he shocked? Cerys squinted as the sun hit the side of her face. 'What date did you have in mind because there's lots of paperwork to sort out and I was going to have a long weekend in Chester with the wife's sister and her husband. We're meant to be going up there Thursday after next. If I need to put it back a couple of weeks that's fine, but really I should let them know as soon as possible. I don't want to inconvenience them more than necessary you see.'

'Right. Sorry. Sorry, I'm not sure yet.'

Stephen sighed. Cerys hadn't seen him on the verge of cross before.

'It won't be for a few weeks at least. You go on your weekend away.'

'Really? Excellent.' He smiled as he rested his elbows on the desk. 'Right then. Will do. Phew. Keeps me out of the doghouse. I'm sorry you're going Cerys. It's such a shame this wasn't the place for you but it's not for everyone, it has to be said. Let me know the date when you've decided and like I said, we'll need around two to three weeks' notice to sort out all the paperwork.'

'There's lots, is there?'

'Oh yes.' He scratched his cheek. 'Now. You've enough in your account to pay for everything have you?'

'What do you mean?'

'Things can seem simple but turns out they're pretty complex once you delve deeper, don't you find? Your reason for going for example, not that it's any of my business, mind.' He held up both his hands, palms facing her. 'But I do hope this is the right decision for you, not because of anyone else. It's only you I'm concerned about. That's the job you see, part of it. I'm to look after your best interests and of course your house, car, income, it'll all be gone. No coming back once you've left you see.'

She would have her clothes, her designer bags, the fluffy towels, duvet sets, plates, mugs, the hand creams and hand washes, body washes, the silver rings she'd bought three of, her coffee machine that was too big for one person to carry. She wouldn't be able to afford a place in London with a kitchen big enough to house it. She'd sell it on e-bay. Voila. There was the deposit to rent a new place.

'And you'll be left with less than nothing of course which could be a shock after having everything.' He looked so sad for her.

'What do you mean?'

'By the time you pay back what you've spent so far that wasn't on absolute essentials which means food basically seeing as we had all your bills covered. You did keep the receipts for everything like Rhys told you to, for *all* your everyday shopping because the fancy bag, all those hand creams, the coffee machine... It all adds up doesn't it?'

'I didn't know I needed to do that.' Her voice cracked with panic.

'Of course you did. He told you to keep receipts for even the smallest thing, and it was in the small print. You did read the whole contract carefully?'

Old habits died hard. She'd burnt the receipts she didn't give to Rhys. Ever since she got a phone call from the bank saying did you spend £800 on this phone and £950 on this money transfer when she hadn't. The lady had calmed her down. The transactions had been flagged as suspicious so please don't worry, they had it under control, the money would be returned to her account within forty-eight hours and she advised burning all receipts from now on, those that had her card details on them, because what will have happened is the criminals got her details from one they found on the pavement or in the recycling.

'We did advise you to check the contract with your lawyer Cerys.'

'I don't have a lawyer. I never have done. Only rich people have lawyers. How could I afford to pay for one of those?'

She thought she'd understood it, most of it. Legal speak was so weird, convoluted, and they'd been so nice to her, always giving rather than taking away. Stephen rubbed his eyes, tired; people aged him.

'Alright then. Well that's a shame. Not what I'd hoped for.' He picked up his phone. 'Sara. Can you be a love and bring in a copy of Cerys's contract. It'll be in the blue cabinet.'

She watched him. He watched his desk. Sara brought in a blue folder and smiled awkwardly at the tension.

'Tea, coffee?'

'No thank you.' Cerys and Stephen replied in unison.

When she'd gone he read section 37. a.1. out loud.

'But I can't afford that. I spent thousands on non-essentials. I haven't got that sort of money.'

Stephen raised his eyebrows like what could he do and she should have thought of that. There he was, the devil destroying her life. He *was* the baddie. They were manipulating and tormenting her, had given her so much and now they'd take it all away so she had less than she'd started with. Or maybe he was double bluffing her. She'd pay for a different lawyer to check the contract to see if that's what the words really meant. All those paragraphs written on purpose so nobody without a legal background could understand them. That would be it. He wanted her to give up so he could have all the money. She wouldn't give him the satisfaction. She pinched her thigh, hard. No pain, no gain. She should have siphoned off some cash each month, put it in a secret bank account, one they hadn't given her the login details for like Sam suggested. She could have spent half saved half and still lived a life of luxury. Stupid, naive Cerys.

'I suppose I'd better have a think. Maybe I can give it longer; I guess I've been a bit lonely.'

'Your call. Let me know when you've decided.'

She flinched at his abruptness, willed the tears away.

~

'I've decided to save some of the money I get each month.'

186

'Ah. No,' said Rhys.

'Sorry?'

'No need. There's no need for you to save anything. Your future's taken care of. What do you want to save money for?'

'I always like to have savings. And I can't spend so much all the time. It makes me feel guilty.'

'Cerys. There's no need. Absolutely no need. We already donate the equivalent of twenty per cent of Thomas's monies to local charities so really, you go have fun with what you're given. Do as you said you would, eh? That's all we ask. Then everything will be fine and dandy.'

Sam was wrong and Cerys had been right. They controlled her, not the other way round. Them more than the money, though that had her too. She couldn't afford to leave. The money she'd squandered now owned her. Unless she stayed. Got a job and saved those wages. Her earnings, her choice, a chink in their armour of clauses. Her phone pinged. Seren.

TWENTY FIVE

Seren lay on the corner of the sofa, back against the cushions, legs stretched out so the soles of her feet were warmed by the sun. It soothed her like the bubbling water at the start of her annual pedicure. The rays stretched over her thighs, up her arms, onto her face.

Usually she'd have to be doing something: change the sheets, clean the cupboards, defrost the freezer so the shelves slid in and out rather than get stuck and need to be forced closed, the door pushed hard with her knee in order to make the seal stick. So hard that one day she'd cracked the plastic on the second drawer down. Now you had to be careful you didn't catch your fingers on it when you opened and closed it, blood blisters beware. Not today though. Not her house. And everything in this house was in its place and perfect.

There was peace. She would enjoy the quiet and let her troubled soul give in to the exhaustion, not by sleeping but by watching, listening, less thinking. She concentrated hard but couldn't hear anything. Joy. Less energy than joy. Contentment. No children squawked or squabbled, no husband asked where his keys were, no mobiles pinged, no laptop whirred, no washing machine beeped, no TV blared, no radio played in the background. No noise at all. When was the last time she'd experienced such quiet? This is what she should have. It was what she'd always needed and that revelation made her happier than she'd been five minutes ago, which she hadn't thought possible.

~

Seren listened to her sister. She refused to agree, smile, sympathise. She would not get angry with her. That's not who she was now. But it was wrong. Cerys had to accept that. It was wrong that she had all this peace, a near limitless budget, a choice about what she did every day and still she wasn't happy. She didn't appreciate it, didn't enjoy it. Instead she moaned and droned on and on. Seren should take her place. She'd adore it, wake up every morning and smile as she stretched her arms above her head, the happiest person on the planet.

'Why don't we go for a walk? It's only light drizzle now.' Seren needed a breeze between them to blow her sister's selfishness away.

'You must think I'm a spoilt brat moaning when I've got all this.'

'No. Not at all. It must be hard getting used to somewhere so different to London. And if it was me I'd have the boys and Mark to fill the space, to make it feel lived in. It's a huge house to stay in on your own. The days must feel terribly long and lonely when you've no-one to chat to. And what's the point of having all this if you can't share it, as in with a new boyfriend, your friends... Not me. Ha. Don't worry, I'm over all that madness. Can I borrow a fleece? Have you got a spare one?'

~

They walked along the woodland path that led to the coastal path, past the dragon carved out of a fallen tree, turning round only when it got really muddy, too slippy for Cerys. They retreated up the concrete path that led to town. Their pace slowed as the hill got steeper. Cerys bent down to tie up her shoe lace.

'Don't look but can you see a man ahead of us, on the corner.'

'Where?' Seren searched in front of them.

'I said don't look, not obviously. The guy in the red top. Can you see him?'

Seren looked the man right in the eyes. He reminded her of paintings of Jesus, an aura so calm there might as well be a halo hanging over him. He smiled, gave a wave, then rode away on his bicycle.

'No.'

'What?'

'There's no-one there.'

Cerys looked up. A family of four had turned the corner, each licking an ice cream that had been promised in order to get the kids out of the house. They'd come to Wales for fresh air and the outdoors, not to sit around the apartment, faces glued to their phones like at home. There was no man, no bicycle.

'I could have sworn I saw him.'

Seren shrugged like it was no big deal.

'Can we get some truffles? I really fancy some. Do you mind?'

They popped into the shop which hadn't re-stocked since the day before yesterday, Cerys's last visit. She was their best customer, had actually increased their profits. Big smiles for the London lady and her friend.

'Still raining is it?'

'Just a bit of drizzle so not too bad, a bit chilly though.'

'You'll be glad to get back to the warmth of London then. When is it you're going? We'll miss you. You'll come back and visit?'

Seren looked to Cerys for an explanation but she was focusing hard, too hard, on the numbers on the till. Seren looked out of the window as her sister paid for their treats, including two chocolate lollipops for her to take home to the boys plus their smallest box of marzipan for Mark, his favourite.

'Oh my god, there he is. I see him. Quick Cerys.'

Seren grabbed the bag off the counter and ran out of the shop. Cerys sprinted after her, down the steps, up the road. But it was an old man pushing a bicycle, dark green socks pulled up over his khaki trousers, a bald head above his unruly beard. He looked nothing like Christ on a bicycle.

'That's not him.' Cerys stood up straighter to catch her breath. 'He's way too old. The guy I see is young with long hair to his shoulders.'

'Are you sure? You know how you are with faces. You've always been terrible with them.'

Cerys was desperate not to crumble into their old sibling roles. She'd treated her sister to everything. She was the master, not the younger one.

'I'm not stupid Seren.'

'I know. Jesus. Chill out.' She walked a foot ahead. 'What did the lady in the shop mean about you going back to London? You're not thinking of leaving are you?'

'Might be.' Sulky teenager. Hello. Hello.

'That's madness. Please don't. Please. What will you do back there? And you've got used to so much. You can't go from having all of this to not being able to pay your rent with no job, no car, no pension. It'd be awful Cerys. Plus think of your house, your beautiful house. You'll never be able to buy one like that at your age, not even a flat a tenth of the size.'

'Always the obsession with buying.'

'A roof over your head makes all the difference to everything, you know that. To not have a home in life... You've been there, the same as me. I don't understand why you don't get it.'

'I guess it takes all sorts to make the world go round.'

'You've got to be kidding me. You'd give up all of this? Seriously? You're actually crazy.'

~

Seren lay the grey Welsh wool blanket over her legs.

'Do you remember that programme when we were young, Fantasy Island? There was this episode where two friends got half a million dollars each or something, to go shopping with, and the deal was they had to spend every dollar, every cent of it that weekend, and whoever spent all of it first got to keep their shopping? At the end of the weekend when there was five minutes left on the clock, they both had to check their bags and each of them found a twenty dollar bill. It turned out they'd each hidden the money in the other person's bag so they could be the winner. They had three minutes to spend it so they both ran across the road to the nearest shop where there was a doll in the window that cost twenty dollars exactly but one of them got hit by a car, not badly, just a bump to the ground. The clock was ticking, the other friend was at the shop door, but instead of going in she turned back to help her friend. The bell went and boom, they both lost everything.'

'Ha. Yeah. They got to keep one of the items didn't they, whichever one they wanted most. One of them chose a real fur lined bowling ball case and we were like don't be an idiot, keep the most expensive thing then you can sell it.'

'Yes. Yeah, that's it. That's the one. God, every time I think about it, it does my head in. I always thought they were both so stupid because the girl who got run over, she wasn't badly injured. She was sitting up, holding her leg, conscious, no blood, and loads of people were around, helping her. If I was her I'd have shouted spend the money, quick, spend the money, don't worry about me I'm fine, hurry up and spend the money then we can split the prize down the middle. They'd still get a fortune's worth of shopping and could sell most of it afterwards so they'd have enough to buy a condo or apartment, whatever they call them in America, or they could keep it all. It's up to them. I never understood why they didn't do that.'

'Because the moral of the story was to put friendship first, before money.'

'I know that. But they were stupid. It could have been a win win, best friends plus shopping. I bet when they got home they were kicking themselves.'

'Seren. You actually waste time thinking about it? You do know it's not real. It was a TV show.'

'Of course I do. Don't laugh at me, I'm not stupid. Just think what they could have had though. They were idiots.'

~

She topped up her wine. Cerys put her hand over her glass.

'No more for me.'

'I can't believe you've become one of *them*,' Seren slurred.

'What do you mean?'

'One of the rich people. But not the nice ones, not a philanthropist who sets up a charitable trust to help others, teaching their children, grandchildren, generations to come that they should use their wealth for good. You're one of the psychopaths, an *I'd love to help you but my lawyer told me not to* one.'

'That's not fair. There's nothing I can do to change things. It's the—'

'Rules. Ha. How convenient. Ooh mister government man, I'm so sorry, I would pay more tax but my accountant told me not to. He told me to do it this way and I can't help it if that means I've paid less tax than people who earn half what I do, a fiftieth, a millionth. Oh honey, I would help you, I really want to but it's out of my hands. What can I say? You know I want to support you like I promised I would, me, me, I, me, me, baby, but it's not up to me. It's up to the people I pay who make decisions for me. In theory they're meant to do what I tell them but I've decided to do what they tell me as then nothing is my choice which means my conscience is clear. Handy that. And even though to you and the outside world it might seem cruel or morally wrong, corrupt even, to my inner clusterfuck of paid-for people it's the right thing to do, so that's that. And in the end what does it all mean? What does it mean my dear sister? Why darling. What it means is you, the one with the lawyers, you'll keep getting richer, all the while reassuring yourself that nothing is your fault because your lawyer, your accountant, your blah-blah-di-blah-blah ones, they insist you follow the rules so nothing is your fault, not ever.'

'That's not fair.'

'Why not?'

'I don't have a choice.'

'What?' Seren cupped her hand round her ear as if she couldn't hear Cerys properly. 'I'm sorry. What did you say? I can't hear you. Repeat please, I didn't catch that last bit.'

'Stop it. You know the rules. I told you at your house right at the beginning. I told you and Mark what they'd told me.'

'Ha!'

'Why can't you just be happy for me?'

'Why can't you just be happy for me?' Seren mimicked. 'Why can't *you* see how wrong this is, how you're treating me?'

'But it's not my fault. I can't help it.'

'I saw Sam you know. Lovely Sam. Sam who wouldn't say a bad word about anyone. She told me that Tom was about to lose his flat because he lost his job and split up with his boyfriend and he's got no family, absolutely no-one, and even though he's paid fifteen years off the mortgage, only ten to go, he could lose everything so they're all putting money in a pot to help him. He's going to pay them back, of course he is, once he's working again. I don't suppose you contributed? I'm surprised they're still friends with you. Do you hear from them much?'

Cerys tried not to cry. She hadn't known about Tom. She used to know everything about their lives. It was too late to call Sam and she didn't want Seren listening in which she would do, always was the eavesdropper. She'd wait until her sister had gone home. Only one night to go then she'd be on her own again.

'What would happen if I stayed four nights?'

'You can't.'

'Don't get your knickers in a twist, I just wondered. I mean what could they do that's soooo bad?' She laughed.

'I'd lose everything.'

'As if.'

'I would. After I bought you the Mulberry bag they said if I broke the rules again, that's it. I'd have to leave here, leave everything.'

'Jesus.'

'It might not be so bad.'

'Yeah right.'

Cerys bristled as Seren rolled her eyes.

'I think I will go home, to London.'

'To visit.'

'No. For good.'

'Don't be ridiculous.'

'Don't speak to me like that.'

'Why on earth would you leave this? That's madness.'

'Not necessarily.'

'Pfff.'

'I'm lonely. I miss my friends. And you guys.' Liar. Seren knew she wasn't anywhere near the top of Cerys's list for love and kinship. 'It's about fighting the fear. I was brave enough to come here, now I need to be brave enough to admit it hasn't worked out and go back. The only problem is they said I have to pay them whatever I've spent on things that weren't absolutely essential so I'd be totally buggered financially but hey-ho, it's only money isn't it? I can get a loan, sell some of the things I've bought, like your Fantasy Island plan. Ha. Maybe it's fate you put that into my head. Anyway, I'll work it out. On some days I wish I'd never gone into the church. I—'

'I'll have it.' Cerys stopped mid pour. 'See. If I say that it makes you think twice. That's what you've got to do, like with an old boyfriend, imagine someone else being with them and see how it makes you feel. Picture someone else living here, driving your car, eating your truffles, you back in London unable to afford a coffee after lunch. It'll make you cross, jealous that they're enjoying what you once had, the audacity of some new person taking what's yours. And you'll know, deep down, that you do want it. You always dreamt of living in Wales Cerys, ever since we were little.'

'You don't get it. No-one does.' She emptied her glass into the sink. 'I'm going to bed. I'm shattered.'

Seren contained her rage as she heard her sister upstairs. She sat on the sofa until the silence lasted long enough so she was sure Cerys was asleep. Then she let loose by whacking a cushion against the designer bi-fold doors again and again and again, part of her wishing they'd break so shattered glass flew everywhere, cutting her skin, making her bleed over the white rug. She grabbed her bag off the floor, pushed open a section of the door, and lit a cigarette.

Something moved at the bottom of the garden. Someone. An upright figure watching her. She wouldn't be a scaredy cat like Cerys. She threw the cigarette down and ran across the grass, but when she got to the bottom of the lawn he or she was gone. She watched the house, lights off upstairs, downstairs on. It was a thing of beauty. Breath caught, she walked back up the slope, snatched the cigarette stub off the patio then went inside, locking the doors behind her. She ran her hands over the worktops, sofa, dresser, chairs. She sank down onto all fours and stroked the floors, the cupboards, hugged the legs of the table. No dirt anywhere. All so perfect. There was a crunch of gravel on the drive. She crawled to the front door, opened it, sprang out to defend with an attack but the bicycle sped away before she could reach it.

Seren lay face down over the bonnet of the car. She embraced the front door, her arms either side of it, kissed the wood before quietly closing it. She stood in the hall, arms wide as she enveloped the whole house in her mind. She wouldn't moan like an ungrateful cow. She would adore it.

TWENTY SIX

Seren led the way.

'Come on. If you're all about fighting the fear now, let's face this one. We won't go near the edges, I promise. I know you hate them. We'll go to the middle of the top bit where we can get a good view. I want a photo for Mark and the boys.' Cerys stayed back, on the flatter bit of grass. 'Nothing's going to happen. Look at all the people up there, little children. That girl looks about three. If she can do it so can you.' Cerys stepped backwards rather than forwards, terrified of heights mixed with edges. She'd stumble when only a few metres high. An escalator made her think she was going to fall over if she didn't hold onto the rail. She'd rather risk a million germs on her fingertips than the chance of falling. 'I thought you were meant to be all brave now, trying new things. I thought you were going to say yes rather than no to opportunities the world opened up to you.'

Cerys started to follow her little sister, who was right. Seren's voice sounded different, calm, like a yoga teacher talking through the ten minute meditation at the end of a class. It made Cerys want to follow her, a snake out of a basket, hypnotised. The wind blew her hair over her eyes. She wished she had a hair tie in her pocket, always be prepared, never be in Wales without one. Step by step she climbed the hill, looking straight ahead, never to the left or the right, only directly in front of her.

'Just a bit further. Nearly there. You're doing brilliantly.'

Cerys was two thirds up, the furthest she'd managed when they were little as she held on tightly to her daddy's hand. She felt like she was floating beside him, her feet hardly touching the ground. It was fine. Nothing was a problem. He wouldn't let anything bad happen to her. She was with her family and blood was thicker than water. One step in front of the other, only look down.

'There you go. I said you could do it. Well done you. And look at the view. It's stunning.'

Cerys froze. The thought of shifting her feet an inch made her balance go off kilter. She'd topple over the cliff, she knew she would. She stretched her arm out to hold onto Seren but couldn't reach her shoulder. They should put a railing all around the side of the cliff. How could people stand so near to the edge, laughing, taking photos, a kiss beneath the grey skies.

'I've changed my mind.'

'Relax. Enjoy the view.'

Cerys did not like where she was. Why did she always do things other people wanted her to, that Seren wanted her to? Her sister laughed, smiled as she kept trying to get the hair off her face but the wind kept blowing it back again. She should have been properly prepared. Cerys shouted to try and be heard.

'I've decided I am going back to London. I love it here, I really do, but I miss my life there too much. Home's where your heart is, isn't it, and for me that's where my friends are. If I've learnt anything from this, it's that. They're the most important thing in the years ahead. I mean, who knows how many we've got left now, fifteen, twenty, twenty-five? I miss the fun too much to stay here. Life's about the people not the money.'

Seren couldn't swallow that news. It was too bitter, potent, more poisonous than any she'd had before, which wasn't how it was meant to be. The half a pill of diazepam in the orange juice was supposed to have made Cerys chill right out and go with the flow, accept whatever Seren suggested. Calm. Open. Willing. But her feelings were obviously stronger than the pharmaceuticals. That wasn't right. The god-damned medicine had given her sister too much clarity rather than too little. Should have given her a whole one.

'Ha-ha, very funny.'

'I'm serious.'

Cerys turned her face towards the wind. Her body juddered as if she'd had an electric shock. Be calm. You will not fall. She would breathe in deeply, live life to the full, and to do that she had to be able to meet up with her friends whenever she wanted and that meant moving back to London. The group chat had confirmed it. So much laughter, more in one night than in the last three months which was what she'd remember on her deathbed, not how many handbags she owned.

'But the money. You said they'd make you pay loads of it back, that you'd be worse off than you were before you came here.'

'I was thinking maybe you could lend me some, just until I get back on my feet.' Seren squinted at her sister. 'Actually, forget I said that. Don't worry. It'll be alright. I've arranged a job interview at my old place, in a different team but on the same money as before, plus Sam said I can live in her spare room for six months just paying towards the bills while I save up for a deposit. And I can sell stuff, though I might keep the Mulberry bag. It'd be hard to let go of that. You can keep your one too.' She took a deep breath as she raised her arms in the air. 'Whoo! It feels good to have made a decision. Freeing.' She waved her arms in the air. 'Woohoo! You were right. It's good we came up here. I feel great. This proves it's the right thing to do.'

Cerys looked to Seren for congratulations, not a hug, not a screeching whoop whoop, merely confirmation that what she'd said made sense. Seren had been furious when Cerys accepted the inheritance, so now she'd be gloriously happy that her sister was giving it up and Seren would be better off than her again, high up on her pedestal looking down upon the pauper.

'Maybe you're ill like mum used to get. Maybe you need to see a doctor,' Seren said.

Cerys winced. That couldn't be what she thought. She couldn't bear that to be her future.

'I'm sorry, Cerys but I think you're making a terrible mistake. You can't leave all this. It's madness. Give it more time. I mean at least get some savings in the bank before you go. Try another six months or a year and I bet you'll love it here and if not, then you can go. But not until next year. And it's the school holidays in three weeks. We were going to visit with the boys, it's all sorted. We've booked a Travelodge for each end of the journey. And we'd planned to come at the end of the holidays too, the August bank holiday weekend. Where will we go if you aren't here? We can't cancel now. We'll lose the money and as a treat we booked two rooms each time so we wouldn't be all squashed together, four of us in one room, no air, no space to breathe. There's never any air when there's four of you in a bedroom. Jesus, Cerys. How could you be so selfish? What day are you leaving? How could you do this to me, to the boys and Mark, without any warning?'

They never knew each other's plans. They weren't that close. She mustn't say that. No rudeness. Be a good girl, Cerys.

'I didn't realise you were coming, that you'd booked somewhere. We hadn't confirmed dates had we?'

Perhaps she was going crazy, not remembering things, seeing Christ on a bike when no-one else did.

'Any time. You said to come down any time. I was going to tell you just before I went home tomorrow, as a lovely surprise like ta-dah, see you in three weeks, not long sis, you'd better stock up on ice cream. For fuck's sake. I can't believe this.'

Seren kicked the grass so hard a tuft flew in the air, exposing the soil beneath it. Cerys's mind was muddied. She felt sick. She always let someone down with whatever decision she made. Why couldn't life be simpler? She drooped her shoulders then pictured Sam's face giving her a look, pfffft, fuck them it's your life, cheeky cow that's not your problem, she shouldn't have presumed to book without telling you. For all Seren knew the Queen could have been visiting Cerys that day. She had to stand her ground.

'I'm sorry but that's not my fault. You should have checked with me before booking the hotel. That's on you Seren. I'm really sorry, but it is.'

Her sister's eyes narrowed. 'You selfish fucker. All my life… All my life I've been worried about you even though you're the older one, saying to Mark that I need to check on you, make sure you're okay, inviting you to lunch even though you never ever invite all of us to your place and we never expected it because it costs so much more to feed four people compared to us feeding an extra one and Christ, we should know because everything we do is for four. Four, four, four, four. What about the boys then? Do you want to tell them? Go on, call them now and tell them their summer holiday's cancelled.'

She held her phone out. Cerys stared at the grass. Seren tried to force it into Cerys's hand but she wouldn't take it. Instead she stepped backwards, away from her. 'All those years when you didn't buy a place. Instead you went out spending money on holidays, expensive make-up, a pair of shoes just because you liked them not because you needed them, meals out with friends three times a week and I bit my tongue thinking there's your deposit, there's the money for a flat right there. You could easily have done it, fifteen, twenty years ago, so easily considering you've only ever had yourself to pay for all your life and if you had, well then that would actually have made all of this irrelevant wouldn't it because you'd have somewhere to go back to. Having a home's the most important thing, you know that. We both know that only too well, shunted from here to there after Mum and Dad died. If you don't have a home what you do have is that unsettled feeling, a great unhappiness inside you but oh no, Cerys knows better. You didn't take it seriously, didn't bother to think about how you'd pay your rent when you reach your seventies, your sixties even. And you would have owned it outright by now, easily. For Christ's sake Cerys, what possessed you? What the fuck's wrong with you?'

Seren screamed the end of her question. Cerys backed further away, hadn't realised she'd messed up her sister's mind so much. Seren laughed. Cerys couldn't keep up with her words. They didn't make sense. Was it Cerys not understanding them that was the problem or were they in the wrong order? Was she hearing things wrong as well as seeing things wrong? There was no Jesus. Cerys laughed. She remembered the kind counsellor from when she was a teenager who'd frowned when Cerys had laughed and laughed so much as if she was having the best memory ever. When she calmed down the counsellor had looked very sad.

'People use laughter to hide pain. Is that why you're laughing Cerys?'

Her smile had turned to crying that carried on past the end of the session.

Her sister was in pain, a very deep pain considering the manic noises she was making. Cerys tried to block out the meanness of the words by telling herself Seren was hurting rather than meaning to hurt her. She reached out a hand. That's what you're meant to do to comfort someone, but what would have been an automatic gesture if she was with a friend was much harder when it had to break through her and Seren's invisible, distancing barrier. They both knew it was there. Always had done. They'd just never spoken about it, not to each other. Cerys had mentioned it to her friends, most often Sam. It was complicated. Until now she'd thought it didn't affect their lives enough to be worth the pain of trying to sort it out. Wrong.

'Please. Don't be cross. I'm going mad here. Look at me thinking I can see Christ on a bike all the time. That never happened in London. And at the end of the day it's my life, not yours, it's up to me how I live it. You don't need to worry about me. I'm fine. I'll be fine once I move back. I'm responsible for me, not you, so whatever does happen... You just focus on Mark and the boys.'

'Is that your Jesus?'

Seren pointed behind Cerys. A man in a red top was standing next to the church, holding onto a bicycle as he watched them. Cerys turned round slowly with her arms out wide for balance. She needed a rail to hold onto. If there was something solid to grip she wouldn't mind so much.

'You can see him? Oh my god,' she wobbled as she laughed. 'You can see him too. You and Sam. Ha. Brilliant.' She raised her hands higher in the air and put on an American accent. 'Thank you, Lord, for allowing Seren to see your treasured son. Thank you for showing her my very own Christ on a bike, Lord God our loving Saviour.'

'That's good timing then.'

'It's perfect. Just the closure I needed.'

'So you don't need to go now. It's another reason for you to stay. He's real. You and I can both see him.'

Seren waved at the man, beckoned him towards them. She needed treats on tap rather than them all lost, the free holidays, fifty-pound presents, a limitless supply of ice-cream, the lack of worry for her sister. Rather than wave back the man looked behind him as if someone had called his name.

'And over there. Look. He's there too.'

'What?' Cerys turned to where Seren was pointing. All she could see was a family of four sitting together on the hill as they looked out at the sea, searching for something on the horizon. It was too early for dolphins. She'd tell them to check again at four o'clock. 'Where?'

'And there. There. And there.' Seren put her hands on Cerys's shoulders and turned her round like when they were little, tea towel tight over her eyes, you had to be dizzy for the start of blind man's buff. 'And there. And there and there. Look, there he is, the Lord Jesus Christ our saviour.'

'Stop it. Stop. I don't like it. Not on the hill. I'm going to fall. Please. Get off me.'

'And there. And there and there. There he is. Hello Jesus.' She spun Cerys faster and faster. 'Don't worry, I've got you. I'd never let anything happen to you. Enjoy the moment. Let go Cerys. Come on. Open yourself up to change. Isn't that what you said you wanted to do, so many times this weekend? Go with the flow and be more daring. Close your eyes and love the fact that there are so many saviours in your life, all wanting the best for you. How many people are that lucky? Round and round you go, like a teddy bear. That attention, it's the most wonderful present ever, worth more than anything your money can buy. Happy birthday to you. Happy birthday to you. Happy birthday dear Cerys, happy birthday to you. Now on top of every lucky thing that's happened, you get the honour of meeting your maker. There he is. And there. Look at the church and the sand, not the sea, close your eyes. Now open them. Look at me, honey pie.'

It was wrong. Her sister was wrong. The man on the beach was wrong. Cerys tried to decide whether to fight or flee. She was fit. She'd been running. She did not like hills or edges or the sloppiness of the mud in the rain. But she had to try. She had to make a run for it. Down the hill, dizzy, lightheaded, her legs crumpled beneath her as she fell over a non-existent edge. Running down a hill was not in her nature. Forwards she tripped. Down with a crack. Onto a rock. Crackety crack crack. A noise that made the tourists turn expecting a broken arm, a figure clutching a fractured femur. But instead she was quiet. A lady reached out to her. No thank you. Cerys stood up by herself. She stumbled too near the edge. As a hand touched her back, over she flew. She opened her eyes to the breeze, too shocked to cry out, too dizzy to know what was happening. Head sore. Blood in the eye sockets. Pushed. No. A slip. Surely. Slippety slip slip, silly Cerys. The old man had been wrong. Water was the secret to a short life, not a long one. People drowned in the sea, slipped in the rain that caused mud slides and collapsed edges.

A woman behind Seren had a funny look on her face like she might be sick. The shock of it. When the two ladies had shouted was it a row rather than a joke? It had looked like a game, sort of, albeit a dangerous one. American accents that called out to

Jesus meant joking around, of course they did. Had the wind thrown the brown-haired one over the rock? It was possible. When the lying-down lady had lifted her head onlookers threw a combined hurrah her way, not unconscious, not dead then. Phew for what their children had witnessed, an accident with a happy ending, something they could learn from, don't run down a slippy hill in Wales, you hear me. They winced at the cut above her eye, an egg bruise already visible, blood dripping. She'd soon have a banging headache, that you could be sure of. The other lady went to help her stand up but she refused the outstretched hand. Confused. Disorientated. The fallen lady got up but stumbled to her right, too near the edge. The other lady went to help her. She got as far as touching her shoulder when that was that. Was it the wind that picked her up and carried her off like a chick from a nest, not tucked in tightly enough? Who saw what happened? Did you? Did they? The whole clifftop inhaled and forgot to breathe out again.

Seren looked round to see who'd noticed the two of them turn into one, a family of four to two to one left on earth. It was good maths, a decent pattern to the numbers. The man with the bike, he was watching. The lady and man on the lookout for dolphins. They weren't. The two men climbing towards her, they'd seen. Their pallor ashen, their faces aghast. God was watching and he could see all her sins. Naughty Seren. She'd better scream. That's what people did when someone fell over an edge. That's what Cerys had done when their mum and dad were there one minute, gone the second after. The lady pulled the man down. She wouldn't check where her sister's body was. Too nasty an image. Bad feelings would abound and she had enough of those to contend with thank you very much. What just happened? She couldn't comprehend it. An accident. It was definitely an accident, otherwise that would make her one of those really bad people who go to prison for their crimes and rightly so, but that wasn't who she was, not at all. No sir, absolutely not. She hadn't wanted anything to happen to her sister. Not in real life. Only in her head and that didn't count. That was top secret. No-one knew what went on in her brain. Thoughts couldn't make things happen. Or could they? Could a person make themselves believe they were due whatever they liked, wanted, needed, so much so that it happened? Cerys had. After all those years playing the lottery. Maybe Seren had too. They were a family with psychic powers like in a film. She was a witch. No. That would be ridiculous.

The voice in her body screamed loud, loud, louder, hands to mouth, hysterical as she stepped away from the edge so she didn't suffer the same fate as the one who'd disappeared over it. Did Cerys feel like she was flying in the moment before she died, all calm from the diazepam? Thank goodness Seren had slipped half a pill in her drink. It was a day of slipping, meant to be. Fate. Not her responsibility.

'We were playing a game like when we were little. It was meant to be fun. We've done it since we were kids, every time we visit, we spin each other at the top. Oh my god. She'd been unhappy but I didn't know how unhappy. No. That wasn't it, it couldn't be. It was an accident. She was dizzy wasn't she? Did you see the bump on her head? She thought she'd seen Jesus. You heard her didn't you?'

The man with the children nodded, knowing he should help, desperate to get away. His wife was more pragmatic. She put her arm around the lady's shoulders and walked her down the hill.

'Run to the lifeguards. They'll know what to do,' she said to another lady near them. 'She bumped her head. She fell. We all saw it. You're in shock, sweetheart.' She squeezed Seren's shoulders then kissed the top of her head as if she was a child. 'You poor, poor darling. What a terrible thing to happen. Was she your friend?'

Cry big girl, cry little one. The man's daughter cried along with Seren. The whole hill top turned into a wailing mass, hysterical.

'No. She was my sister.'

TWENTY SEVEN

They wrapped a red woollen blanket round her shoulders and surrounded her in sympathy, while she imagined that if she lived in the house that over-looked the beach there would be enough space so she didn't have to see the boys every minute of each day. A haven for a bedroom with an ensuite and a walk-in wardrobe, space for arm chairs as well as a bed, or what about a day bed? That would be both comfy and stylish. When the boys were at school she'd lie back and read. They'd be happy. The boys would have their own bathroom. They loved it there: the space, the beach, the garden ten times the size of their plot at home, big enough to play football on. There was already a trampoline and wetsuits that fitted them hanging in the utility room. It was fate, meant to be. The house was waiting for them, a ready-made answer to her prayers. God had answered her secret prayers. He was real then. Maybe there really was a Jesus. Christ on a bike watching from the church and a top of the morning to you, young man. She was not Irish. She was not Welsh. What was she? A monster. No. Her sister had fallen. It was a terrible tragedy. Jesus saw. He knew.

~

A man and a lady were standing in front of the house when the police car dropped her off. Of course they knew each other, them and the police, tense greetings all round, hushed tones that suited Seren fine. Such a small place where everyone knew everyone else's business. She played dumb. Best be in shock.

Anything you say might be taken down and used in evidence, that's what they said on TV. She didn't know what had happened. Her mind was a mush of meanderings. They led her inside the house, gentle and full of kindness. It would be fine. They were good people. There were so many witnesses. The view really was beautiful.

'I'm Stephen. I believe we've spoken on the phone.'

His eyes were cold. That. Nasty. Man. What did people do in films when they needed to hide a feeling? They looked up as if they didn't know what was happening. She scrunched her eyebrows together. Too much. She loosened the frown a little and wobbled her lips when she realised she would never see Cerys again, the same as her mum and dad, as Gwen. She started to shake. People got lost so suddenly. That wasn't what was meant to happen. The things you dreamt and worried about, that you imagined when you were out running, they weren't meant to come true. Was it a good thing that it had? Had she made it happen? Was she some sort of crazy psychic lady who could tilt the world and change the future with her mind? There was a thought. There was a power.

'I'll make some tea.'

Cathy put the kettle on, Cathy put the kettle on, Cathy put the kettle on, we'll all have tea. Seren sang the words in her head rather than out loud as then they'd think she was a crazy lady, not as crazy as Cerys telling everyone she was being followed by Christ on a bicycle though. There was the proof that she did it to herself, had flown off to meet her maker. It was nothing to do with Seren. Cathy handed her an orange mug. Seren would pretend to sip the calming camomile she hated the taste of.

The drink went cold. Cathy rinsed the mug before putting it in the dishwasher. Miele. Fancy that. Very fancy.

'We shouldn't leave you alone.'

'I'd rather, to be honest.' They stared at her. 'So I can call my husband, and her friends, be near her things, feel close to her. I'm fine. Honestly. You go.'

~

The empty house was useless at calming her brain that wouldn't stop whirring. Seren sang quietly as she cleared away the two plates from the cake that Cathy had found in the cupboard for her and Stephen, they hadn't eaten since breakfast. Imagine eating at such a time. Heartless. Seren takes it off again, Seren takes it off again, Seren takes it off again, they've all gone away.

And so they had. There were the women in her life, all gone now. That's what her dad would have said, laughing, loving that phrase. The mother, the sister and the mother-in-law who was more of a mother than the dead one ever was, all gone away, leaving Seren with what. Three boys. Two boys, an adult man, and her. She was there too but what to do, to do what. She sat on the sofa, watched the sun set through windows that were so vast it felt like there was nothing she couldn't spot in the world. A wideness to be embraced and adored compared to the narrowness of her terraced home. Seren didn't fear the darkness like Cerys had. She stood in front of the windows and surveyed the land. Her land. Whose land? Who owned it now? Was it in some trust or did it still belong to Cerys?

Where was her sister? Seren half expected to see her ghost staring from the bottom of the garden, arms reaching out to grab the baddie. But Seren hadn't pushed her. Cerys had slipped. She hated edges and it was a tragic accident, same as their parents. That's how it would be referred to from now on, the phrase she would use and let others run with as they spread the news by phone, messages, emails, on and on across the planet, the universe. And it was Seren who was the victim. They'd all see that. Left on earth to deal with the triple tragedy. She scanned from left to right then skywards. The stars knew where Cerys was. They'd watched the earth longer than man had lived on it. They got it. Whatever was up there got it. Seren rose up. She flew over the mountains and across the midlands, higher over the skyscrapers down to south-east London where she watched

Mark. She needed to tell him what had happened. They'd expect her to call her husband. And he was the first person she wanted to talk to but first she needed to process it more, work out what had happened, plan what to do, how to mould the right future.

She walked through the house, opening each door, checking under each bed, inside each wardrobe, behind each chest of drawers, slowly, methodically, leaving a room then quickly opening the door again to catch a ghostly Cerys who'd come back to haunt her. But she wasn't anywhere. Or she definitely was not there. She was in a room in another building. Unreachable.

Seren sank down on the thickly carpeted floor, so soft compared to the hardest wearing hessian one they'd bought for her other home. Her home. Wales was not hers. Not yet. Would it be? Should it be? What had she wished for? What had she done? Now she was inside the daydream it felt too complicated. If it was a dream. Maybe she was hallucinating on drugs paramedics had given her after she'd had a car crash on the way to visit her sister and she'd wake up in hospital and have to go back to the same, more of the same of the last eleven years of daily awakenings. In her imaginings there'd been no confusion. Cerys would be gone, the details murky, main thing being it hadn't hurt her and she was dead before she hit the ground etcetera. There'd be a phone call from Stephen to Seren where she cried before pulling herself together and rushing down the motorway. And there she was at the funeral. There was the book in the foyer. This time she signed it. And it was with her older sister's blessing, as if Cerys had gifted Seren the future she needed, that she deserved. Her sister was sharing the gift with her, the gift she'd had enough of and it was okay because she was happy now in heaven with their mum and dad. Cerys remembered them better than Seren did. She'd had more years with them and they'd been close and felt love so it was right that she was the one back with them leaving Seren on earth, alive, for the family, with her family. She'd keep the family going.

She changed the sheets on Cerys's bed but it felt wrong to sleep there while she was barely dead. Dead and not yet buried in the pretty churchyard which had been her final wish, something she'd been looking forward to so that was a good thing. Where was her body? They'd rushed Seren away so she didn't have to experience the upset of seeing it wrenched off the rocks and up the cliff edge. All the pitying stares from strangers. Truth be told, she liked the stares when she noticed they were directed at her. Except for his. Christ on a bike who watched her closely. She looked back at him, straight in the eye. They locked eyes. He wasn't all *poor you, lady,* not like the others. Was he a witness? A witness to what, a witness to nothing. Nothing to see here, move along, move along people. Seren breathed deeply and stood tall. There was strength in her yet. There was a life in her that she would make the most of. She would not sleep, of course she wouldn't. She'd sit in the living room, embrace the outside world, soak it right up. She refused to be frightened.

~

As the sun rose, Seren worried that Mark would suspect foul play and go all Sherlock on her. Which wasn't fair because she hadn't done anything. She needed to shake off the numbness, feel the raw pain and cry. Cry like a lost soul alone on the earth, one of those rarities who had absolutely no family left to be with. She built herself up to near hysteria. Ring ring. Ring ring. Ring ring.

'It's me. Sorry to wake you so early. Oh Mark, something terrible's happened.'

~

He was kind, of course he was. And Seren wept true tears because it was a shocking tale, an awful end to a life, such a tragedy. The platitudes they reeled through: Cerys's new start, it wasn't fair, she was just getting to enjoy life, winning then losing before she had a chance to properly relish it.

'I know. I know. It's heartbreaking.'

Seren did not tell him that Cerys had planned to leave her Welsh wonderland. No-one needed to know that. Sam, she'd be told the opposite of her last chat with her best friend, that Cerys had decided to stay longer after a visit from her little sister. They'd spoken to a man she thought was Jesus and it turned out Cerys looked like his aunt who'd died the previous summer, that's why he kept staring at her. It was uncanny. Cerys's imagination had gone into over-drive from being alone in the house for too many hours of the day. The relief to finally speak with him. They'd all smiled, laughed. She decided to stay and relish the Welsh countryside.

'That's the word she used, relish?'

'Yes. Why?'

'It's just it doesn't sound like Cerys.'

Seren believed the make-believe conversations she was writing in her head, the words and stories flowed so smoothly. There was no-one to tell her the events she now pictured hadn't taken place. I am right and you are wrong. No, that didn't happen, this did. Let's move on. Some people. Honestly. Even if you showed them a video of them doing the thing they denied, they'd still say it hadn't happened. They were usually the nasty bastards in life. That's what Seren had discovered. She didn't want to be one of those people. She wasn't. Look at her crying. That meant she was a kind soul, one of the goodies. Goodie, goodie, yum yum.

Mark cried too, which she hadn't expected.

'I'll tell the boys. Oh god, they'll be devastated.'

'I know. It's awful. Thank you. Thank you so much. I love you.'

'I love you too. Always and forever.'

Death made a person love more, even if it was momentary. Or hate more, detest and rage. That was a big one, made more difficult by the need to keep secret the feelings that were pummelling your heart and brain, because you weren't meant to talk ill of the dead. Definitely don't say out loud all the awful things you're thinking. If you did, people would look at you like you were an evil one. Whichever route the grief took, that knee jerk reaction on answering the call was always the same, being told they were dead was followed by a shock of tears, followed by the actual grief that could be the pure *I loved them, I loved them, I'll miss them so much* or the complex *I loved them, I hated them, I wanted to love them but look how they were, how could a person be like that.*

Whatever type of grief it was, death frazzled the brain, drove you to the edge of insanity. Two in a year. That was a surprise. As was her not being able to manage the emotions the deaths had stirred up. Seren had always been so good at controlling how she felt, but Gwen's death and her will had thrown that out of the window, then Cerys's inheritance and death confused her brain so the world was a blur. She wouldn't sleep, of course she wouldn't. She changed into the running kit she'd brought with her. When in doubt, run. She sprinted down the garden, over the road, back and forth over the beach until her legs felt like jelly. A dog ran after her, snapping at her heels but she was faster.

'Frank! Frank! Frank!'

The runner and the dog both ignored the owner.

~

After five missed calls, she rang him back, her head clearer, the coffee machine conquered. Today she loved them all so much. The heightened emotions had brought out the best rather than the worst in her. She loved everyone on earth and she'd loved Cerys and Gwen and she'd make life good for her family from now on. That was her duty.

'What about the funeral? Should we bring the boys? Sorry. Sorry to upset you more. I shouldn't have asked yet.'

'No, no, it's fine. Of course you should ask. I think they're too young, don't you? I was thinking I'd go and you stay in London with them. I mean, it's the second funeral in such a short space of time and I don't want to leave them with friends this time, not when it's their aunty. I'll only feel happy, be able to focus on it, if you're the one who's with them.'

He cried at the thought of not being able to say goodbye to his sister-in-law. There there, Mister.

'She'd understand. Try not to feel bad about it.'

Seren comforted her husband. She saved him from the pain of having to see the body in the coffin, the image that never left you once you'd been exposed to it. Coffins were so final. They always made her cry. She would suffer for her family to protect them. She'd sit alone in front of the open coffin. Good girl. Selfless Seren.

TWENTY EIGHT

Cerys's phone had been tucked inside the zipped pocket of her navy fleece when she and it hit the rocks, tumbling down the cliff together. Tumble sounded kinder than thrashed and bashed, pummelled against the rock face. The screen was smashed as much as her body. Although it turned on, there was nothing to see, nothing you could read. All of the content was inaccessible which meant Seren couldn't contact Cerys's friends, couldn't let them know about the funeral. That was fate then. Not her fault. She couldn't control it. It was not of her choosing, nothing to do with her, no-one could lay the blame on her for that one.

They organised it quickly. She overheard Stephen and the accountant boy in the driveway before they got into their cars. The older man apologising on the phone as he said tomorrow was the only day the Reverend could come and it would be a quiet service, a quick one. Look at them thinking they could get away with her not knowing, not going. They wanted to sign the book themselves no doubt. She could function enough to drive. She would be there. Surprise surprise, people.

~

Stephen, Rhys, Cathy, Louise and David sat in the front two pews as the Reverend gave his eulogy. In the name of the Father and the Son and the Holy Spirit. Amen.

'Amen,' the five of them chanted.

215

There was to be no singing even though Stephen was partial to a good Welsh hymn. But there wasn't time. Father Jones had to be in Aberporth by ten thirty for one of those modern mid-morning weddings where they celebrated with a big breakfast instead of a disco and posh dinner.

They filed out of the church, busy, busy, things to do, places to go, people to see. It was nearing peak holiday season. Stephen kept touching the book that was tucked under his arm as if to reassure himself he was still holding it.

'No-one's tempted I take it? Ha.'

Rhys laughed, half nervous, half to keep his boss happy. Cathy frowned as she hurried outside. Louise was tempted to say yes please at the thought of a Celine bag, a shopping trip to the Liberty's shop which was near Carnaby Street according to Google maps, so beautiful inside with all the wood panelling. It was alright for her mum. She used to live there and had tired of those places. It wasn't fair that Louise hadn't been given that chance, not even for a weekend.

'It's so expensive and smelly, dirty. Why would you want to? Wales is much more beautiful, trust me.'

David hurried his niece out of the church, sensing the stirring thoughts where young people believed they were infallible. It was always the same, ever since the beginning of time. Louise was glad once she was in the fresh air, out of the way of temptation rather than inside the stale nave. None of them wanted to bring the bad luck on themselves and it was always bad luck, the local equivalent of a bad omen if you read the name and said a prayer, like seeing one Magpie, walking under a ladder or forgetting to touch wood in order to ward off the bad things that can happen. The young ones had to be reminded by their parents not to try it, just look at how many had gone wrong, the short time they lasted, all of them, not once was there an exception.

'You don't want to risk that do you, to die so soon for what, a new bag, a new car, a temporary thrill that's gone as soon as it's arrived really.'

It was always the same. Humans were so predictable.

'I don't understand,' said Louise. 'She had everything. Do you think—'

'It's certainly disappointing, I'll give you that,' said Stephen.

'I don't know why we expect any of them to be different to the ones that went before them anymore. It always ends up like this.'

'Not always,' said Rhys. The girl called Layla had lasted nearly two years and they'd all relaxed a little, happy to be accompanying a good rather than tormented soul. She and Rhys had kissed. Which was against the rules. He'd nearly, nearly but not quite, cooked the books for her until he realised he was being used and it had turned out Stephen was right, he was always right, when he said it was best not to get involved, best to see them as a number not a person, that made it easier through the ages. Now they had to get ready for the next one.

'I suppose Cerys didn't do quite what we expected,' said Stephen.

'The sister did.'

'Hmmmm.'

Gethin rode across the field towards them, the tyres of his bike bumping up and down, side to side, over the grass.

'Sorry I'm late. Shit. Bloody bastards. I came out of Aaron's and there was my bike, gone. The little shits had cut through the lock. I had to borrow one from Dylan. Has she been yet?'

Louise smiled at her love. He was enough for her. Him and her in their cottage by the sea. Her mum was right. People who owned more weren't happier than them, not in the long run, and when she went down to Cardiff for the day it had felt too busy, not enough clean air to breathe so God knows what London would be like. When she walked on the coastal path each evening she overheard visitors say they wished they lived where she did, so she was already living a blessed life. The picture of Cerys and her sister on the hill made her cry. Cerys wanting to leave had been a fair enough choice. It shouldn't have turned so ugly.

'I keep feeling so sad for her.'

The rule was everyone should share their feelings before they became extreme emotions.

'Not again Lou. How many times.'

'Now Cathy,' said Stephen. 'It's fair enough. You can't expect her to be as hardened as we are.'

'What now?' said Louise.

'We wait.'

'And see who comes to visit.'

'But we already know who'll come.'

'I keep thinking I should have done something.' Gethin chewed the skin at the edge of his index finger. 'I saw them. I could tell something bad was going to happen. I mean, I watched her so that I could protect her and instead—'

'No. You watch to see, that's all. That's your job. You're not to do anything, you know that. We're like documentary makers, Gethin. We can't get involved, that would be wrong. It would change everything and that's not our place, it wouldn't be right, not at all. Young Dewi being proof of that, saying her name for God's sake, what on earth got hold of him? Anyhow, we provide. We tell them the rules and it's up to them what they do with that information. If it messes with their heads, so be it. That's not our fault. They're in charge of their own minds and they're responsible for the decisions they make when they're here. What they do with their friends, their families, that's up to them, not us. We must never change the path they've chosen, not ever. You know that. We have to leave them to their own devices.'

'But the sister was mean, rotten. I think she's deranged.'

'Not our business. We mustn't change the natural order of things, the history they're creating. Some people are bad, no matter the parenting, schooling, the mentoring. Some people blame the world no matter what they've been given rather than just get on with it. What she—'

'Talking of getting on with things.' Cathy tapped her watch. She didn't understand why young people got phones out to check the time rather than wear something that didn't need to be pulled out of a pocket or a bag and re-charged every evening.

'But aren't we getting involved now?' asked Louise. 'Doing this when she's not even—'

'She's coming,' said David.

TWENTY NINE

Seren hired a car to drive to the church. Not the smallest or the cheapest because soon money, money, money would be coming her way. All she could picture was the book to sign, her biggest priority. And Cerys to grieve over of course but the book... It had to be there. It was one of the rules. Cerys had emphasised that. It was always left for the next kind person to sign, the lucky unknowing champion. Everyone who signed it would also be buried in the churchyard and so it went on: sign, inherit, live, die, get prayed for, sign, inherit, live, die, get prayed for.

She would be the only mourner at her sister's funeral. No-one else had been invited. She hadn't been invited. Seren would say a prayer especially for Cerys then write her name, address and kind words on the yellowed sheet of paper. And she'd take a photo of it with her phone in case they tried to make out like she hadn't done it. She didn't trust that Stephen man. Not. One. Bit.

She'd told Mark the date of the service. After a moment's guilt she persuaded herself she'd made the right choice, in fact she'd made things easier for him, the boys and Cerys's friends. Her selflessness made their lives less stressful and in the future, when they asked why they hadn't been invited, she'd explain it was organised so quickly, had been out of her hands. Those Welsh people did it, them there strange people, and anyway, it was so far to travel, they were all so busy with work and as they hadn't found time to visit Cerys when she was alive Seren had presumed... Dig dig, guilt guilt from Mrs passive aggressive. Seren had assumed they wouldn't be able to come all that way in twenty-four hours. When was the last time they'd called Cerys, had a catch up? Squirm. Bitch, bitch. She was a star to call them out for what they were. She was the loyal sister. There was Sam of course. But it would be too late by the time she questioned anything. Everything would be sorted and as a distraction she'd organise a memorial service in London. They'd all hug Seren as they appreciated the kind sister making it easier for them, grief without the long journey, food and drink on tap, all paid for by her. Generous to a fault. She really was wonderful, such a kind lady.

Seren would do good things with her life from now on. She wasn't a bad person. People needed to understand that. Mark and the boys would love her so much when they realised what she'd done for them. And it was for them, for her family, her only relatives in the world. They had to understand that she'd only offer to leave them in order to make their lives better. It was the ultimate sacrifice. The purest love of a wife and a mother. If Mark didn't understand, so be it. She'd sign the book. It would all be in her name. She'd be independently wealthy with no further need of his wage. Either they came down to Wales or she'd come down and they could visit in the holidays. That would work best. Simple.

~

A lone grey car sat in the car park, the same model as the one that would soon be Seren's. She'd learn to live with the brightness and it would be so comfortable on the motorway, a pleasure to drive, that's what reviewers had written when she googled it. She couldn't see the owner of the grey one. Ten a.m. was early for the service. From what she'd overheard it was the only time the vicar could come as he church-hopped around the county in the same way Seren bus-hopped to and from work back in London.

It was good there was no-one else around. That was the best thing about Welsh beaches. They always felt empty and wild like a beach should. She had to be the only person to sign the book. She was not in the mood for sharing.

Seren was amazed at how calm she felt as she approached the church, proud of her strength in the face of such adversity. Her parents would be proud of her too, like last time, the way she'd held her head high at their service, double coffins, two for the price of one, madam. The metal door handle screeched when she turned it. A visitor book lay on the table opposite her, bound in brown leather, attached to the dark wooden table with a chain, a shabby string of red silk marking the open page. She got a pen out of her bag but there wasn't a column to write her address in, her prayer. It was filled with compliments, no room for the earnest message she'd prepared. That wasn't right. She concentrated hard. *And then on the way out there was the book so that's when I signed it.* She needed to copy exactly what Cerys had done.

The coffin was closed. Cerys must have been disfigured by the rocks, lipstick and powder not enough to hide the wounding. The wicker coffin sat in front of the altar made from good Welsh slate. Wicker chosen as young people nowadays liked things to decompose without hurting the planet, and Cerys had been young compared to Thomas and there'd been enough hurt without the earth flinching from the pain of one more wooden box being lowered inside it.

Seren ran her hands over the altar but felt nothing, not like Cerys said she did when they visited. Had her sister somehow been more Welsh, more in tune with the country, having spent more time there when she was younger? Her with more years on the Welsh earth than Seren. She imagined the corpse like Cerys had described Gwen, a muslin cloth dulling the features, her cheekbones jutting out. Good bone structure. She'd been lucky to have inherited that. They both had good bones, strong enough to withstand the challenges life threw at them but not rocks from a height, the smash of a slippage. No-one's bones were built to beat that.

Seren was tempted to open the lid and peek. She hoped whoever had prepared her sister's body had painted a rich red paste on her lips. That was what she always wore in her twenties, contrasting with her pale skin and dark hair. When she reached her forties she'd stopped wearing it.

'I'm too old for red now, don't want to draw attention to myself. I'll leave that to the younger ones.'

Seren didn't understand. She still wanted people to notice her when she walked into a room. Once she was pretty, stunning they said. Now she'd be able to regain some of what she'd lost. She could afford designer clothes and facials, a nutritionist and a personal trainer. Oh happy realisation. On such a sad day. She'd never hear her sister's voice again. That thought darkened her mood. She did not like it. It didn't have to be like this. Such a tragic accident. She would make sure good came from it so Cerys's life wasn't wasted.

'All you had to do was share. It was so simple. Then God would have blessed you rather than taken you. It wasn't rocket science, Cerys. God bless. In the name of the Father and the Son and the Holy Spirit.'

'Amen.'

She jumped at the man's voice. There in the middle of the aisle stood Jesus dressed in white trousers, a white T-shirt, brown Birkenstocks, light brown wavy locks that rested on his shoulders, beard and moustache neatly trimmed. Good cheekbones and the bluest eyes. He was rather beautiful. No wonder Cerys had noticed him. Not that the Son of God would have actually looked like that. Such nonsense.

'You're real then,' she said to the young man who looked right at home, as he should do in his dad's house.

'Of course.'

'You scared her you know.'

'I meant her no harm.' He held his arms out, playing the part. Bravo, Mister.

'Yeah, right.'

Christ looked scathingly at Seren. His eyes narrowed as he judged her. She couldn't bear that. How dare he? Look at all the bad things his dad had done, even if his son was a goodie. None of them were absolute angels. She pressed record on her phone and said a prayer for her sister out loud so he could hear it too. There was her official record. Now to sign the book and move on from the churchyard.

He would have to let her pass. Christ wasn't allowed to be violent, not like the crusading Christians. Hopefully. Who knew what he was like in this day and age? A nutjob obviously, thinking he was Jesus Christ on a bike for heaven's sake. She put her keys in her fist just in case, two fingers through two steel rings ready to punch, defend, kick him in the balls if needed. You never knew; there was always the good and the bad in any religion.

He sat down in the pew furthest to her left so she couldn't reach him or vice versa. Seren hurried out, her pen at the ready but the book still wasn't there. That wasn't how it was meant to be. Did Jesus have it? He must at least know where the book was stored. Perhaps he was holding it back from her because he thought he'd seen her do a bad thing when she hadn't. That's not what happened. Her sister had slipped. She hated edges, always had done, ever since their parents fell, ask anyone. It was a tragic accident.

Seren returned to the main part of the church. Jesus man was gone. In his place sat the mean man Stephen, and on his knee sat an ancient leather book. She was right to have been wary. He was the one with the power. A figure rose up from behind the slate altar. Christ beneath his cross, the sun casting coloured shadows on him through the stained glass window. No. He was not Christ. Christ hath not risen. Bob Dylan had, dark curls surrounding his twenty-something face. Stephen stood beside him. They could be father and son, two sets of curly hair, one grey, one coal coloured. Both ignored her. She coughed, which felt a cliche but would have to do. It was all she could think of.

'Can I help you?' Stephen asked.

She did not like him, not one bit, but she had to learn to deal with him if he was to play a part in managing her future. And the young one. The gatekeeper and the bookkeeper, that's what Cerys called them.

'That book should be in the foyer.' She nodded at what was in his hands.

'The what?'

'The entrance.' She half turned and pointed, not taking her eyes off them.

'You mean the narthex?'

His smirking grated. Nasty up-himself fellow.

'That book under your arm, shouldn't it be on the table in the entrance?'

'No.'

Flummoxed. It was all about the rules wasn't it. That's why Cerys couldn't share. They'd taken it out of her hands, these people, that's what she said. It wasn't her fault. It's what she'd been told to do by the solicitors, the lawyers, the accountants. She had to do what they said no matter how much she didn't want to and she had morals, she was a good person. Honestly, if she could share it all she would, for the love of god of course she would. So the people commanding her, those with all the letters after their names, they had to follow the rules too. That was a rule in itself, otherwise they'd be damned for eternity and what was it about, what had it all been for. What the hell was happening?

'Yes it should.'

'No.'

'Liar.'

'Now then—'

'You do. You have to put it on the table and anyone who prays over the body inherits the house, the car and the monthly money. Cerys told me all about it. You have to do what you did in the past for new people in the future. It's a cycle. You can't mess with fate, with what's meant to be. That'd be wrong. You're not allowed to.'

'You did,' said the bookkeeper.

'No.'

'Ha. No. No. No. No. No. No. No,' sang Stephen in a choral scale. His pitch-perfect baritone bounced off the white walls. 'We seem to have reached an impasse, my dear. Best move on, let it go now.'

Rhys laughed, then sang along with his master.

'No. No. No. No. No. No. No, my dear,' they sang. Higher. 'No. No. No. No. No. No. No.'

Seren pressed her hand on the edge of the pew. She imagined the wood was her anger as she pushed down on it.

'Don't you dare *my dear* me,' she shouted. All the alliterations. She was reminded of something, someone, somewhere. Her scream silenced the singing. Stephen's face turned very serious.

'I think it's best you leave. Go home to your family, Seren.'

'I'm not leaving until I sign the book.'

'There is no book to be signed today.'

He looked sorry for her which made her even angrier. It was her right, her future he was holding onto. How dare he keep it from her.

'Yes there is. I can see it under your arm. Why are you doing this? It's not fair. I'm a good person, I am. I don't know how what happened happened, but it did and here we are and that's fate, and me being here now is what Cerys would have wanted, keeping it in the family. She told me that lots of times. She said I wish you'd inherited it with me Seren as then it would help all of our family. She loved the boys, and Mark. She saw how hard we worked all the time, running to stand still. She wanted to help us. She wanted to share it and now she's gone fate has decreed that I'm the one who should get it.' Seren shrugged as if there was nothing she could do about what was happening. It was out of her hands. 'I need to make sure that what she wanted more than anything, happens. So please. Put the book on the table and let me fill in the details. I said a prayer over her body. Those are the rules.'

'No you didn't.'

'I did. And there was a witness. Jesus boy heard me. He was here, he'll tell you. And I recorded it, a video that I've sent to myself already. Incontrovertible proof, you see.' She held up her phone.

Stephen and Rhys stood on either side of the coffin. They lifted the lid. Seren walked closer to see inside. There lay an old lady, very old, very wrinkled, happy to rot as her time had come. Seren forgot to breathe. With all that was happening she forgot that her body needed oxygen. When her lungs remembered she made noises like she'd broken through the surface of the ocean after too long a free dive.

'Where is she? What have you done with her?'

'She's in hospital. No-one ever said she was dead, Seren.'

Must. Remember. To breathe.

'Which hospital?'

'Ah.' They put the lid back on the box. 'I'm afraid that I can't tell you. As her guardian I need to protect her.'

'I'm her sister.'

'I know.'

'As her next of kin you have to tell me.'

'No we don't.'

'Who's we? What we is it? Who are you all? What game are you playing?'

'It's not a game Seren. And to be quite frank, I'm pretty insulted you're calling my life's work that.'

'You mess up people's lives.'

'No we don't.'

'They do that for themselves,' piped up Rhys.

'Yeah right. You keep telling yourself that.'

'What exactly did I do wrong?' asked Stephen. 'Tell me. I manage a trust. People inherit the wealth. A lottery win, most would say, with no bother and worry because we do all the paperwork for them. If they choose to accept it, all they have to do is enjoy life. And before they sign the papers they're told all the rules. There's no rush for them to sign, no time limit. In fact we encourage them to go away and sleep on it, to think carefully, to talk to their family and friends before making a decision. There's no pressure on our part. It's all up to them. And as for us, we're merely bystanders. We never get involved apart from to make sure the rules are followed, and they're simple enough rules, we make sure of that so everyone can understand them no matter their thinking, their education. So how is it you think I, or rather we, are the baddies?'

She'd paid too much for the hire car, not the cheapest one, the second most expensive one that she'd never usually even contemplate hiring. All to come to the funeral of a no-one.

'How is she?'

'Not well I'm afraid. She's in a coma, not an induced one. They're not sure how long she'll be like that for.'

'As in days? Weeks?'

'Years perhaps. It's very hard to tell. She's definitely alive. She can breathe on her own, although there's nothing to see as it were. The content of her brain is inaccessible but it's still there. That's what the doctors said, that her memories and her feelings, they're all within her, the outside smashed, the insides working. If we can get her booted up again she'll have a future, so we mustn't give up on her no matter how long it takes. The most similar case the doctor read about was a boy in America who woke up after nineteen years. Isn't that amazing? So there's hope. Don't give up on her. And don't worry. We'll make sure she's properly looked after. She's getting the very best care money can buy and there are enough funds so it can stay that way for however long she needs, fifty years if necessary.'

Seren's throat burnt as she swallowed the bile that had jumped from her stomach into her mouth.

'I want to see her.'

'Sorry. Not possible.'

'Of course it is.'

'No.'

'I'm her sister. I have a right.'

'No.'

'You're awful people. Terrible. You should be ashamed, the way you treat people.'

'What you did to your sister, we've got it on film,' said Rhys, fed up with the accusations. 'There's a copy in the clouds, with him upstairs.'

He laughed at his joke and waved his hands in the air like one of the hippies tripping out at Woodstock in that famous documentary.

It made no sense. There was nothing to see, nothing to get on film. It had been an accident. A court scene came to mind. Who would believe Seren over a solicitor and an accountant with Jesus on their side? She wouldn't win that battle. Pick your battles wisely. That's what mums said to each other when their kids wanted stuff, kicking off about this or that, their homework, what they were wearing, a refusal to eat their tea. It had to be the same with her. She must be careful with this battle, make sure it was one she could win. It would be close, even though morally she was in the right and overflowing with enough anger to fuel a long fight. Detestation. Was that a word? How she felt about them and her invalid sister.

'We'll see!' Seren stormed down the aisle, desperate to have the last word.

'You need to be out of the house by nine o'clock tomorrow morning. No later please. It's one of the rules.'

She flew round.

'Fuck you. Fuck you and the control you have over everyone. I wouldn't want to be part of all this even if you did pay me.'

She laughed at the ridiculousness of what she was saying, at how freeing it felt, only stopping when she saw Stephen raise his eyebrows like he didn't believe her. 'It's true. And I don't want to know if Cerys wakes or dies. You can have her. I don't give a shit about her.'

'Yeah, right,' Rhys mumbled.

'I mean it. I don't want to hear from you no matter what happens, no matter that I'm her only next of kin on this planet. She's drained me my whole life and now I don't have to worry about her any more. Brilliant. That's great as far as I'm concerned. Even if she dies I don't want to know about it.'

'You don't want to come to her funeral?'

'Nope. Never.'

In that precise moment she didn't but just after she said the words she knew she might change her mind in the future. She wouldn't give them the satisfaction of knowing that. Her mind had been warped by death, wills, people. People drove her crazy. She needed to think, work out what to tell Mark. She thought of Cerys in a coma, a ventilator coming out of her mouth which was wrong because he said she was breathing okay. Was it better for her to be alive or dead? If it wasn't for modern medicine she'd be gone, her body in the wicker coffin. Seren screamed, straining her vocal cords as she shouted, 'Fuck you! Fuck you Stephen and God and Jesus and every-fucking-one of you.'

The gatekeeper and the bookkeeper remained calm. It wasn't the first time: it wouldn't be the last. She ran all the way to her luxury hire car.

'Did you get that?' Stephen called to the back of the church.

'Yep.' Gethin emerged, hair now tied up in a bun. He swiped and pressed different parts of the screen on his phone. 'There we go. It's all backed up now.'

'Blessed be the modern technology,' said Stephen.

'Hallelujah.'

All three of them put their hands in prayer position and nodded.

THIRTY

Four new phones ordered, one for each of them, a second Mulberry bag, small, for the evenings, the hire car, new plates and cups and bowls, all matching, new towels, a watch for Mark, an 85-inch smart television for the family to enjoy together. All paid for with her credit card the night before the dreadful morning. A frenzied attack of consumerism where she'd wondered should she wait but no, she was always so good, always waited, had been so frugal her whole life for Christ's sake. Unlike her sister. Lesson learnt. Lesson learnt looking at her. Live for the now and go for it. Except it turned out that was wrong, not what she was due. The gods were against her. God, the big one, him and his son conspiring, watching, judging. Now she understood why Cerys wished there were curtains and blinds in the living room, a double layer between her and them. They were watching her. All of them. Every single one. People had plotted against her, decided they knew what was in her brain when they didn't. How dare they, motherfuckers.

~

She tried to cancel the orders but the premium postage she'd picked meant they'd been processed with the highest priority, madam. She had to tell Mark because the packages would arrive at their house before she did. It had been a moment of mad grief, actual craziness. She worked out what to say. *Please don't worry. It's all going back. They'll take everything back so don't worry. Please. Just leave it with me. Don't shout. I'll sort it out.*

Promise. I always keep my promises don't I? I always sort out everything for the family.

The day's car hire and delivery charges came to two hundred and seventy-three pounds. Much as it irked, money for nothing, she could take that hit. Though there was also the four nights of two rooms a night that had been booked and paid for in August, their summer holiday. It wasn't fair that Cerys had made them lose that money, especially considering how much she'd been given, the strength of her bank account. Seren calculated the total cost on her phone. Sod that for a game of soldiers.

She found one of Cerys's large suitcases that had never been used, bought for a planned escape to the sun in January. She filled it with Egyptian cotton sheets, duvet covers, pillow cases, all never used. When it was full she took a second large suitcase, god knows why Cerys had bought two when she was on her own in life, and she filled that one with hand lotions, bath oils, the expensive truffles from the fridge. There was still room. She was still owed money. She checked for jewellery but couldn't find any. She opened the kitchen cupboards and picked out the Anthropologie cups, mugs and plates, wrapping them up in used but still fluffier than any that she owned towels. Then she found the Mulberry handbag in ox-blood leather at the bottom of Cerys's wardrobe. That would doodle-do considering its value. The cases bulged when closed. But it was fair. It was right and what she deserved: her lost money plus a little extra for the inconvenience, the trauma.

She messaged Mark:

Someone cloned my credit card. Bastards. Don't worry, it can all be sent back. Idiots forgot to change address. Duh. Bank people called me, all under control. They said it's pretty common. Too tired to think. This on top of everything. Turning phone off now. See you tomorrow. Give the boys a big kiss from me. Love you xx

She put on Cerys's black fleece, cagoule and waterproof trousers, slipped a set of keys into the zip-up pocket. She

232

dragged the suitcases to the bottom of the garden and sat on one at the bottom of the hill. She waited. She watched. Now who had the power?

~

Cathy handed the inventory to Stephen.

'It was empty when we got there. She'd taken all the towels and duvet sets apart from one, some of the plates and mugs and all the lotions that weren't open. Plus the maroon bag. Anything that was expensive basically.'

He sighed. 'To be expected, I guess.'

'And there's a set of keys missing. Do you think she's got them? Or they might have fallen along with Cerys.'

'Best we change the locks, just in case. Remember Mr Johnson.'

'No problem, I'll call Timpsons. What about the stuff she stole?'

'Let's leave it. They're only things. If they give her pleasure so be it, though to be honest I think they'll cause more pain than joy in the long run. Can you imagine the guilt you'd feel each time you used them? Let her keep them. Owning piffles rather than the house, that can be her purgatory.'

'I'll head back and lock up then. Louise and Gethin should be nearly finished with the cleaning. At least we'll all get a break for a while, especially you. You work too hard you know, trying to make it perfect for everyone. You're always telling us it's up to them what they do with their fortune but we can all see how much you worry, too much if you ask me. And what do you always tell us? You can't control how happy they'll be, how they'll handle it.'

~

Front door shut, key in the lock, a red Royal Mail van pulled into the driveway.

'Alright Cathy. Got a parcel for you. It's a bit bulky. Want me to carry it inside?'

She unlocked the door and the postman carried it through to the kitchen where he put it down on the worktop, leaving after she'd signed his tablet. Cathy chose a vegetable knife to sever the tape. She pulled off the bubble wrap.

Eight glass ice cream dishes, the kind that restaurants served a knickerbocker glory in, and eight long-tailed silver spoons that reached to the bottom of them. A kit of luxury sauces and sprinkles in glass jars rather than plastic.

Cerys had been there the shortest time of any of them. Which felt wrong. She'd seemed nice, eager to be liked, nervous for her new adventure. Cathy rinsed the glasses – not worth putting the dishwasher on for only them – dried and put them away neatly in a cupboard. There was nothing she could do about it. Nothing any of them could do. They weren't allowed to advise or get involved. They just had to make sure the rules were followed and it was up to the beneficiaries what they did with their winnings.

A door shut beside her, a purposeful clunk rather than the wind. She didn't turn round. She knew. There was trouble ahead from the trouble behind. She gave the base of the tap one last wipe then went to open the knife drawer at the same time as she hung the tea towel over the oven handle.

'Leave it.'

Nothing so dangerous as a mad lady, man, child. Limitless strength and no off switch, only the on. Cathy didn't smile. She hadn't been friendly before so no need to start now.

'Where are your keys?' asked Seren.

'They're on the table.'

'Who else has a set?'

'Stephen.'

Seren knew he would. That's why she was clever in asking. It was good the cleaning lady was honest, poor dumb servant woman.

'I'm going to live here now. It's not fair that I can't. I'll stay and look after the place for my sister until she wakes up.'

'You're not allowed.'

'Because of the rules.'

Cathy nodded.

'You shouldn't play God. It's not right, acting all *we're rich so we can do anything we like.*'

'We're not the rich ones. The people we work for are. It's them who can do anything.'

'But—'

'They don't have to accept the money. They don't have to come.'

'Rubbish. No-one could say no to what you offer, not when life costs so much.'

'Not true. Someone did once.'

'Who?'

'None of your business.'

She stared at the cleaning lady. 'You can go now please. Thank you.' Always be polite to the staff.

Cathy picked her bag off the chair and walked to the door, her back to the sister, relieved to make it outside, into her car, out of the drive. She pulled into a parking spot on the other side of town, safe with the doors locked. Her hands shook as she pressed on Favourites.

'Stephen?'

~

Seren dragged the sofas in front of the bi-folds but they weren't tall enough. Someone could open the doors and jump over them. She needed a camp, her own camp where no-one could get her. The fridge was empty after their cleaning but there was water on tap, of course there was, and you could survive for ten days on that. She filled glass after glass and mugs meant for tea and coffee. She carried them on a tray to the master bedroom, lining them up on the floor, on top of the dresser, a glorious variety of heights, widths and colours, every surface covered. She heaved the suitcases up the stairs and across the landing. Her things. That's what she wanted to be surrounded by, and inside there were the five boxes of chocolate truffles fulfilling what would have been Cerys's dream of having no choice but to live off sugar. It was all working out so well, as water was the best thing to drink with sugar. It was what chocolate tasters sipped when they were on the job, and if Jesus came he could turn it into wine which was handy. She emptied the wine cooler which was built into the corner of the marble island in the kitchen, resting the bottles on their sides next to the bed, which wasn't made now the cleaners had been. Easily solved. She picked the sheets with the waffled edging, fluffing air between the feathers before she lay the duvet back on the bed.

Still no sign of the baddies. Time to play a game, make them wonder whether she was downstairs or upstairs. She carried six dining room chairs into the hall and stacked them so they blocked the front door. The racket of a tumbled-down chair jenga would warn her they were coming. The utility room. Lucky she was so good at remembering things. There was always more to think about, a need for her brain to be wired rather than tired. She took the two remaining dining chairs and jarred them against the back door. It looked pathetic, not strong enough to stop a child let alone a pack of adults, but noise was what she was after. She knew she couldn't stop them entering her house, but at least she'd hear them coming.

Seren stopped in the living room and turned her head slowly. There was Christ, holding onto his bike, the rain flattening his hair against his skin, making his red T-shirt stick to his torso. The Lord hath risen, he cometh again. Fine. She would fight him, and his father. Her rage at the injustice of it all, the early deaths of Gwen, and her parents. Look at the fuckers on this world and up in the heavens, all of them conspiring against her. She wasn't unreasonable, hadn't asked for more than she deserved. Other people got things so she should too. That was fair. And that was all she wanted. Parity.

He didn't move. She stepped to the right. He didn't edge sideways. She grabbed a chef's knife and pointed it at him from behind the sofa.

'Go away.'

'You don't want this,' he shouted.

'Yes I do.'

'No you don't.'

'Get off my land!'

'You have children. Go back to your children, your family.'

'No!' she screamed.

The boys had drained her. Enough. They would not take her future. The vase she threw at the window smashed against the glass. She ran out of the room and up the stairs, screaming even though no hand tried to grab her, no claws gripped her feet pulling her backwards. She made it to the bedroom where she slammed the door shut, roaring as she dragged, pushed, pulled the bed in front of the door but it took so long as it was heavy, too heavy and slow to move. Any minute that Christ on a bike man was going to open it and get her. Success. The door was blocked. Too slow. He was too slow. She caught her breath as she fell onto the bed. She lay on her back, triumphant, ecstatic.

'Fuck you motherfuckers!' Her feral cry bounced off the ceiling as she danced a jig of joy – water, chocolate, wine, a bathroom, a bed fitted with expensive sheets, a window to spy from and no-one able to get her. Alone in a luxurious world of her very own making. Bravo Seren.

THIRTY ONE

Mark asked one of the mums at school to look after the boys. She was reluctant, felt unable to say no due to the circumstances, wished Seren's husband's brothers lived closer because this was a job for family rather than friends. She didn't know them that well and wasn't so keen on his sons.

'Definitely only one night, because we've got friends coming the day after?'

'Absolutely.'

He didn't sound sure. Everyone knew their two fought and grumped, were little shits according to Jenny. Rumour had it they'd driven Seren crazy. She was always moaning about them. Rumour had it she was lazy, one of those *couldn't be bothered* mums.

~

Seren ran a bath with the taps on their lowest setting so she could listen out for intruders. It was too slow for her impatient mind so she turned the hot tap up to its highest setting and closed the ensuite's door while she stood guard in the bedroom. She opened and shut the bathroom door every minute to check the water wasn't overflowing, turning the tap off once the bubbles were a few centimetres from the top. She put her foot in the water, pulled it straight out, skin burnt red, drained some of the water then topped it up with cold. Before she submerged herself she stood near the door to the bedroom, holding her breath, listening. To nothing. She knelt on the floor and peeked over the windowsill. Jesus was at the bottom of the garden talking on his phone. The steam from the boiler pipe that heated the water for her bath had given her away, of course it had. She couldn't submerge herself now because this was the time he'd attack, knowing she was vulnerable. Unless he thought she'd been having a shower. What to do. *Think, Seren.* She pulled her cases into the bathroom. And the duvet and two pillows from the bed. The mattress wouldn't fit, more's the pity. The cases took up too much room, so she emptied them of what she coveted most: the Mulberry bag, the truffles, one set of towels. Then she remembered she needed water to survive because she couldn't drink bathroom tap water, or could she? Was that allowed or did it poison you from dead rats in the tank, dead sheep in the stream, the boy with dark hair who got ill on their Duke of Edinburgh expedition. Everyone told him not to drink from the stream, how dangerous it was, but he wouldn't listen, he knew better. Now she had to make things better but there was danger all around, even in a stream that looked so pretty. The beautiful bathroom with its decadent bubbles wasn't the place for her to hide. She pulled the duvet back into the bedroom but it caught under the door. She pulled harder and harder but it wouldn't budge.

'Bastard. Bastard duvet destroying my bastard life. I have a plan and you need to get out of there now, you utter cocksucker.'

All the anger from the too-soon-dead people channelled through her, their anger mixed with hers, she was sure of it. She pulled with a superpower strength, not caring if the cotton ripped, but it wouldn't shift so she kicked the door that was stopping her from moving forwards with her plan. When the door didn't budge she banged on it with her fists and palms.

'Motherfucking fucker.'

The skin on her palms turned blue from the bruising. Three bones in her fingers split apart.

~

The front door wouldn't open. Stephen checked Mark. His manner was calm. The police were behind them, just in case, in a kind way. It was part of their job, one they were good at, helping a family work out how to deal with a member whose mind had broken.

'I don't want her sectioned. I'll get help for her. I'll deal with it.'

They nodded. It was his call unless she got violent. The husband looked fearful when the pile of chairs tumbled to the floor.

~

Seren turned triumphantly to face the bed. She knew they'd come. She'd have bet money on it. If a bookmaker had given her odds of 100 to 1 and she'd bet a thousand pounds or ten thousand pounds, what about that then. She'd have won a million pounds plus she'd be given back the ten thousand pounds she put down so that would be her and them, all her family, sorted, and she could leave the house because she'd have her own fortune, enough to buy her own Welsh cottage. Jesus was still at the bottom of the garden. They were in front and behind but they wouldn't get her because she was a genius. *More water Ma'am? Why thank you James, just what I need.* Her butler bowed as he exited through the wall.

Her eyes were tired, but her brain beat them open. It was lucky she hadn't slept. She might have missed her enemies advancing.

'Seren. Seren honey it's me, Mark. Can I come in?'

That was not what she'd expected.

How did he get there so quickly? Who was looking after the boys? And more importantly, who was at home to sign for all the parcels? She couldn't bear to have to go to some depot to pick them up. There was no time for that. It was too exhausting and she didn't like to queue. Tears threatened to weaken her. She would not let them.

'Seren?'

Mark tried the door but it only opened an inch, enough for them to see the top of the bed that was blocking it. The policewoman went downstairs to check the windows.

'You're meant to be at home! You idiot. You absolute idiot. I told you they were coming. I told you the parcels were coming and now no-one's there to sign for them and that means I'll have to queue to get them and I hate queuing, you know that. I hate it. I can't bloody stand it, such a waste of time, hours of my actual life I'll never get back again.'

If she was lithe enough she'd have run up and down each wall but tricks had never been her gym thing. She ate three vanilla truffles in a row then felt sick. Fuckers making her do that, two hundred and forty calories for nothing. She checked for Jesus. He'd gone but a lady and a man wearing black suits were carrying a ladder across the patio.

Seren moved the truffles and two glasses of water and a pillow for comfort into the bathroom. The door wouldn't shut because of the still-stuck duvet. She pushed it as far as it would go and did cry this time because she'd tried so hard, planned so hard, worked so hard her whole life and now she was so tired when she needed to be utterly energised, ready to fight them. If she was a gangster in a movie she'd snort a line of cocaine. Checking the cupboards Seren found three disposable razors, no scissors, no scalpels, no knives. They would have to do and she must remember to slash rather than stab. She practised in the mirror.

'You want some.' Slash. 'Leave me alone.' Slash. 'It's my house. You're trespassing. Check the book, bitches.' Slash across the throat you fucking bastard. 'He knows what I'm talking about. It's the rules, not my fault. Ask him.' She pointed to the fallen man, blood spurting out of his neck. Uh-oh. Dead he was of no use to her. Who cares. She'd slash them all until she was the only one left standing.

'Seren.' The door opened two inches towards her. She pressed her foot against it. They were quick. Up a ladder, in a window, bed moved, bish bash bosh madam. 'Can I come in?'

She stood in a fighting stance, her legs apart, knees bent and unlocked, ready to get them, unable to make sense of their whisperings.

'Seren?'

She glimpsed the nasty man. In her house. How dare he! Attack is the best form of defence. Always attack your enemy. She ran but the door made it awkward to get out and the duvet made it impossible to find speed so it was more of a stumble than a scary approach, though the roar seemed to put the fear of god in them. She laughed as she lunged at that little man, the same height as her, slashing the razors from left to right but a hand got her and she was on the floor and it was very sad the voices said, so sad, such a sad thing, they'd get her help, thank you for all your help, sorry for all the trouble, no problem, it's no problem, there's help out there, I know, thank you, it's been a tough year, my mother died too you know, she's not been the same since. We're so sorry. That's terrible. Here's the doctor. So awful. Such a hard thing to bear.

'Mark!' She hated the brown leather shoes in her eye line. She hated him, the traitor. The loser. Lost. All of it was lost. Everyone and everything gone now.

THIRTY TWO

Postcards dropped through letterboxes. From Walthamstow to London Fields across to E9 down to Greenwich then West to Beckenham, the chain ending at Wimbledon. A beach in Wales, bright green handwriting, *visit soon, it's so beautiful, I'll treat you to delicious ice cream, double cones all round.*

They would message her later that day, that night, the next day if they remembered. Sam replied straight away:

Let's get a date in the diary. Loves ya honey.

Undelivered.

~

Stephen, Rhys, Cathy, Louise, Gethin and David sat in the two front pews as Reverend Jones gave his eulogy. In the name of the Father and the Son and the Holy Spirit. Amen.

'Amen,' the six of them chanted.

They filed out of the church. Stephen handed the vicar a bottle of Penderyn whisky as a thank you for his trouble, his kindness for popping by on a non-Mwnt day, then he placed an old leather book on the table at the entrance, a pot of pens beside it in case a solitary pen rolled off and was lost, forced into a dark corner by the wind.

'I feel guilty,' said Cathy, picturing the unused ice cream glasses, bought for the nephews presumably, lined up ready for the next owner.

'You heard what she said. She didn't want to be told. She was adamant about that. We played it to you.'

'I know. It's just... She was upset, wasn't she? She wasn't well. What if she didn't mean it?'

Stephen hadn't told any of them about the letter he'd received, apologising for her swearing at him, the lunging. She was doing well now, almost compos mentis on some days and the medication helped, though it made her very tired. The note asked for the family to be told when Cerys woke up, or not, they loved her so. He could tell the words were forced. He was sure of it. Seren would always be a money grabber and the point of the inheritance was that it was given to kind souls. As the guardian it was his job to ignore the fakers, the groupies, the wannabes.

'She did write once.' Little white lie. 'But I can't let her inherit everything, not after what she did. A person mustn't be rewarded for acting terribly, that wouldn't be right. And she's not well. If she said a prayer for her sister, who's to know if she'd really mean it?'

'I thought we weren't meant to make decisions like that. We're not meant to influence what happens, shouldn't get involved.' Louise squinted as she waited for an answer.

Rhys looked directly at Gethin who'd bent down to tie up a shoelace that hadn't come undone. He'd given Cerys the subtlest of warnings but she hadn't understood it so that didn't count as meddling because it hadn't changed anything. Surely.

'You're right,' said Stephen. 'And I haven't before but we all saw what she did.' They looked at their feet, the gravestones, the field, the sky; not the scars on his cheek and his hands, Seren's razors inches from deadly. 'What sort of world would it be if a person was rewarded for being greedy, nasty, rotten? What would humanity evolve into if one was seemingly rewarded for such behaviour, if that was hailed as the way to get on in the world?'

'I'm not saying it's right, I'm just saying we're not meant to get involved. Like documentary makers.'

Louise was fed up with people saying one thing and doing another. She and Gethin had always been so good. They didn't even help themselves to a posh fork when the drawers were crammed full of them because the people who inherited the money wanted to buy more stuff they didn't need. She'd always left well alone because that was one of the rules and now look at the boss man acting differently. Stephen's shoulders sank.

'I'm sorry. I've failed you all.'

'No.'

'No.'

'No,' added Cathy. 'You did a good thing Stephen. If you'd reported her, shown the clip from the cliff to the police, she'd be in prison by now, so you saved her from that, and her family from more suffering. You did a kind thing, really you did.'

'I don't know. Not getting the wealth will be her own worst life sentence, waking up each day knowing she'd come so close to it.' He sighed. 'At least she doesn't know Cerys is dead. That will save her from more pain, hopefully. We're meant to do good on this earth, aren't we? I mean, what's the point if we're not doing good with it? That's why we all pledged to help others.'

Rhys put his hands in his fleece pockets. Louise shivered as she spoke.

'So we are acting a bit like God then, like she said?'

'No.' Rhys frowned at Louise. 'We're just making sure they follow the rules. All of us must follow the rules all the time, do what we're told to do. That's what we agreed when we said we'd work on this. What happens isn't our responsibility, same as how we take responsibility for the day-to-day away from them. The point of the rules is to make life easier, not harder. If they don't see that and don't appreciate it, well that's their problem, not ours. It can't be. We're not gods, not at all. We're not all-seeing all-knowing, as much as we try to keep up with what's going on, Gethin and his mates keeping an eye on them. We're only human so there'll be some errors, of course there will. It's impossible for that not to happen. But as long as we do our best, well that's good enough and none of us should lose sleep over it. We mustn't beat ourselves up about it. At the end of the day what they do, it's their choice, that's the whole point. We merely document it.'

'Someone's coming,' said Gethin, finger on his lips. Shush now.

'Right. Action stations everyone. Good points well made, Rhys. Good. Very good. Are we all okay then, happy to go on?'

The group nodded, moved into position.

THIRTY THREE

Magdalena ran into the church to escape the rain. Her boyfriend sulked in the VW van, seething that they were in Wales rather than Portugal where it was twenty-eight degrees and sunny. He'd checked. It wasn't fair. It had been her year to choose where they went on holiday and she'd always wanted to hire a camper van to go on a road trip round the west coast of Wales, dropping in on the towns where her great-grandparents on her mum's side were born. Every morning and afternoon he showed her the Algarve's sunshine icons. Five years into their relationship, he mostly annoyed her. Not great. Not what she'd dreamed of.

She froze, her breath shallow at the shock. There was a coffin, no lid. All alone. No order of service on the pews, no sign of anyone. Feet visible, white trainers with three navy stripes, Adidas. A young person then. She didn't want to see the face that was hidden in the depths of the wicker. Eyes down, she walked sideways in front of a pew to light a candle, as she'd been taught to do when she was little. She knelt down on a cushion to pray for the departed.

'In the name of the Father and the Son and The Holy Spirit. Amen.'

~

A door banged shut. Magdalena shivered; the damp denim of her jeans stuck to her thighs. The church was calming with its white walls and powerful grey altar. Good. Welsh. Slate. That's what her mum used to say at Christmas when she got out her best dark grey slate coasters. Magdalena's phone beeped. She replied *coming now* even though she wanted to stay longer.

A lady smiled at her. The photo was framed in wood, the same colour as the table it sat on. Cerys. Such a lovely name. If her baby was a girl that's what she'd call her. In front of the photo sat an old ledger. Her phone beeped again as she read the note inside it. Her shoulders drooped, her heart weighed down with sadness. Such a tragedy. She looked too young, and the poor thing, not having any friends or family. Was it because she'd never married, not had children? Was she an only child so there were no nephews or nieces? She didn't look old enough for all of her friends to have died already. It must be a photo from thirty years ago or something. No-one that young could have absolutely nobody to care whether they were alive or dead. She quickly wrote down her name, address and the prayer she'd said for the dead lady, then ran over the grass to the car park. Water soaked through her trainers into her socks, so they squelched as, head down, she didn't see the man in a red cagoule, standing next to his bicycle.

~

Stephen slipped inside the church, took the book and Cerys's photo, wrapped them in a plastic bag to protect them from the rain then tucked that bag inside his briefcase. He sat in the pew nearest the doors, nodded hello to the grave diggers as they pushed the coffin down the aisle. His chin drooped as he dozed.

'All done,' Grave Digger One called through the door. 'We'll be off now then.'

Stephen stirred, yawned, stretched. '*Diolch*,' he called back. '*Diolch yn fawr iawn.*'

Reverend Jones sat beside him, a glass of whisky in each hand. He passed one to the solicitor. They clinked their glasses together, took a synchronised sip.

'She has a strange energy, the new one,' the Reverend said.

'You think?' Stephen drank. 'Na. She'll be fine.'

The lady was in need of a fresh life; Stephen could feel it in his bones. They could help her. Him the conductor, the others his orchestra. A break in the clouds let the sun shine through the window above the altar and, when it lit up the aisle, the Reverend stirred.

'That's my cue to be off then.' He took Stephen's empty glass. 'I've a christening in Penbryn at five-thirty. One of those new-fangled ones where they serve a dinner instead of a buffet lunch. What's that all about?' He shook his head. 'You got your keys?'

Stephen nodded.

~

Stephen locked the church door and pushed his shoulder against it to make sure it was properly closed. He strolled to his car, not minding the wet, used to it. He was Welsh, therefore he was waterproof. Once the heaters cleared the condensation from the windscreen, he switched the wipers to their fastest setting and reversed, headlights on full. At the entrance to the car park he flashed them twice. Gethin raised an arm in thanks. Stephen checked his rear-view mirror, indicated, then turned onto the road. He drove at the same speed as the boy on the bike, lighting the way ahead of them. Mirror, signal, manoeuvre. Always follow the rules. They were designed to keep a person safe: a good thing, not a bad thing. Why was that so hard to understand? She would be different, the new one. Of course she would. She'd paid for her parking and stuck to the speed limit the whole way home, according to David. She'd settle in fine.

He pressed Play and let the voices of the Treorchy male choir surround him. He joined in with the singing. All would be well. Complex but harmonious.

249

Acknowledgements

A huge thank you to Kevin and Hetha at Bluemoose Books - it's a dream come true to have *Christ On A Bike* published by you; to my lovely editor, Lin Webb – I've really enjoyed the gentle trimming of words and addition of commas; and to Fiachra McCarthy for the brilliant cover design – I absolutely love it.

Thank you to Jo Fottrell for reading and feeding back on an early draft, and Sue Flood for reading those first fifty pages. Diolch yn fawr to Emily Jones for checking the Welsh text; to Rhian Owen and Siân Owen, for the chats about Welsh phrasing; and to Ian Owen, for all our holidays and walks across the wondrous mountains, coastal paths and beaches in Wales.

Thanks to the writers, book bloggers, and friends I've made on BookTwitter and Instagram, for your encouragement and support, and to the other Bluemoose authors whose brilliant books I really recommend you read. And finally, thanks to Carys, Erin and all my lovely friends – your faith in my stories means the world.